PANTHEON

BY AUSTIN WEN

 FriesenPress

Suite 300 - 990 Fort St
Victoria, BC, V8V 3K2
Canada

www.friesenpress.com

ISBN
978-1-5255-7155-8 (Hardcover)
978-1-5255-7156-5 (Paperback)
978-1-5255-7157-2 (eBook)

1. YOUNG ADULT FICTION, DYSTOPIAN

Distributed to the trade by The Ingram Book Company

To Oliver, who helped me begin.

For Abby, who kept me going.

And for my mom, who stood with me till the end.

PROLOGUE:
A STEP TOWARDS DARKNESS

YEAR 2035

Reine strode along the broken cobblestone path, straightening her back and keeping her chin raised in order to appear confident. *Perhaps too confident*, she thought. She relaxed and shifted her weight into a more casual position—until she saw a shimmer of air dart suspiciously behind a broken-down apartment. *Huh. Starflight is probably using me to train her newer cadets. Even the ones with stealth abilities reveal themselves with their stupid mistakes.* Starflight liked to keep an eye on her—especially after last year's events . . . she tried not to think too much about it. The metahero tailing her right now was what she should be focusing on. Inexperienced or not, letting her guard down with cadets nearby could be deadly. She had to assume they would be as bloodthirsty as their master—the most ruthless, most *unhinged* hero of Valmount City.

She stopped walking and looked about her. *Hmmm . . . right or left?*

She had reached an intersection in the park, and remnants of crumbling buildings littered either side of the road. It was actually an abandoned neighborhood that had lived a brief life as a wrecking yard before losing even *that* purpose; most people couldn't afford cars anymore. The torn-up automobiles that hid among the houses were the only clues left to hint at the neighborhood's former existence, and she knew the buildings discouraged residency with their protruding nails and rusted interiors.

Reine pictured the map she had committed to memory. The park was a symbol of the state the world had fallen into, but even a neglected junkyard had its uses. She jogged along the sides of a curving path and moved further and further away from the city. Hopefully, by the time the metahero caught on, Reine would already be weaving through a sea of steel and cement.

Starflight had ordered her placed under constant supervision after the metahero had murdered Reine's parents, though not without reason. *They had . . .*

Reine refused to think about it. She wouldn't give in until she had gotten her revenge.

The problem was that the woman Reine was trying to kill happened to be the chief commissioner of the Metahero Force in Valmount City, who was an extremely powerful metahuman to boot. Starflight was always on the lookout for new recruits, and though she didn't outright admit it, Reine knew that the hero must have detected some latent power in her. Why else would she continue to spare her life?

Reine felt her muscles tense again: the route she had rehearsed over the course of several jogs was finally approaching. There was no backing off once she started. She would either lose the metahero and reach her destination . . . or die trying. *Pantheon's academy*, she thought, preparing to escape. *That's the place my parents were going to send me to if I developed any abilities.* The academy had one of the only large-scale metavillain training programs they knew of. There were plenty of crime families or shady organizations to join instead, but those treated recruits as cannon fodder instead of apprentices; only the lucky survived, and Reine didn't exactly trust fate to do her any favors.

She and her parents had lived as thieves, forced into a life of crime after the Great Enhancement caused a chain of events that reduced the world to mass poverty and discrimination—especially against the metahumans. Superhero tropes from the world before the Enhancement, which Reine had never lived in, split their morality into black and white. The metahumans hired by the government to hunt their own became "heroes," and the rest were forced into the role of villains.

Taking a last look at her mental map, Reine suddenly dove into one of the vacant apartment buildings that lined the crumbling street. Frantic footsteps followed her. Now there were at least two pursuers. She felt her heart begin to pound, but she concentrated on keeping her breathing steady.

Win with your brain. Not your heart.

The two metaheroes closed in on the building, unaware that she had already escaped outside through a hole in the wall. Reine heard a rush of conversation as she observed the two trainees dropping their invisibility and splitting up. Both were wearing dark purple uniforms, but one had pretty eyes that sparkled like diamonds.

She started to sprint away. She might have a head start, but metahumans who could use their Goethan—which was what allowed them to manipulate the world—had unique powers, and they also gained an overall enhancement of all physical abilities. She didn't know how it worked; only that they could circulate the mysterious, fog-like substance as if it were spiritual blood.

Her feet felt like lead as she ran as fast as she could. Living in the city wasn't exactly good for her health; being under the constant stress of finding her next meal and avoiding people who wanted to stab her took a toll on Reine's body.

Red door, broken down but still intact, blue roof . . . she reminded herself, refreshing her memory.

Behind her, the constant shouting of panicked heroes chased after her as they threatened, begged, and reasoned with her to come out from wherever they thought she was hiding. She was glad they were inexperienced. If Starflight were chasing her, Reine would be dead before it even started.

"There," she breathed as she slowed down and risked a glance at the instructions hidden in her pocket. "It should be in this area." *After all that sneaking around, finding my parent's map . . .* She still remembered the excitement she had felt the day she had unearthed the key to her escape: instructions written on the back of an annotated map of the city—a map she had helped her parents steal.

Every second day of January, a villain will be sent to meet with potential recruits, she recited to herself in her head. *Do not reveal the location to anyone else.*

Reine hoped the person meeting her would forgive the extra baggage she had unwillingly brought along. Maybe they would even get rid of them for her.

Come on . . . Come on! A red door . . . Where are you?

She was so busy inspecting a roof—the paint was peeling off—that she didn't notice a third pursuing trainee until he was an arm's length behind her back. Then it was too late. Golden sparks erupted from his fingers, and Reine felt a telekinetic force grip her brain. It didn't hurt, but there was a feeling of pressure, as if her ears were on the verge of popping

"Don't move," the cadet said, trying not to appear smug but failing miserably, "or I'll give you a brain hemorrhage you'll never forget."

Seriously?

Reine resisted fighting back as the cadet's two friends finally caught up. One of them opened a government-issued phone and began to type something—probably a passcode—while she stood frozen. Death was no stranger to Reine, but that didn't mean she wanted to die with her brain squished into pulp. She had heroes to kill.

She thought, *Maybe I should resist. Who knows how Starflight will react—*

"I normally don't interfere . . ." a man growled flatly, **"but that was an unforgivably terrible threat."**

All four teens jumped as a tall, broad-shouldered stranger appeared out of nowhere. Reine didn't know how to describe it, but she felt a sense of gravity from him, as if his every step were loaded with power. A translucent shroud of golden mist shone like stars against his black skin, and she was suddenly shaken by the fact that there might be people more dangerous than Starflight in the world.

The fortyish-year-old man looked them over with a bored, blank face. His very words radiated with meaning, and even the flat tone of his voice could not conceal the intent behind them. This metahuman was meant to be obeyed.

"I—we . . ." the guy who had captured her stuttered, sizing the newcomer up, "we're on official business for the Metahero Force. She's under our jurisdiction."

The man's eyes flickered towards Reine, and she suddenly knew that this was not just any normal recruiter. It was the original himself—

"It's Pantheon!" one of the cadets whispered, having reached the same conclusion at the same time. They all took a step back. Everyone knew him. He was the principal of the most powerful metavillain academy in North America, but before that, Pantheon had dabbled in a bit of everything. A mob boss, a gang leader, the one who had single-handedly stopped the government from experimenting on metahumans . . . even the most powerful government officials knew his name.

"No way it's him," the smug guy scoffed, and his confidence slowly returned when the mysterious metahuman didn't reply. "Why would he come to this junkyard? He's obviously a fake."

So fast that Reine barely caught it, the cadet whipped around and pointed a finger at Pantheon. She felt the force on her brain loosen. As if redirecting the energy, the hero tried to do the same thing to Pantheon . . . but the man just shrugged. The cadet cried out as his own power flung him backwards. He collapsed on the ground. The Goethan flared around him like an aura before dispersing. Pantheon didn't waste any more time after that. Vanishing and reappearing behind the cadet who had first pointed out his identity, he twitched his index finger slightly in a beckoning gesture. Her pretty eyes glazed over, dead. Reine could have sworn she saw a golden mist fly out of the body before it collapsed.

"Christine?" her friend gasped, checking her pulse with a shaking hand. His disbelief turned to anger. "You—you killed her. You killed her—"

Is this really what I want?

Reine turned away before Pantheon broke his neck with another impassive twitch of his hands.

"**Useless,**" Pantheon remarked. "**It's a wonder he was even considered a metahuman.**"

Ignoring the remaining cadet, the man stared Reine in the eye. Her left hand crept involuntarily towards her short hair, trying to run her fingers through it, but she forced it down. The habit always popped up when she was nervous.

Careful, Reine. Show your strength.

She approached the guy still lying on the wilting grass and pulled a cable tie out of a side pocket in his uniform—all meta-heroes had them—then bound his hands with it, striking him in the back of the head when he tried to resist. It wasn't a cruel attack; just enough to stun. Pantheon looked on silently. She hoped it meant that he approved.

"Here," Reine said to Pantheon. "I was trying to return this." She handed him the map, and he turned it over, reading the words with the slightest display of surprise. Pantheon didn't ask her where she got it. The message was clear. *He doesn't care if I stole it. Only that I'm here.*

"**Haven't seen this in a couple of years,**" the man told her, putting the sheet of paper in his pocket. "**We've moved on to electronic copies now.**" His tone finally turned serious. "**Why do you want to be a villain, Reine?**" he asked. She was shocked until she realized her parents had written her name on the map.

"**What can you contribute to my school?**"

Reine tensed even more, mulling the question over. She was tempted to say, "whatever you want," but that made her seem like the type of person who lacked direction. If she wanted to lead a team to kill Starflight in his academy, she would need all the leadership roles she could get.

And what about all my abilities? The years of martial arts with my father . . . all the knowledge my mom passed on to me . . . She breathed out. *Just tell him the truth.*

"I guess . . ."

Reine suddenly felt extremely frustrated at her inability to explain her need to get revenge. It wasn't exactly that she wished for justice—her parents were already dead—it was the simple fact that she had loved them, and that Starflight had taken it all away. Avenging them was the only thing she lived for. What else was left?

"I guess . . ." Reine hesitated again, before a flash of inspiration struck her, "I can kill Starflight for you."

The words left her mouth before she realized that it might not be prudent to make such an impossible promise, but she had already spoken. You didn't just take back a vow of that magnitude. With a smile, Pantheon laid a hand on her shoulder. **"Very good."** He nodded approvingly. **"Now for the young man to meet his fate."**

With a slight flick of his finger, a spark of Pantheon's Goethan landed on the tied-up hero's head; Reine had almost forgotten about him.

"What? No," cried the hero. "Stop! Please!"

A chain reaction of explosions spread across his body as his Goethan reacted violently to the villain's, Pantheon's power being so potent that even a drop of it was enough to overpower his. Reine caught one last glimpse of his squirming figure before she and Pantheon teleported away in a shower of sparks and left the cadet to join his teammates in death.

"No."

CHAPTER 1:
THE EARLY WORM GETS EATEN

THE PAST: 6 YEARS AGO

Beep, beep, beep, beep . . .

Reine groaned and slammed her hand down on the alarm clock. Even though she was used to waking up at 5:30 in the morning, the sound still drove her crazy. A few rays of sunlight made her skin tingle; the sun was barely awake, but Oliver was already standing by the window of their room, bright as ever.

"Nice weather we got here!" he said, throwing open the curtains. "You ready for some training?"

Reine mumbled incoherently. Now the sunlight was marking a prickly square on her face, and her dad's cheerfulness didn't help. He was wearing his only pair of black dress pants and a checkered shirt—he had even combed his messy black hair.

She tried gathering her thoughts. *What's happening again?*

Reine rolled over and got to her feet, shakily. It wasn't that she didn't like practicing—it was just so early! Her muscles felt as stiff as stone, and there was an aching nag in her head that she couldn't place. *The perils of sleeping on the floor,* she thought, *and a thin mattress.*

"C'mon," Oliver urged. "There's no time to waste. Shortened schedule today, remember?" He left the room, Reine walking slowly behind.

Skipping with energy, her dad laid down a thin mat and hung up a punching bag in the living room while Reine drank water from the sink. Their apartment only had two rooms—a bedroom and a living room—but it was enough for their purposes. Her mom, Amy, was still lying on her side with the blanket muffling her ears, so Reine let her sleep; she always needed it after staying up so late.

"Give me a minute," the girl yawned softly, "I'm going to splash some water on my face."

She left the apartment and made her way to the communal bathroom down the hall. There, she ran her entire head through the water dripping down from the rusty faucet. Her short hair had its perks. After the lukewarm liquid had rinsed away all the grit of the day before, Reine dried her hair with a towel, letting the remaining dampness evaporate in the dry air. She had learned the hard way that sticking her head into the shower meant getting much more than her head wet, and the sink in their living room was too small.

"Reine?" she heard her dad call down the hall.

"Alright. I'm coming!" she yelled back.

Oliver winced at the volume of her voice, but since none of their neighbors complained, he let it go. She never remembered his warnings, anyways. There were about five others living on their floor of the three-floor apartment, and each one had retaliated in their own way. The one next door had kept banging on their wall until Reine's mom banged back. Her dad had to patch up the hole afterwards.

"Good. Then let's get started with some stretches," he ordered as she reentered the apartment. "Oh, and try to do five more pushups than last week."

Seriously?

Reine complied, grumbling a little. She knew the sooner she started, the faster it would go away, but it was really the familiarity of the training that kept her going. She and her father had been going through this routine for as long as she could remember. Every two days, instead of boring textbooks, she got to let out her inner warrior.

"Remember," Oliver continued sagely, "always use what I taught you for retaliation, never to initiate trouble. You shouldn't fight people for no reason, but never let yourself be pushed around. You can't let people think you're weak, or they'll be stepping on you for the rest of your life. So hold yourself with pride, and use your abilities wisely." He gave a wink. "Got it?"

Exasperated, Reine made an "okay" gesture with her fingers. Her dad always said the same old thing whenever they had a training session . . . as if she would forget something he repeated so often. The sentiment seemed really important to him, though. He had told her he first learned modern wushu because he thought it would be fun, but it wasn't until after the Great Enhancement that he really got into it.

As she threw two rapid punches, Reine exhaled through her teeth in bursts; this was supposed to contract the diaphragm and chest, allowing her to hit better. With a quick jab to the left, she struck the punching bag her dad had given to her for her seventh birthday.

"Good job, Reine! Nineteen more, then move to kicks," Oliver directed.

She smiled proudly, and her innocent look seemed out of place against her serious demeanor. Though Reine was only nine, her father made it clear he expected hard work and grit from her. It was a work in progress.

"Sure!" she replied in between breaths, not pausing to wipe away the sweat.

Reine continued punching until she got into the same rhythm as the music her father was playing through a speaker. The speaker was a relic of their past, when they had still been able to afford these things.

The songs are so weird. What kind of person sings about pine-apples and pens?

"Just ten left!" Oliver encouraged.

The lyrics slowly faded away as her mind drifted, thinking about the shortened training time her dad had promised. The routine had become so familiar to her now that she could let her mind wander and still maintain perfect form. *Dad's job interview, right? Mom won't let me stay home by myself, so I'll have to go with them . . .*

Reine had been surprised last night when her dad mentioned he needed to apply for a new job—something about not wanting to live dishonestly anymore. That didn't happen often. As registered metahumans, it was hard for anyone to hire them legally even if they wanted to, and no one did. Only heroes had all the rights of a normal citizen.

"Kick higher!"

Reine reluctantly raised her aching muscles. She didn't understand why her parents didn't just become heroes themselves. Maybe it was because the job was too violent? Being former teachers, she guessed they didn't see much of it in their line of work.

But they do steal stuff, you know, she thought to herself. *They don't think I notice, but sometimes, I see them sneaking out of the house with crowbars and knives.* It didn't bother her that much. She understood the necessity of stealing food to survive, and her parents knew better than her. They understood subjects like biology, physics, and whatever poetry was, so why not life?

"Time to go," Oliver said, shrugging on a jacket. "We have a job to do—at least, I hope."

CHAPTER 2:

TIMES ARE HARD FOR METAHUMANS

THE PAST: 6 YEARS AGO

Reine had guessed that her parents would insist on bringing her along to the job interview. It kind of sucked, but she knew there was no point in arguing when it was two against one. Her mom was going to make her study chemistry or something.

She looked up at the cloudless sky. It seemed so clear now that she couldn't believe it had once been filled with smog, or that there had been places where people couldn't even go outside. She had never experienced it herself, of course, but her mom's stories were enough to paint a vivid picture.

Reine held onto her mom's hand. "What job is dad trying to get?" she asked.

Her mom chuckled. "Nothing special yet, honey. This store is owned by an old friend of his, so they might trust your dad enough to give him a position as the cashier."

They were sitting against the wall of a grimy grocery shop with dust-caked windows. Broken trunks of severed palm trees ruined the symmetry of their healthy counterparts. Hanging from the shop door, a misshapen sign reading "Los Angeles" swung in the breeze.

"The owner uses nostalgia to bring in customers," Amy explained once she noticed her daughter's gaze. "The government doesn't like it when people mention Valmount City's original name, but it's not like they're going to arrest anyone who says it."

She pulled out a battered biology textbook from her backpack, and Reine reluctantly took it. She began flipping through the pages without much interest. Why did she need to know how her joints worked, anyway? She wanted to be with her dad, finding out about his new potential workplace.

Reine risked a glance at her mom. She had closed her eyes, still tired from last night's heist. The little girl quietly set the book down and crept towards the store's front door. There would be time to read later.

Muted shouting was coming from inside the building.

"Get out of here, you metahuman scum! We don't want your kind in our shop."

Reine tensed, eyes wide, as she stood up and smeared a hole in the window's grime and looked inside, the dust making her sneeze. Her dad was standing next to a balding man, who was arguing with a group of customers congregated near them. Behind the two, she could make out similarly angry employees.

"He's harmless," the balding man protested, "My friend here just needs a job."

Reine panicked when she saw an employee step forwards with his fist raised. "And you think we have enough space for him? KP, we don't make enough money already."

The employee's protest was met with cheers from his fellow workers, and the shop owner stepped back helplessly. Emboldened, a woman with a horrendous amount of makeup slathered on her face chimed in.

"Hey. Don't tell me you you've forgotten the destruction metahumans caused when they were free to mingle with us," she accused. "Or are you disrespecting all the people that they killed?"

It was the final straw. Nudging a few people out of the way, her dad strode towards the door, trembling a little as jeers and insults hurt him more than he expected. He raised his hands defensively. Reine wished he had explained that all the deaths caused by the metahumans were mostly from them losing control or protesting against government testing, but she was more concerned with getting out of the way as he slammed the door behind him.

"These people," he growled to Amy, trying to keep his frustration contained. "When Kuo Pao agreed to hire me, his other employees told all the customers about my . . . unique circumstances." He shot a glare at the store. "And then the bastard—"

"What did you call me?" a voice snarled.

Reine had to admit she felt a bit scared when a knife-wielding maniac stormed out of the shop, throwing the door open so hard that it unbolted from the wall. She heard her dad take a deep breath. They all knew using Goethan right now would get him arrested.

"Let me deal with this," Amy said quickly, and moved to tie her brown hair back to show that she wasn't holding any weapons. "We don't need to fight." She checked behind Oliver to make sure there were eyewitnesses watching from the window, and the aggrieved man relaxed a little, unsure of what course of action to take. Though government law allowed people to attack metahumans under the guise of self-defense, they couldn't just stab a normal citizen. The man didn't know if her mom was a metahuman or not.

"You a metahuman or not?" the guy asked Amy, deciding on the most obvious path to enlightenment.

Reine didn't think too highly of the man's intelligence, but at least he was straightforward. She moved a bit closer to him.

Amy raised an eyebrow at her husband. "You think I should tell him?"

Oliver shrugged, and the man brandished his knife threateningly. "If you all aren't going to give me an answer, then I'm going to take it as a yes—"

Reine kicked him in the stomach. It wasn't just some random attack. Still warmed up from her morning exercise, she threw a roundhouse kick, arcing her legs to strike him with her feet. The man stumbled back. He had definitely not been expecting her to hit him.

"What the hell was that?" the man demanded, regaining his stance and adjusting his sweat-stained tank top. "Lying metahumans. Your kind doesn't deserve to live—"

He lunged forwards, and Reine tripped over her own feet in a sudden panic to get away. He was faster than he looked. She twisted as his hand grabbed for her, but he managed to snag a fistful of her loose T-shirt and throw her to the ground. She hit the street chest-first. Reine rolled over, feeling the cold asphalt rub against a spot on her back where a jagged hole had been torn from a previous fall and an unfortunately placed nail.

Great. Just what I need: more holes in my shirt.

She tried to get up, but the man was walking towards her again and she froze when she saw the knife in his hand. Her legs seemed like they would give way anyway if she stood up. She bared her teeth, feeling like an ant about to be squashed. His hand was reaching for her shirt, and—

Reine's mom suddenly backhanded him so hard that he flew into the windows behind him. A collective gasp rose up. People who had been standing behind the glass where the man lay cursed, but his crash hadn't broken the glass or hurt anybody.

"Let's get out of here," Oliver grumbled, pulling Reine to her feet. She was still gaping at her mom.

"Are you—"

Amy put a finger to her lips with a wink at Reine and let the golden glow fade from her hand. She smiled back. The bystanders were leaving now, either because they were afraid or ashamed that one of their own had attacked a child.

"I don't know . . ." Her mom asked her dad as they walked quickly away, "Should we be worried about them reporting this to the metaheroes?"

Oliver shook his head. "No. We're registered metahumans, but Reine isn't, and he attacked her instead of us. She still has rights. If the heroes come, we can claim it was self-defense."

They walked home in silence. The confrontation had disturbed them more than they liked to admit, and Reine was trying to wrap her mind around metahuman discrimination. She wanted to say something, to ask why the mean people were being so unreasonable when they didn't even know them, but nine-year-old minds weren't made for philosophical discussions. Her dad didn't seem to want to talk to her, anyways. He was fidgeting with his wedding ring, the way he always did when he was deep in thought.

"Why did you guys register as metahumans?" Reine asked after they had arrived home, latching onto a subject that was more concrete. "They're only being mean because you always have to tell everyone about not being normal. Can't you just have lied or something?"

Amy put her hand on Reine's head and ruffled her hair.

"It's not that simple, honey. We thought it was for our own good back then, and, well, maybe it was. The government has gotten a lot more corrupt since then. You'll understand when you're older."

Reine huffed indignantly. "You'll get it when you're older" seemed like every adult's explanation when they were too lazy to give her an answer.

She hesitated, "Oh, and Reine? I know you were trying to protect us, but please don't jump into the fight like that next time. He's three times your size. We can handle it."

"But—"

"The point is that I'm proud of you for doing what you did. You just need to think about the consequences before you act out."

Reine gave up and tried to act suitably chastised. She didn't want to argue until her dad was forced to speak. He seemed tired enough. *I don't want to give up my TV privileges, anyway.*

"I'm sorry, Mom," she replied meekly. "I won't do it again."

Amy seemed satisfied. "Alright then. Now go back into the apartment while I talk with your dad for a bit. We need to discuss some stuff about finances."

Reine grinned, all pretenses gone. She leaped up the stairs and checked the keys in her hand. If she was fast enough, she might even be able to catch an episode of *Wonder Abby* after making lunch.

Outside, Oliver looked over their list of bills with Amy.

"We're going to need to plan another heist soon," he said.

CHAPTER 3:
A TRIAL OF THE MIND

"What . . ."

Reine could have sworn someone had punched her in the face. She rubbed her eyes to clear the grit away, trying to figure out why she was lying on the ground. Her memories weren't cooperating yet, so she stood up and stretched, observing her surroundings. The room she was in resembled something you would find in an insane asylum: padded walls and floors, with a fixed security camera in the corner of the room. It was clearly designed so that she couldn't hurt herself if she tried.

But why would I . . . ?

A flash of understanding came over her, and Reine remembered what Pantheon had said after he had brought her back to his school.

I have to take an entrance exam to get in. The final pieces of the puzzle were clicking into place.

Pantheon had led her through a retractable wall of unpolished rock built into the walls of a small hill before directing her down a flight of stairs and several underground tunnels. When Reine explained that she didn't know anything about controlling Goethan yet, Pantheon had given her a day to learn the basics from an instructor. They had taught her about how to enter the third level of the subconscious, and though she didn't have much time to practice, she recognized a lot of the steps from when her parents had shown her with the hopes that she could learn.

I really hope Starflight was right about seeing some potential in me, Reine thought. *Pantheon's tests are not known to be lenient.*

Getting rid of the residual taste of the drug they had knocked her unconscious with, she finally stood up and took a look around, making sure to check both the ceiling and the ground for threats. The only entrance or exit she could see was a wooden door on the far side of the room.

Huh. Way too obvious.

Letting her posture relax a little, Reine moved to run her hand through her hair, but . . . couldn't. She frowned. Her left hand was frozen, as if someone had disconnected her motor neurons to it or something. She wiggled her fingers on her right hand: it seemed fine.

Is this part of the test?

Leaning in, Reine inspected her left hand . . . and it slapped her across the face.

"What in the world?" Dumbfounded, Reine stared at her left palm like someone had somehow switched their hand with hers.

SLAP!

She reeled back, more shocked than hurt as another stinging smack landed on her cheek. There was nobody else around, but it was obvious someone was controlling her body. The security camera suddenly seemed much more sinister to her. She didn't know much about how Goethan manipulation worked, but maybe a metavillain didn't even need to be in the same room to ambush her with their powers.

She started to sprint towards the surveillance device. *If I can just disconnect or even break that thing . . .*

Reine's stomach unexpectedly caved in as her left hand slugged her right in the stomach, causing her to stumble and fall onto the padded flooring. She found something deeply disturbing about hurting herself against her own will.

Okay. So that's obviously not going to work. Maybe use the stuff the instructor taught me?

Taking a deep breath, Reine went through the procedure for entering the third level. She panicked as her mind drew a blank. Cramming wasn't exactly the best strategy. *Focus, Reine. This is exactly like the tests Oliver used to give you. Just relax and try to remember the retrieval cues you planted when you were memorizing the steps. It's basic psychology!*

She shrugged away the pain and attempted to picture the exact scene that had happened when she had accessed the third level. The instructor had been talking about submerging herself in her subconscious—the state of mind essential to all Goethan usage—in a spotless classroom with desks pushed to the side. As she struggled to recall every detail, her teacher's words became clear.

"Now start cycling Goethan to your heart—"

"Stop fooling around! I honestly don't understand why Pantheon keeps bringing in these useless city rats."

Reine's left hand shot up again, this time aimed at her nose, but she was more surprised by the voice shouting inside her head. She ducked her head just as her fist flew past.

It's a mind-controller, she realized, starting to feel for the golden substance naturally generated in her mind. *I wonder if they can read my thoughts.*

She managed to get a grip on the Goethan in her brain just as the left arm came at her again. It smashed against her body, but Reine pushed through, cycling the Goethan to her heart in an attempt to connect with the third level of the subconscious. It felt like moving air by flapping her hands.

How long is this process going to take?

Unfortunately, the arm seemed to know exactly what she was doing because it twisted itself behind her back, turning her vision red as she bit back a scream. It was too late. Her concentration broke, and it was all Reine could do to grab at the weirdly angled limb with her other arm. The feeling of the Goethan inside her heart disappeared as she struggled against her own strength. She tried to imagine the arm was heavier than lead. Was that how the third level was supposed to work? She didn't even know if she was submerged in her subconscious yet, but there was nothing else she could try.

Concentrating on her possessed appendage, Reine willed it to stay still. *Come on . . . Come on . . .* **Do not move.**

Reine's vision tilted as her head got hit by what felt like a sledgehammer. Her adrenaline spiked, and she realized with a sinking feeling that her arm was free again. The mind-controller must have let it go.

"Okay, enough," she said in an attempt to buy time, "this test doesn't measure potential. It's just an inaccurate knowledg—"

As if electrocuted, Reine's entire body froze up, completely ignoring her own commands. She couldn't even speak!

"Mnnn," she grunted helplessly. She started to feel for the Goethan in her body again.

"No."

Reine's eyes would have widened in shock if they could. The voice felt invasive, as if it were coming from a primal part of her brain where she kept all her most instinctive functions. She shuddered involuntarily, trying to shake it off, but it only grew stronger.

"*You disrespect me by wasting my time when you don't even know the proper steps to defend yourself,*" it continued. The voice was slathered in contempt. "*You deserve this punishment.*"

As if mocking her, the tester gave her a full ten seconds to try to enter the third level before he made his—it was definitely a he—first move. She couldn't, of course. There was a reason practice was important.

Reine's head moved an inch. She gasped, confused by the slackening of control, but she prepared to shout for help anyway. There was no point in fighting a battle she couldn't win.

"What a coward."

Instead of listening to her, her mouth opened and savagely bit her tongue. The salty pain of iron permeated everything. It was like a disease, multiplying by the second. Reine tried to scream.

Funny, she thought deliriously. *Wanting to scream? It's usually the other way around.*

She was beginning to suspect the mind-controller was doing this out of malice instead of purely academic reasons. It made sense, in a way. Why else would someone agree to torturing teenagers for a living?

Reine felt the same slackening of control all across the rest of her body. Before, the development would have excited her, but now there was only dread. *It's not that bad,* she told herself. *Just survive like you always survive. You've endured worse.*

She gritted her teeth and silently struggled as her limbs twisted and all reality seemed to warp. It hurt, but not to the extent that anything was broken. Bruises she could suffer.

CRACK!

A wave of black dots darted across her eyes, and Reine had to summon every bit of her willpower to stay conscious. *If you can't beat this guy, how are you supposed to defeat Starflight?* she asked herself while entertaining the notion that maybe she was never destined to do either.

Suddenly, Reine was tempted to just give in, to let the darkness take her. Sure, she would never get to join Pantheon's academy when she woke up, but anything was better than this!

Or is it?

The thought reminded her of a different kind of strength—the cold, emotionless one she had learned to rely on when her parents' death had left her with nothing to live for but revenge.

I came here to learn how to be a villain, she reminded herself. *To make my parents proud. Do I honestly think the school is going to take me in after this?*

She gripped the Goethan in her mind and used its power to push against the darkness until it receded, becoming an insignificant speck in the distance.

No. They won't.

Reine felt a certain satisfaction at the simple logic.

It's time to make them proud, Reine, she told herself. **Do your best!**

She took a deep breath and went over the last steps of her routine. It was hard, especially since pain wracked her body, but Reine worked them through one at a time, never stopping.

Now picture your heart . . . please let this work . . . and let power cycle through!

It was as if a firestorm had blazed through her chest. The pain was suddenly cleared, pushed aside, and forgotten.

Reine entered her subconscious.

Let's get to work. She could see the entire blueprint of her body. *Hmmm . . . seems like I'm going into shock*, Reine mused. It was like looking down on an interactive diagram. Before, she would have been disturbed to see every part of herself labeled in such detail, but now it was just . . . natural.

Reine searched for the location of her spinal cord. Finding it, she started fishing around, trying to determine where her somatic nervous system connected with the brain. A memory of a textbook page slid into her awareness.

It controls voluntary movement, so all I have to do is . . .

Reine reached for the Goethan in her heart and willed it to stop sending and receiving messages to her brain.

Nothing happened.

Damn it! If I don't stop me from hurting myself soon, I'm going to pass out no matter what!

She found the glowing clump of power in her heart again and moved it around, trying to determine what she could do. Metahuman powers were fickle. Though all metahumans used Goethan to fuel their abilities, they each had an assortment of different functions. Reine had been hoping she was some sort of all-powerful reality warper, but for all she knew, she could easily have the power of twirling her eyebrows instead.

I'm so close! It wants me to use it in a specific way . . . I just need to keep searching.

She thought back to the only time she had ever displayed anything remotely metahuman-like before. The incident occurred about three years ago, and she had dismissed it as an accident, or perhaps wishful thinking, especially when taking in the fact that it was the night her mom was murdered—but then again, maybe it wasn't just luck.

It would be terrible if my power turns out to be changing my voice, though, Reine thought. *Considering all I managed to do was imitate Starflight's tone for a few seconds, I'm not feeling too confident right now.*

Nonetheless, she was sure she was getting closer to the truth. She could feel it in her Goethan. The golden, misty substance was speaking to her in its own way, its purpose becoming clearer and clearer as she played around with it.

And Reine understood.

She drew on her knowledge of biology and created the semblance of a spinal cord injury at the top of her spine, not expecting anything to form. To her amazement, her somatic nervous system instantly stopped communicating with the brain, thinking it had actually been damaged.

So my power is illusions? Hmmm . . . maybe body-related illusions—what was that?

She had bought herself a little time with her trick, but the mind-controller was definitely still in her system. She could feel his presence like a growing burn in her submerged state, and he was trying to cause damage.

Gotta set up a few defenses, but first . . . Exercising great care, she checked to make sure that her autonomic nervous system wasn't affected. *I definitely don't want my heart to stop.*

No problems. Satisfied, Reine zoomed in to the diagram of her body and focused on the head. She needed to take some precautions before fighting the invader. Her instructor had briefly taught her about the flexibility of Goethan, and how each level of the subconscious allowed the metaphysical substance to affect different things in the physical world. It explained why she could move Goethan from one part of the body to another. Since the golden fog didn't interact much with her physical self, there was no need for a physical vein or valve to transfer it.

So I can use the third level to defend myself, even if I don't draw on my illusionary abilities, she thought. *Because my power allows me to affect things with Goethan inside my body, I can just like . . . bash the guy with it or something.*

She paused. Reine still didn't know what form—if there even was one—her assailant would take, but she could feel his Goethan clumped up in her mind. That meant there must be something she could fight.

Reine gathered up her power.

And if I can try . . . then I can succeed.

The invader struck, this time with far greater power than before. Reine could feel his fury grating against hers like a whetstone grinding down metal.

Okay. Got to plug the brain stem here . . . some more Goethan there . . .

She felt like she was a commander waging a war. Her heightened mental processing speed from the Goethan helped a bit, but it was all she could do to constantly defend, plugging up spots and reinforcing them when they weakened. She had the home advantage—her brain was a factory for making Goethan, after all—but her opponent was many times more experienced.

I can't keep doing this, she thought, growing tired. *I need to try something else before he gets through.* Desperate, Reine decided to push back. She ignored the exposed feeling she got from coalescing all the power barricading her spinal cord. *Better to attack than to defend, right?*

The mind-controller responded in kind. He had concentrated all of his Goethan at a single point in a last-ditch effort to destroy her entire arsenal; his power sparked and smoldered when it clashed against hers, as if rebelling against her very nature.

The winner of this fight will win the war, she realized. *And he obviously expects to overpower me.*

She couldn't disprove his logic, either. Though Reine's body was constantly producing power, she was becoming too tired to use it. The instructor had warned her about this—something about "Goethan weakness."

Focus, Reine. He's striking from the left.

She tried to surround the invader like a white blood cell with her tendrils of gold, but his Goethan just shrugged them off, casually slipping through with a practiced movement. Reine growled. She twisted around. He lunged, and she managed to block him off before some of his Goethan could slip through to the rest of her body.

"You're putting up a better fight than I expected," the mind-controller admitted grudgingly. *"Not many people hold out this long after I get into their system. They either beat me quick or fail."*

Reine was surprised by the fatigue in his voice. With a start, she realized he might be as tired as her, especially if he wasn't used to prolonged fights. The invader was afraid of losing to time.

I can exploit that! Umm . . . With a blast of concentration, Reine wove a sloppy illusion of her spinal cord, but with all the parts in the wrong places. She made sure it was only a visual one. She didn't want to accidentally trick her body into thinking it was dying.

"What . . . what is this?"

Under normal circumstances, the mind-controller might be able to feel his way around her illusory maze, but he was panicked now. He didn't have the luxury of time to search, and Reine knew it. She separated a small part of her Goethan from the rest and sent it flying at her enemy. His power immediately formed a shield in the direction of the attack, the front of it hardening to deflect the incoming Goethan, but . . .

Like a mirage, the flying missile of power dissipated just as it reached the invader's defenses. She could almost picture the confusion on his face when it dawned on him too late that it was a trap.

Reine instantly smashed all of her power into his undefended back, dragging every last dreg from the depth of her mind and heart. Around her body, the illusions she had created broke one by one as they fed the fuel of her attack. Miniature explosions erupted at every point of contact.

Reine burned, but he burned too. *And who's the one with more power to spare?*

CHAPTER 4:
AN UNSURPRISING TRAGEDY

THE PAST: 4 ½ YEARS AGO

Reine balanced on the edge of the couch, pretending that the floor was filled with dangerous metaheroes. It had originally been lava, but then she had decided that heroes were more dangerous.

"Where's the remote?" her dad asked. He didn't like to spend money on luxury items because he thought stealing was unethical and dangerous, but both he and Amy had agreed that they needed a way to watch the news. Thankfully, a TV set wasn't very expensive. Reine cocked her head. His voice sounded weird, too bright, and his smile seemed forced.

Reine's mom reached out and passed her hand through the couch with a burst of Goethan. She blushed. "You scared me earlier when your experiment made that loud . . . bang. I fused the remote with the sofa by accident," she explained, half of her arm slightly transparent. It moved around freely, as if the couch didn't exist. "I'm just disentangling the atoms now."

Her voice sounded weird too. It was kind of subdued.

The explosion had scared Reine. She'd been sure that their neighbors would come yelling at them, but they didn't. That had happened last time. Hopefully, his experiments wouldn't be as violent in the future. She still didn't understand what he was making, but whatever it was sounded . . . deadly.

"Wow, Dad," Reine said sarcastically. "So it's your fault!"

He raised his hand in mock surrender.

Amy muttered to herself as she worked. "Hmmm . . . something trapped there? Ah . . . wait . . . damned hydrogen atoms."

She finally retracted her hand and held up a remote. "Done," she said with a satisfied grunt. "Now, who's ready to watch TV?"

"Me!" Reine cheered while her parents rolled their eyes.

Everyone got comfortable and sprawled on the couch. Amy's head was resting on Oliver's shoulder, so Reine didn't hear what her mom whispered to him before she turned on the TV. The words had sounded like ". . . be fine." The familiar theme of VBC news—a division of the Valmount Broadcasting Corporation—blasted out, prompting Oliver to turn down the volume.

"I hope our neighbors didn't hear that . . ." he muttered to himself. "They almost killed me last time for making popcorn."

Watching the news was a family tradition that Reine and her parents celebrated every day at 4:00 p.m. They used it to teach Reine about current events, since she couldn't go to school anymore. After all, the world wasn't a safe place. Crimes ravaged the poorer sections of the city, and the only result of a metahero interfering with a crime was unnecessary collateral damage—fighting fire with fire was not a good idea when the fire was replaced with the ability to blow out every window in a city block. Reine knew she was actually one of the lucky ones; at least her parents were former teachers, and even though they were also metahumans, they had useful enough powers to survive the stigma surrounding them.

The danger out there doesn't bother the rich neighborhoods near the center of the city, of course, Reine reflected. *Mom says they're all either extremely powerful metavillains, metaheroes, or government leaders who live there. I guess you can get away with anything if you have enough money.*

On the TV screen, a masked, leotard-clad woman walked in from the side. *Starflight.* She had on the gleaming eagle-shaped pin that all government metaheroes earn after graduating from their training program. Reine scratched her head, remembering the time she had asked her parents why they didn't just replicate the design in order to fool people. They had explained that the eagle pins had special properties that could only be produced by a metahuman named Geostone.

"Starflight's the head of the Metahero Force," Oliver warned Reine. "So it's probably going to be propaganda."

Reine nodded without taking her eyes off the TV. Starflight started talking to a meticulously dressed news anchor, who listened with an attentive grin. She turned to face the camera.

"I'm here today with Starflight, the most powerful hero in Valmount City!" the anchor brightly announced.

Beside Reine, Amy frowned, and darted a glance at her husband's face. He twisted his ring, marring his usually calm demeanor.

The news anchor cleared her throat. "I recently reached out to Starflight because I wanted to learn more about the burglary that she had prevented. From what I heard, the facility was a bank that held the money of the most influential government figures of the decade!"

The anchor's expression turned grave and she stared at Starflight. "Is it true that this entire operation was performed by a group of metavillains as a form of protest, and that it occurred in the richest section of the city?"

The masked hero shrugged in a nonchalant fashion. "It could have been. Yes." Smirking at the camera, Starflight continued, "But with the completely amateur approach those criminals took, even the police could have resolved it—"

Oliver clicked off the TV with a growl. He was breathing hard.

"Hey!" Reine complained, pouting. "I was watching that."

He ignored her, and handed the remote to Amy. "Here. Look at something else. I'm going to take a nap."

Groaning in frustration, Oliver stood up and strode towards the bedroom like an old man. Amy got up too, as if she wanted to comfort him, but thought better of it. Instead, she closed the door quietly after he exited.

"What happened to Dad?" Reine whispered to her mom. "Is he alright?"

Amy ruffled her hair. "Don't worry, honey. Your dad just isn't on very good terms with that woman, okay?"

Though she was only ten and a half, even Reine knew there was more to the story. But . . . seeing the state that her dad was in, she decided not to press her mom for information. She changed the subject.

"So . . . can we watch something else?"

This seemed to revitalize Amy.

"Sure," she said, turning on the TV. "I've been wanting to show you this documentary for weeks."

She started to browse through Hare'O with the remote, and Reine cocked her head thoughtfully. Hare'O was an internet streaming service that her parents never allowed her to use.

"It takes money to stream something," they had explained when Reine asked if they could watch a movie. "Best just to watch what's already being shown on TV."

The concept confused her. They spent a lot of money on textbooks, so why not more episodes of *Wonder Abby*?

"Found it," Amy said, putting her hands on her hips. "We're learning about the origin of metahumans today."

Reine perked up. "Really?" She loved the mystery that surrounded the existence of Goethan. The world before metahumans was so different that she couldn't imagine it even with the help of her dad's stories, so it must be pretty incredible to have such an impact.

"Of course. First, I'm going to tell you the basics, so you'll have some context for the video. Then we'll watch the documentary." Amy raised an eyebrow. "That sound good?"

Reine nodded.

"The first metahumans started appearing about ten years ago," Amy began. "I know you didn't experience the chaos that ensued because you were too young, but things weren't always like this." She spread her arms with a flourish, indicating the life they lived. "Can you picture it, Reine? A world where everyone was normal, where anyone could cross a street without being mugged?"

Reine shook her head. It was like trying to imagine a world without toilets.

"Not to say that there wasn't conflict or death. We had our fair share of problems too! It's just that . . . compared to now . . . the world was a whole lot better."

Amy hesitated for a second, reminiscing on the past. "Anyways," she continued briskly, "I just wanted to tell you that after the metahumans appeared, our government decided that we were too dangerous. After all, with all the potential damage that we could—and did—cause, it was easy for them to turn us into scapegoats." She exhaled, "I just wish they wouldn't lump us in with those monsters who actually committed the crimes. It makes it almost impossible for us to find work these days.

"Anyway," Amy concluded, "I'll leave you to watch the video now. If you don't understand anything, just come find me. Dad and I have to work on planning another protest—I mean project." Amy left, closing the door behind her.

Reine turned her attention back to the TV. After a minute of logos and advertisements—*Is everything made by Disney these days?*—the documentary finally began. Words started appearing, spelling "Metahumans: A Study" on the screen. Reine yawned. She was tempted to skip this part, but who knows what she might miss? The scene transitioned to a "mad scientist's" lab with a whoosh. The lab had stalactites hanging from the ceiling, and you could see strange liquids set on stone platforms with chains attached to them. As mysterious music started to pound, the camera slowly zoomed in on the back of a man's head.

"Hello," he whispered excitedly without turning around, "you're just in time to help me examine the model of a metahuman's cerebrum!"

The camera followed his pointed finger to land on a plastic-looking brain, and then focused back on the scientist's cheesy smile. He spoke in an overly enthusiastic voice. "I'm Professor Klay, and today we'll be learning about the Great Enhancement! The 'GE' happened ten years ago. No one could have missed it. Not only was it broadcast across numerous news channels, but the federal government announced that it would gather the country's brightest scientists to build a lab devoted to investigating this phenomenon, as well." He paused, pointing at the camera. "Not to mention that the research facility was subsequently pillaged and destroyed by a mysterious metavillain! The point is that some metahumans are immensely powerful. In fact, even though only one in about one thousand people is a metahuman, they're still managing to surpass the number of crime-related casualties for normal criminals."

Professor Klay heaved himself out of his chair and started jogging towards a projector screen. "But what makes these people—these metahumans—tick? How did this whole thing happen in the first place? To answer that question, we'll need to look at my trusty chart of a metahuman's mind." He gestured to the screen as it flickered to life. It displayed a normal human brain, but with one big difference.

"A common misconception of today's generation is that the Great Enhancement only affected the people we call metahumans. That is far from the truth. In fact, everything with . . .

awareness, from plants to human beings, naturally produces at least a small amount of Goethan."

His teeth gleamed. "This brain here . . . it's brimming with Goethan: a golden, mist-like substance. Much more than an unenhanced human possesses. What's interesting about this stuff is that it's half-grounded in reality, and half . . . not. You see, this strange material is constrained within the body—unless it's expelled from specific points like the heart and lungs. These Goethan points determine how the Goethan will be used."

With a wave of his hand, the screen changed, reading, "Fact Time!"

"Anyway," Klay continued, "here are a few things that scientists definitely know about metahumans. One: the more 'golden fog'—or Goethan—they have, the more powerful they are. Two: metahumans access this power through what they call the 'subconscious.' Though this is not proven, they definitely do enter a calmer and more concentrated state of mind when using their abilities. Three: most metahumans have only one specific power, and oftentimes it's useless. However, even though it is unknown if this uselessness is due to a mental limitation—since their brains are literally using their imaginations to change reality—or a Goethan limitation—maybe everyone's Goethan is unique and does different things—it is an established fact that the power they possess could range from having unbreakable fingernails to creating earthquakes."

The professor took a deep breath. He talked amazingly fast. "And now, if you'll excuse me, I must find my esteemed colleague to put on a demonstration."

As he walked off to who knows where, the video on-screen was replaced with a slide containing the three facts. Reine paused the documentary. She needed to write a few notes down before she forgot. She took out her piece of notepaper and pencil and rapidly jotted down the most important points.

"Yup . . . Three facts . . . Goethan? . . . Mist-like . . ." After she was done, Reine started the video again. It was very interesting, if not downright world-changing. Why hadn't her parents shown her this earlier?

On the TV screen, the list of facts transitioned back into the lab. This time, the camera focused on the backs of two people. One was Professor Klay, and the other was a man wearing . . . a really weird costume.

Reine couldn't stop herself. "What the heck is that?"

Not only did he have on a weirdly distorted donkey mask, the man had also donned a too-small T-shirt with spiral patterns swirling around.

"This," Professor Klay explained, as if to answer Reine's question, "is Charles, a.k.a. Telikiman. As you can guess, he has the power of telekinesis!"

Charles gave the camera a winning smile. "I am here today to demonstrate my awesome abilities," he proclaimed. "Behold as I lift up that duck!"

Lights flashed as a duck walked in. It immediately started floating towards the ceiling, where a spinning fan was located.

The panicked bird waved its wings to slow its ascent.

"Poor Abby," the professor laughed, "I guess you better *duck* your head."

Reine cringed, both at the animal cruelty . . . and the pun. "Mom?" she yelled. "I'm going to turn off the TV."

"What?"

"I can't watch this anymore."

Amy walked out of their bedroom, and Reine caught a glimpse of Oliver hunched over a couple of papers before she shut the door behind her. Her mom paused the TV. "But it's good for you."

"It's stupid." She crossed her arms. Amy opened her mouth to tell her off, and Reine quickly added, "I've been thinking about why Dad was so mad. It's because of the failed burglary we saw on TV, right?"

Her mom's expression was guarded. "It's a protest, honey. And maybe—well, that's part of it—but there's something else too. I don't think you want to know."

"C'mon! I can take it."

"Reine . . . fine." Amy sighed. She bit her lip. "You know how your friend Hae-Jin was coming tomorrow to train with you and your dad? She's not coming anymore because . . . It's Hae-Jin's father. He hanged himself in their living room while she was out with her mom."

Reine let the shock wash over her. It broke like a wave on rock.

"Is she okay?" Reine asked.

"Who?"

"Hae-Jin. Is she okay?"

"I'm sure . . . they're still mourning, but her mom is tough. She won't give up on her."

Reine nodded. She wasn't angry at Hae-Jin's dad, or particularly sad about his death, but she understood. The same thing happened in her preschool before it was shut down. One of the parents had turned out to be a metahuman like Hae-Jin's dad, and the rest was history. She got it. Some people just died when they had enough—it was a fact of life for metahumans. Reine *did* feel a dizzy sorrow when she tried to imagine what Hae-Jin was going through. She couldn't picture a world where her parents weren't helping her fill up the empty hours of the day with their interesting challenges and caring chatter.

Reine scowled and looked at Amy. She would do all the worksheets in the world to keep her parents happy, and no metahero was getting to *them* after she learned to fight better—to . . . hurt better.

Her mom looked back sadly.

CHAPTER 5:
MEETING NEW PEOPLE CAN BE WEIRD!

YEAR 2035

Reine smoothed out her shirt as she walked briskly down the underground hallway, then turned left through an arched opening. She knew she should be "leisurely touring the school," as the nurse put it, but there were a million other distractions that nibbled at her mind. Like the fact that she was covered in bruises . . . or that she had almost failed her entrance exam.

You need to rest, she scolded herself. *Your interview starts in thirty minutes.*

The school's interior walls were made of perfectly cut rock, as if someone had vaporized the excess stone and dirt instead of digging it out. She didn't know if it was true, but there was no denying the meticulous effect it created. The entire building was a symbol of Pantheon's triumph over nature. Even with almost everything made out of natural materials, it was still completely artificial. Kind of inspiring, really.

I wonder if he made this place himself, she contemplated. *What is his power?*

Reine had left the infirmary half an hour ago, promising to come back later. There were black-and-blue spots in places she hadn't even thought were possible to get bruises in. The nurse only agreed to discharge her because she didn't have any broken bones. Everything still hurt like hell. As Reine continued to pace around the corridors, she winced at the soreness in her legs until she couldn't stand it anymore and sat down. Unfortunately, that just left her alone with her thoughts, and she spent the next twenty minutes panicking about what she would do if she were kicked out of the academy.

I better get going to the meeting.

The truth was that Reine didn't know if it were possible for her to survive another year in the city. Not only would Starflight want retribution for her dead cadets, but Reine also had no other backup plan, nothing to look forward to. What was the point of living if you spent the rest of your life stealing and begging for food?

She suddenly remembered she was supposed to ask for pain medicine from the second infirmary in the north hall, but Reine didn't care; they were only contusions, and she had bigger worries. *Like the fact that you almost failed the entrance exam!* The thought popped up again for the hundredth time. She didn't even try to suppress it.

Wincing, Reine finally reached Pantheon's office. She started to turn the door handle with her bruised hands, and then stopped.

What if m—

"**Come in!**"

Reine jumped. Pantheon's voice was so filled with authority that she didn't know if she was ever going to get used to it. Starflight's presence was already intimidating enough, but he was something . . . more.

"**No need to be nervous,**" the man continued. Reine could imagine the impassiveness etched across his face.

She cursed under her breath. *First impression . . . ruined.* Plastering on a grin—she imagined it looked more like a grimace from the pain—Reine walked through the door.

It was a pretty cozy place. Two comfortable-looking armchairs sat in the center of the room with a cluttered desk and a roaring fireplace. Briefly, Reine wondered how he managed to get the smoke out with no chimney.

"**Hello?**"

Damn it.

Reine jerked out of her reverie to see Pantheon raising a questioning eyebrow at her.

"Uh-um," she stuttered, "Uh, hi?" She hated that she couldn't think of anything else to say, but something about the villain was putting her on edge. The room was so charged with Goethan that the air itself seemed to crackle, reminding her of the night of her mom's death. *It's just a trick, Reine. Snap out of it.*

"Sir?" The word felt unfamiliar in her mouth. "I was given directions to come here by the nurse."

See? That wasn't so hard.

"**Of course you were,**" Pantheon replied. "**Now focus, please. We've wasted enough time already.**"

Reine complied; he didn't exactly seem to be in the mood for pleasantries.

"**Good,**" he continued, gesturing to an unoccupied armchair in front of his desk, "**We are here to discuss your test scores.**"

Reine straightened her back and stepped lightly to the seat and sat down. *Remember,* she told herself. *Just let Pantheon do the talking.* Being raised as an only child with no friends had done nothing for her social skills.

"**You were paired against Samuel, correct? Was his last name Miller?**"

Reine nodded. After the test, she had asked for more information about her assailant, but the nurse had only given her his name.

"**Hmmm . . .**" Pantheon continued absently, staring at his laptop screen. "**Ah . . . here it is. I found it.**" He turned his screen around so that she could see.

"**As you probably have guessed, Samuel had the power of mind control.**"

The villain gestured at a small line of text on the monitor. "**More specifically, Samuel had the ability to control your muscles through the brain.**" He gave Reine a pointed look. "**Do you understand what that means?**"

She quailed under his gaze. "Um . . . No?"

Pantheon's voice seemed to grow more dangerous. "**It means that he could have killed you before you even knew he was there.**"

Damn it. I should have attempted to access the third level as soon as I woke up.

Pantheon continued indifferently, "**Instead of playing around with your limbs, he could have gone directly for your heart.**"

"Bu-but . . ." Reine tried to argue. *So I made one* mistake. *Is that really so unforgivable?*

"**But what?**"

Reine gritted her teeth. "Nothing."

The corners of Pantheon's mouth drifted ever so slightly upwards. "**Of course,**" he said, amused. "**It was also very impressive that you managed to defeat Samuel with so little training. The potential is definitely there.**"

Reine's hopes rose like a balloon.

"**In fact, I find your power quite fascinating. What is it again?**"

"I'm not so sure myself," Reine replied excitedly. "Probably something to do with illusions."

Though she didn't show it, her heart felt like it was about to burst out of her chest. This was her chance! Pantheon opened a file on his laptop again.

"Hmmmm," he pondered. "It seems that my analysts think you have the power of biological control under the category of 'Illusionary Manipulation.'"

What the hell does that mean?

Before Reine could ask, Pantheon continued explaining. "Don't worry about understanding anything now. You'll learn about it in class. Suffice to say that you have the power to create any illusion related to the body. Got it?"

Reine had already stopped listening. *Did he say . . . class? Have I passed?*

"Got it?"

She nodded numbly.

"Good, because I'm only explaining it once. Now go." Pantheon gestured slightly at the door. Reine didn't need to be asked twice.

"Though your lack of skill *is* quite unforgivable . . ." he called after her. "If only you had started your education earlier . . ."

She froze, her heart skipping a beat.

"But then . . . what else is school for, than to teach the inexperienced?"

Reine would have kicked him if her body didn't ache so much—and if he couldn't snap her like a twig in retaliation.

An hour later, after she had been assigned to a dorm room in dormitory three with a roommate that she hadn't even met yet, and unpacked her meager belongings—a few sets of clothes, a water bottle, and some old food—while also gathering toiletries from various places in the underground facility, Reine was exhausted.

But that didn't mean she wasn't nervous.

Damn it, Reine, they're just people. Who cares if they don't like you? Walk into that classroom like you belong!

She took a deep breath. *Yup. Just school. Sure, it's a villain's school, but it can't be that different . . . right?* Not that she's ever been to a proper school either . . .

Scowling, Reine pulled open the door to her first and—for now—only class. Her schedule wasn't established yet, so she still needed to pick her courses. A couple students glanced up with interest as she entered.

Relax, she told herself. *It's the first day of the school year. They're just looking for their friends.*

She glanced at the left wall of the classroom—shiny rock lined with shelves of graphs and tablets—in order to avoid making eye contact with anyone as she found an empty desk. She never saw the teen walking in the opposite direction until it was too late.

"Oh, sorry. Let me help you with that!" The pretty young woman held out her hand. Reine picked herself up but accepted the notebook when it was given to her. She usually wouldn't have been bothered by something as small as this, but her jumpy nerves made it seem more serious than it was.

"It's fine," Reine replied quietly and brushed herself off.

The other students in the class were staring at them as if their conversation were the most interesting thing they had ever seen. As Reine tried to ignore them, their stares turned to glares, and she stepped back, confused.

"You're not supposed to talk to Sky—" a guy spoke up, stopping when his friend shushed him. Everyone seemed conflicted.

Reine looked around her. *What is going on?*

"She's new, so she doesn't know," another person whispered, her voice small but audible in the silence. "We have to give Sky a chance, anyways. Wasn't that part of the deal?"

Reine wanted answers. She strode towards the nearest student but hesitated when he turned away. She didn't push it. When everyone had lost interest and returned to their chatting, she pulled the young woman out into the hallway.

"Who are you?" she hissed. "Is this a social norm or something?"

The stranger appeared disoriented, but then quickly recovered. It was a weird transition. Though the other girl looked nervous, Reine swore she saw something calculating in her face.

"Hi!" she said, shaking Reine's hands vigorously. "I'm Sky!"

Reine stopped herself from pulling away and sized her up. Sky had ginger hair, light freckles, and mischievous green eyes. Probably younger—maybe fourteen. *She's definitely someone I would remember . . . if I had seen her before.*

"Do I know you?" she asked, mentally preparing herself for an attack.

"No," Sky responded cheerfully, "but I know you." She stared at her with hopeful eyes.

Huh. That enthusiasm is definitely faked. She doesn't strike me as dangerous, though—just desperate.

Reine ran her hand through her hair. Maybe if she could ask the right questions . . .

"I'm your roommate! I was watching you while you unpacked," Sky said.

Never mind about that.

"Wait," Reine said. "You were stalking me?"

"Of course not!" Sky pouted, offended. "You just walked in while I was practicing my power!"

Of course. So obvious.

"See that?" Sky said, pointing at a small notice pinned on the opposite side of the hallway. "What does it say?"

Reine narrowed her eyes, but the tiny text eluded her. She shrugged. "No idea."

"Well. To me it says, 'Playing reruns in the *Wonder Abby* club,'" Sky said, gesturing to a room further down the hall.

"Huh," Reine said. She decided to trust her on it. "How could you have seen me in the dorm room, though? I was behind a wall." *Does she have x-ray vision too?*

Sky stared at her in disbelief. "I also have super hearing, you know, and all the rest of that stuff. When I heard footsteps pounding in my room, I obviously had to go investigate. So I just looked through the blinds of our room's window, and there you were!"

Note to self: close the blinds when you're trying to do something secret. "Well . . . that explains it, I guess." Reine hesitated, feeling like there was something she wasn't getting. "Nice to meet you, Sky."

Sky laughed. "Nice to meet you too."

Opening the door, they both turned back to find their seats, but Reine was slower. She was still kind of dazed from the conversation. It felt weird to speak with someone her age—well, a little younger—so casually. Mostly, when she met someone new, it was because she was climbing into their room under the cover of night.

Something caught Reine's eye. *Wait . . . is that . . .*

She could see the hint of a scar peeking out from behind Sky's hair. Reine had mistaken it for a birthmark, but it was actually a burn of some kind on her neck.

Seems to be mostly healed though. Must have happened at least a year ago. Suddenly self-conscious about staring, Reine found her seat in the corner and sat down.

You know . . . I just realized something, she thought as her heartbeat slowed. *She never explained why our classmates were so angry at our conversation.*

CHAPTER 6:

WHAT IN THE WORLD IS THE SUBCONSCIOUS?

YEAR 2035

"Hello, students, and welcome to 'The Biology of Metahumans.' Today, we'll be reviewing some basics for the newcomers . . . and the idiots who can't remember anything despite having been in my class for the past few years," the teacher said, straightening his blue bow tie and suit jacket as he chuckled to show he wasn't being serious.

Sky smiled when everyone else started to laugh. *Typical Mr. Nidek, always starting off class with a joke,* she thought. For some reason, she felt better this semester . . . more hopeful. Not like one of those sappy romance novels where the protagonist feels like she's about to fly off into the infinite reaches of space while her heart bubbles with joy—but instead, a general sense of optimism.

After all, it's been more than half a year. Maybe they'll finally forgive me for my father's death. She opened her backpack. *Maybe even I will.* Just thinking about him reopened an old wound, literally. The scar at the back of her neck throbbed. Though an entire semester had gone by, she still felt as if the healing process was far from complete.

Be optimistic, Sky, she chided herself. *Look on the bright side! That new girl—what was her name again—is another reason to be happy. She could be the one to finally stop the school from shunning me. All I have to do is make a good first impression, and my new roommate won't suspect a thing. She doesn't know about the bet after all . . .*

"Hey, Mr. Nidek," a nasally voice piped up, "why are we wasting time on stuff we already know? I'm sure *anyone's* parents would have at least taught them the basics!"

A sullen-looking girl beside him nodded in agreement. Sky wasn't fooled by her apparent lack of involvement; she was putting him up to it. Even though he was annoying too, Abby was way worse than Asher. He had at least been nice until the bully persuaded him to join her friend group.

Sky groaned silently. During the winter break, she had almost managed to wipe all knowledge of them from her mind, and would have liked to keep it that way. *What asshats! Having powerful parents doesn't mean everyone else does.*

Mr. Nidek gave Asher a warning look. "Hey. Haven't we talked about not mouthing off in class? You're . . . what, fifteen for heaven's sake?"

Sixteen, actually. He was held back a year for failing to protect his partner on a mission.

Asher ignored the jibe with a sneer. He had heard it way too many times. "You still haven't answered my question," he replied.

Mr. Nidek twiddled his thumbs, obviously debating with himself. Sky knew he was conflicted about whether to give in to Asher's request because this situation had already played itself out *way* too many times.

Just ignore him, will ya? She wanted to say it out loud, but that would only damage her already-failing chances at ever having someone talk to her again. Most of the students in her class might not like Asher, but they hated her even more.

As she expected, the teacher ignored her silent suggestions. Instead, he turned back to the class. "Fine." He rubbed his forehead. "I might as well introduce our new student then."

He smiled at Reine. "Would you please stand up so that everybody can see you?"

She did. "Um. Hi. I'm Reine."

Oh, so that's her name. I wonder what her power is . . . It must be pretty good for Pantheon to let her in at such a late age.

Oblivious to Reine's discomfort, Mr. Nidek continued by raising his voice to drown out Asher's complaints. "This is Reine, our newest student. To answer Asher's question . . . yes. Her parents have already taught her a lot about biology and history, as shown by her use of it during the entrance exam."

I heard she fought Samuel. That guy is sadistic.

"Unlike you, however," Mr. Nidek jabbed, built-up resentment from last year breaking through. "She scored an average of 9.3 .. . and she didn't even have anyone to teach her 'the basics!'"

Out of the corner of her eye, Sky could see Reine scowling at the praise. *Doesn't seem too easily flattered,* she noted. *Or maybe she doesn't like Mr. Nidek using her accomplishments for his own ends. It's going to be tricky to prove Abby wrong.*

Asher muttered something that might have been "whatever."

"That's what I thought," Mr. Nidek finished. "Now, as I was saying . . ."

He booted up the projector, and Sky got out her laptop, ready to take notes.

You know, Asher has a point, she thought to herself as she waited. *Everyone here seems to have been in this class since they were ten. Why didn't Reine's parents enroll her in this school?* She paused.

Maybe it's because—

Mr. Nidek's voice interrupted her train of thought. "Alright, class, get out your computers to take notes. You may use paper too, if you want."

Sky sighed. From the corner of her eye, she could see Reine pulling out a pencil. *The fact that people still use paper instead of electronics never fails to surprise me.*

The teacher pointed at the screen and pulled up a list with his remote.

"For many of you, this chart looks familiar because we went over it last year. Don't worry—it's not the same. Not only have I added extra details and information to the different levels of the subconscious, there are also several new levels that we'll be going over today."

Instantly, the class filled with soft muttering. Sky wished she could join in on their conversations.

"But," Mr. Nidek continued cheerfully, "We still have to review last year's material first. So if you bear with me on this, we'll be moving on to more interesting stuff in no time." A few half-hearted boos rang out from where Asher was sitting, but stopped when the entire class turned to glare balefully at him.

Some people were just too annoying.

"Quick recap: who can define the levels of subconscious?" Mr. Nidek asked, clapping his hands to get their attention.

A student, Annette, raised her hand. She was wearing a beanie and a sweatshirt with egg-shaped designs on it. She was wearing a beanie and a sweatshirt with egg-shaped designs on it. "Um .. . An ascending scale from one to ten that measures how deeply submerged you are in your subconscious?"

"Completely correct," he said and beamed proudly. "Ten being the most immersed, and one being the least. Now," Mr. Nidek continued, "who can tell me what these levels of subconsciousness do?"

"Do?"

Sky and her classmates turned to look at Reine. She shrank back, embarrassed.

Oh yeah. She's homeschooled right? Probably just used to asking her parents without raising her hand.

"Do," Mr. Nidek confirmed without missing a beat. "As you may know, each level of the subconsciousness lets you access certain aspects of your powers. These powers vary for everyone, but the general principles are mostly the same. Anyways . . . would someone like to give it a shot?"

Twenty hands went up.

Scratching his chin, Mr. Nidek stared in contemplation for a second. "Um, Isaac."

Isaac, Mr. Nidek's son, stood up and glared at him venomously. Sky was shocked by the amount of hate in his eyes. She guessed some things never changed.

"Well . . . the chart says that the first level allows you to manipulate your surroundings with your powers, but it only applies to inanimate objects," Isaac explained without much inflection. "The second level gives the ability to affect any life-forms that have little or no cognitive functions, such as plants or insects. However, smarter and more complex creatures can also be influenced; it just takes way more power. From what I've experienced, it also extends the range of the first level of the subconscious."

Isaac glanced at Mr. Nidek questioningly. He nodded and motioned for his son to sit.

"In case you guys didn't know, once you enter a level of the subconscious, you won't come out until you release your hold on it. This means that it's possible to be in both the first and second level at once."

Well . . . for everyone else, yes. Not for me. Sky felt the back of her neck prickle. The wound had damaged one of her Goethan outlets: points in the body where you could expel Goethan to produce a specific function. They didn't look any different—at least not physically—but were connected to the metaphysical in a way that pioneers of metahuman science were still investigating.

She sighed. In her case, the point at the neck was where the second level acted through, so she couldn't access its uses even if she submerged her mind.

Not that it's that important . . . why would I need to sense plants and animals anyways?

She propped up her head with a hand.

From her seat at the edge of the classroom, Sky could see Asher opening his mouth. *He's probably going to complain about the amount of time the explanation is taking,* she thought dryly.

The teacher tried to cut him off before he could start. "Of course, the more levels you are immersed in at once, the harder it gets to concentrate. Without training, you most likely won't be able to enter the first level and keep it open for more than a minute! Moreover, the higher the level, the harder it is to connect with. Most metahumans can only enter the fifth level, and no higher."

A student raised her hand, but Asher beat her to it. "But it takes so long to immerse yourself, Mr. Nidek," he complained. "Even if you could go through all these procedures at high speeds without getting distracted, your enemy will have shot you before you can finish."

Mr. Nidek smiled wearily. "Good point, Asher, but we'll be going over that later in the school year. For now, you'll just have to be content with this."

"But that's exactly what I'm talking about," he replied, throwing his hands above his head. "Why are we reviewing this useless stuff if we could just learn better things now?"

Groans permeated the room as Sky shook her head. *I swear . . . if that guy speaks again, I'm going to kill him.*

"Anyway," Mr. Nidek said, "Isaac, would you please tell us about the third level?"

"Sure." He kept his voice neutral and stood up again. "Unlike the first two, this level allows you to directly affect your own body with your power. Most people find this useless because their power—say, the ability to control the weather—does not benefit their anatomy in any way, but it's still extremely effective at defending yourself from other attackers because it is the only level that allows you to manipulate Goethan within the confines of your body."

"Of course," Isaac added, "it is also the only instance when the Goethan is in physical form."

He shot another glare at his father and sat back down. Sky knew he was trying to spite Mr. Nidek for not living up to his expectations, but did he have to be so harsh? Sky understood the pressures of being overshadowed by her dad's legacy; Isaac had the same problem, but reversed. People didn't believe in him because Mr. Nidek had only ever reached the fourth level. No amount of ingenuity could outweigh a bad power and weak Goethan capacity, and it was one of the reasons why Pantheon had forced him to teach instead of working in the city. It didn't help that Isaac had high ambitions.

Asher suddenly exploded. "And why don't you just explain everything else to us, know-it-all?" he said, obviously disgruntled at being ignored by the teacher. He turned to Isaac. "You should know, being the son of that useless coward."

At the front of the classroom, Mr. Nidek's face turned a deep shade of red. "That's enough, Asher," he said. "Don't insult Isaac just because you're mad at me for bruising your ego."

Asher's lips drew into a snarl. "But it's true, isn't it? You're teaching him things that you're not teaching us!" He accused.

Mr. Nidek's body quivered as he tried to restrain his anger. The man was gripping his whiteboard marker like a lifeline. "I said, *that's enough.*"

Sky noticed that Isaac didn't seem to share Mr. Nidek's rage. He ignored them both and studied something on his laptop—which infuriated Asher even more. "I'm insulting you, not your father, moron."

Sky turned away to look at Reine again and tried to ignore their bickering. She imagined what it must be like to transfer to a new school. *I really need to get to know her better. Should I . . . no.* She shuddered. Deep inside, Sky felt kind of guilty about her deceit. Sure, Abby was the one forcing her to become more coldhearted with her evil game, but that didn't mean she was completely faultless . . . *Argh. Don't think like that, Sky! No matter what, you've got to win that bet.*

She rubbed the back of her neck out of habit. A semester with everyone ignoring or jeering at her had been . . . well, terrible. After all, what use had they for a villain that was no better than a metahero? She had brought down one of the founding members of Pantheon's academy, and even worse, refused to die when it happened. So what if that person had been her dad, saving her out of love? She was a failure anyhow—one who didn't deserve to be acknowledged.

Sky sighed, thinking back to the time when her isolation had just begun. The silence had only lasted a week back then, but she had already been restless for human attention. Her classmates had chosen to desert her at the worst time possible. Just when she needed a shoulder to cry on, to accept her father's death, her "friends" had all abandoned her. It was like a nightmare come true. *No*, she corrected herself, *not just a nightmare. Something even worse.*

When Abby had confronted Sky in the hallway at the start of the semester, she was given a choice. It was foolish to accept, but how could she say no?

"What do you want?" Sky asked defensively, hoping against hope for a nice conversation. "I have to get to class, you know."

The girl laughed. Abby was the kind of person who was more likely to stab you in the back than say hello, so she either had a plan up her sleeve . . . or just wanted to torment her. Sky suspected the latter. Her reputation was in such tatters that even a double-crosser like Abby wouldn't be punished for roughing her up a little.

"It's not like I'm not doing you a favor," Abby answered in an infuriating tone. "No one wants you in their class, anyway."

Sky winced, but not from Abby's comment. Sky had already heard too much of the same thing from the likes of Asher and his cronies to be affected. Gingerly, she felt the bandages around her neck. They were scratching the burn wound again.

"I better go get some more salve," she muttered to herself, ignoring Abby. The girl could wait if she wanted to talk.

Abby evidently didn't feel the same. "Are you even listening to me?" she demanded.

Sky didn't reply. Instead, she started to walk away, hoping to alleviate the burning in her neck as soon as possible. A throng of people stopped her immediately. They had formed a ring around the two students, obviously sensing a fight. She growled in frustration. Abby was a known troublemaker who preferred to sabotage rather than fight. That was what made her so dangerous. If Sky appeared weak and backed off from a known coward, she could kiss her chance at regaining respect goodbye. On the other hand . . .

Sky turned to face Abby, sensing an opportunity. They both straightened their postures unconsciously.

"You think I don't deserve to be in this school?" Sky challenged, more for the benefit of their spectators than Abby.

"That's right," the girl replied confidently. She turned to the surrounding people. "Right, guys?"

Sky's heart sank when they glanced at each other, and then nodded, but she forced a smile anyways. Anything to project strength.

"Like I care," she bluffed to them, "I bet you're just angry you weren't there. *I'm* the one who actually fought Starflight."

Abby's laugh was vicious. "Fought? You mean helped her like a good little . . . 'metahero?'" she asked mockingly.

The people around her immediately started chuckling—and for good reason. It was the worst insult you could give someone. The laughing turned to jeering.

"Like you're one to talk," Sky shot back. "What does a backstabbing snake like you know about bravery?"

Abby's smile turned to a frown. She knew that she was a turncoat but didn't want to admit it.

"What are you jabbering about now?" she answered instead, feigning innocence. Sky's blood boiled when the spectators decided to support Abby for the second time that day, yelling things like "liar" and "what *is* she talking about?" in a hundred different shades of sarcasm. She seethed, knowing there was no way she could win them over.

Those asshats, she thought. *Might as well teach them a lesson then.*

Sky rushed forwards and punched the bully in her face.

An audible gasp rose from the spectators; they hadn't expected her to go so far. Breathing hard, Sky ignored the throbbing pain in her hand and Abby's dazed groan. She didn't even stop to wonder if a teacher was nearby. The whole week could damn itself to Pantheon's wrath for all she cared.

Excited murmuring intensified behind her. She turned around to face the disturbance, just in time to avoid Abby's attack. The girl stumbled wildly towards her and tried to claw at her face. She missed by a mile. Sky concentrated on entering the first level. Judging by the way people were scrambling to get out of Abby's way, her destruction powers were definitely activated.

Sky grimaced. The lowest level that could let you affect humans was the fourth level—a level that Mr. Nidek promised to teach them sometime this week—but Abby's powerful parents had already tutored her in private. Sky's suspicions were confirmed a second later when Abby's hand skimmed another person's hair and it dissolved into dust.

The student's horrified scream was wiped away with a blast of clarity as Sky entered the first level of the subconscious. She frantically moved her Goethan reserves to the brain, where she could use it to detect inanimate objects.

"What are you going to do now, Sky?" Abby gloated.

She had escaped the crowd and was now directly facing her. Her hands crawled with disintegrating ash—still Goethan, but gray. Sky gave her a pained smile. Abby's powers required her to touch whatever object she wanted to destroy, and if there was one thing Sky was good at, it was dodging other people's attacks.

Closing her eyes, she extended her senses to the air around her. Though she couldn't detect Abby with only the first level, Sky could use the movement of the air to alert her of her opponent's every move. "Better smart than strong" was what her father used to say.

The teacher's here.

Sky cracked open an eye to see Mrs. Wu wading through a sea of students to get at them. That was good. All she had to do was survive until she arrived. Narrowly dodging a lunge—she could feel Abby's movements a second faster than normal, but that didn't mean her reflexes were on par—Sky started running towards the teacher, who was now threatening them with suspension.

"Get back here, coward!" Abby screamed as soon as she realized her failure. "We're not done yet."

Sky didn't stop. "Nope," she yelled back.

"It's your fault!" Abby seethed. "You took Eajesuth away from us. He died saving you because you were too weak to save yourself, and now our school is suffering the consequences." She turned to the students around them. "How many of you were recruited by him? Rescued by him? He gave us a home, and Sky ruined it."

Sky scowled as she slowed to a halt. "It's not like that," she said, unsure. She turned around. "Look. I tried, okay? He was my dad, and I—I just couldn't."

It was Abby's turn to walk away; she had regained her composure. "You see?" she asked, capturing the attention of the people around her. "She's not one of us! She's not ruthless or strong or even brave. She useless."

Sky's face flushed red. "Okay. I get that he was important to you as well, but don't speak to me like that. You don't—you can't know what it was like. I loved him."

Abby turned around. They glared at each other, and Sky noticed a tear in the corner of Abby's eye. *This isn't all an act,* she realized.

"Then how about this?" Abby offered, turning away. "If you can show you're a true metavillain, I'll make sure everyone forgives you for your father's death." She paused. "Next time a new student arrives, you have to befriend . . . and then betray them."

"What?"

"But if you fail . . . you'll publicly apologize to the school for not having the guts to hurt someone, then leave forever. Deal?"

Trapped by the gaze of her fellow classmates, Sky could only nod.

A shout from Mr. Nidek yanked her attention back to the present.

"So you want to know how to access each level through a shortcut, huh? Well, why don't you show me your mastery of the third level first?"

Asher smiled smugly, and lightning rippled between his fingers, "Maybe I will."

Sky scratched the back of her neck. The air was thick with ozone. *Mr. Nidek better not get hurt. Asher's unskilled, but he can control the weather. Our teacher doesn't stand a chance.*

As if blatantly ignoring Sky's advice, Mr. Nidek made a gesture with his palm at Asher. "If you can defend against this, I'll give you the password to the archives myself."

"Sure." Asher was cocky—he had obviously realized the same thing as Sky. "Bring it on."

Mr. Nidek smiled back.

Asher doubled over and started coughing, water coming out of his nose and mouth. Mr. Nidek was condensing water molecules from the air in his lungs. It slowed as he used them all up, but returned full force when Asher gasped, bringing in a fresh lungful of water-laden air. From her corner, Sky winced as Asher's face scrunched up in concentration, then turned to panic when his attempts were broken by a coughing fit. Her classmates had the same reaction as her; they weren't *completely* heartless.

"Uh. Mr. Nidek," Sky said. Everyone was so nervous that they didn't even glare at her. "I think that's enough."

He continued staring at Asher's struggling form as if he hadn't heard her.

"My point is," she continued cautiously, trying again, "I mean . . . c'mon, his face is turning blue! And he's lying on the ground!"

Mr. Nidek brushed her comment off again, shrugging. He was too angry for rational decisions now.

Sky turned to her classmates for help. She disliked Asher as much as they did, but that didn't mean she was willing to see him die. She glanced at Reine. Her roommate looked resigned, as if she would like to help, but knew it was too risky.

"Guys! He's dying. Do something!" Sky pleaded.

Damn. No reaction. They're either too shocked—or just plain ignoring me. Growling, Sky rushed forwards. If her classmates weren't going to help, then she would have to help him herself.

"Reine," she shouted and pulled her roommate up from her chair, "Go call the nurse using that yellow button near the door."

Reine stood up reluctantly, but wasn't about to refuse to save someone's life. Determination replaced the hesitant expression on her face.

"Fine," Reine said grudgingly, running off.

Now for the teacher. Sky ran in front of Mr. Nidek and waved her hands tentatively, hoping to break his concentration along with his line of sight. Nothing happened. *Damn, the guy is already too immersed. I'm going to need to try something a bit more . . . violent.*

She took a deep, rattling breath. "Sorry about this."

Using a Muay Thai head kick that she had learned in the mandatory self-defense class, Sky's foot arced through the air. It seemed to happen in slow motion. Her brain struggled with an instant of self-doubt, guilt, and worry as she watched her foot approach his face. She almost pulled it back—just a little lower, even—but managed to follow through instead.

Mr. Nidek's body hit the floor with a thud. The force of the kick had snapped his jaw shut with such a loud snap that every kid winced. He was knocked out cold.

Wow. Did I just . . .

Sky sat down, shocked. *Did I just kick a teacher?*

The rest of the day passed quickly for Sky, and her classes seemed to end in minutes. She knew what she did was a punishable offense. She didn't care. Sky felt a sense of euphoria.

People were just looking at me! she realized giddily. *And they weren't even glaring!* In fact, one person had gone as far as to say a tiny "hello." She smiled to herself. *I'm still going to have to win the bet, of course. Things aren't going to change after only a day of work. But* . . . Sky laid down, feeling hope blossoming in her mind.

Maybe . . . just maybe . . . It'll be better this semester.

CHAPTER 7:
THE MORE YOU STEAL, THE MORE YOU LOSE

THE PAST: 2 ½ YEARS AGO

Reine glanced around nervously as she snuck through the streets, keeping an eye out for any metahumans that could be hiding in the dead of night. Rivulets of rainwater flowed into cracks in the concrete. Her parents followed closely behind, concealed in shadows. They were going to rob a house.

Looking left and right, Reine made an "all clear" sign behind her back. She was anxious, but also exhilarated. A slight breeze carried the last drops of yesterday's rain—it was just after midnight—onto her jacket. There was something magical about a robbery. Her parents only stole out of necessity, and Reine did too, but she tried to enjoy it as much as she could. There was no room for guilt or indecision if they wanted to succeed. She needed to think of it as normal, not taboo.

Reine took a deep breath and motioned for her mom to begin cracking the lock to the door. Her role tonight was to be the scout, and she was relieved that the operation was going so smoothly. Amy nodded in affirmation, sweat gleaming on her face. Reine grinned. She felt the same way. After all, this was no ordinary robbery—it was an attack on Starflight herself.

As she watched her mom work, phasing through the door to turn the lock on the other side, Reine thought back to a few months ago, when her parents had first told her they were villains.

"Reine, we're going to reveal a secret to you, okay?" Oliver asked.

"Sure," Reine replied and brushed a pamphlet to the side. She had been working hard on studying the political situation in Valmount City. It was pretty interesting to compare the propaganda of the government against the illegal stuff that the meta-villains and their allies spread.

Her dad sat down on the opposite side of the dining table that doubled as his workbench and Reine's desk.

"The thing is," he continued hesitantly while Amy looked on, "we haven't been totally truthful about what we do for a living."

Seriously? They waited till my twelfth birthday to tell me this?

Reine decided to play along. "Um . . . what?" She raised an eyebrow, finally able to use the move she had perfected after hours of practice. It was fun to see her mom be on the receiving end of it for a change.

"Well." Oliver paused. "I mean . . . how do I phrase this . . . um . . ."

His wife finished for him. "We benefit off others by occasionally taking goods from financial institutions and places of residence. We also use it as a form of protest."

Reine had to stop herself from laughing. "You're robbers," she replied flatly.

Her mother winced and said, "If you want to put it that way . . . yes."

"You're robbers," she repeated again, disbelievingly, "and you didn't tell me?"

Her mother reached out to try and comfort her, but Reine batted her hand away.

"We've been training you for a long time now," Amy told her desperately. "I'm sorry, but we had to!"

Reine shook her head, "I know that! But what I'm trying to say is . . . I totally support your decisions."

The answer was so unexpected that Oliver and Amy both stopped dead. Reine could almost hear the gears turning in their heads.

"So you knew all along?" her father asked cautiously.

"Of course!" Reine replied, disguising her amusement with exasperation, "I had my suspicions, and it's pretty hard to hide your equipment when there's literally two rooms in the apartment."

"And you're okay with . . . our choices?"

"Of course I'm okay with them! I've been looking at the news articles you gave me, and basically every metahuman is either a corrupt and murderous law enforcement officer or a thief. The metaheroes take most of the taxes and kill even the smallest of 'criminals' for money, so I already knew you guys would never go that low."

Reine paused as a thought struck her. "Just asking—why *did* you decide to tell me? I mean . . . sure it's my birthday, but did you really think that spilling your secret criminal lives is a great present?"

Oliver grinned sheepishly and cleared his throat.

"Not quite," he said, determined to take back his role as the parent. "We just thought twelve means you're old enough to start helping us with our operations, and it gives us enough time to start training you before we attempt to rob our biggest target yet."

"Recently we discovered the location of a house in the richer areas of the city," Amy said excitedly. "It's one of Starflight's smaller bases, but it's perfect for our purposes. I feel no guilt stealing from that monster, and we might even get enough money to live a normal life for a while."

Reine wondered if they were the ones playing with her. "Starflight? That metahero you guys hate? The one that's on every TV channel for killing villains all the time?"

"Yup," Oliver said proudly. "The house may not contain a lot, but its unimportance also means that there won't be many guards, if any."

Amy grinned. "Revenge is going to be soooo sweet . . . and we want you to taste it too."

Now Reine was standing in front of a building she had never been in but knew like the back of her hand; repeatedly looking at and sketching the floor plan allowed for that. They'd bought the building's information from a bitter but trustworthy villain, paying almost the same price to keep his silence. Her parents basically treated the map like it was made of pure gold.

Honestly though, we might have overplanned a bit, Reine thought. *It is just a house, after all. Even if Starflight owns it.* She ran through the skills she'd gradually picked up from her parents' training in her head—nothing major, just basic stuff like sneaking around and surveillance equipment evasion—and crept cautiously through the open doorway her mom had created.

"Everything clear?" she whispered to her dad.

He nodded slightly. "I scrambled the proximity sensors with my powers, and your mom already took out the two guards."

Without the threat of being watched looming over her head, Reine darted up the stairs with her dad and turned left into the control room. As planned, Amy had knocked out the guards with a few enhanced tranquilizer darts her husband had created.

"Good job," she said, kissing him on the cheek. "They worked perfectly."

Reine smiled. Her dad occasionally invented weapons based on his own abilities. Being a metahuman who could nullify the power inside anything—be it Goethan in a metahuman, or electricity running through the security cameras—Oliver thought it was more ethical to use nonlethal weaponry.

She assessed her surroundings. It had been hard to judge the details or even the size of the building outside in the dark, but the rooms inside Starflight's house were all illuminated by multiple light bulbs. She marveled at the waste of electricity.

"Anyway," Amy said, and Reine stopped staring at the chandelier, "let's get to work searching the house for anything worth stealing. We only have four hours until sunrise."

This shouldn't be too hard. I was expecting the base to be some sort of hulking warehouse or something, but it's nothing more than a big house. I guess Starflight only cares about her main headquarters.

"Maybe less," Oliver added. "My tranquilizer darts will only knock them out for three hours, so we need to move fast. Plus, we can't take any chances. If someone comes to check on this base, they'll alert Starflight about the disturbance."

Reine nodded grimly; she understood the risks. With a final "good luck," the three thieves parted ways, the patterned carpet muffling their already quiet footsteps.

As she trudged through the house, Reine felt fear replacing her receding adrenaline. They were in enemy territory, after all. What if her parents were wrong and missed a guard? Even worse, what if they had triggered an alarm, and didn't know it? *Shoot.* Just thinking about it made Reine shudder. Starflight would be on them in a second.

With a grunt, Reine popped quietly into a bedroom and took an alarm clock off the nightstand; the one they had at home was breaking down. She also snuck a few golden bracelets off the dressing table before exiting back out the door. Her backpack was quickly getting heavier, and she felt a pang of guilt. If the world she lived in was unjust, did that make it right to steal?

We already discussed this, Reine told herself sternly. *Steal now, question your morality later. No point in getting distracted.*

Out in the hallway, she pushed open another door with a creak and peeked into what looked like a study. A wooden desk sat on the far left side of the room, and bookshelves stocked full of binders lined the walls. Walking slowly—and a little confused about where to start—Reine decided to take a look at what was on the desk. *Probably nothing important,* she figured. Starflight wouldn't keep classified information in her smaller bases, would she?

Nevertheless, Reine's breath grew shallow as she neared the table. Such an important room was bound to have booby traps, right? What if Starflight had planned for this? Maybe . . . it would be better if she left the room alone. There was plenty of other stuff to steal after all. But . . . no. Almost unwillingly, as if her body had already decided what to do, Reine crossed the rest of the room in two large strides until she stopped right in front of the desk. On it was a piece of paper depicting Valmount City and the land around it in big broad strokes. *Huh . . . are those lines outlining a path?* Cautiously, Reine picked the map up to get a better look. *Yes! They are!*

She slowly started tracing the black line with her finger. It ended, after going through a winding path outside the city, at a black dot labeled "Rendezvous for Pantheon's Academy."

"Pantheon?" Reine whispered quietly to herself, "Wow. Isn't that the owner of the school my parents were talking about sending me to?"

There was more text on the back, but she was too distracted to read it. Everyone, regardless of social status, knew about Pantheon. His name was whispered throughout the city on a daily basis. Even Starflight couldn't catch him, and she was the leader of the entire Metahero Force!

Reine paused. So why would Starflight leave such an important document in one of her less-protected bases? Reine knew how hard it was to find information about Pantheon's academy, particularly if you were a hero. Her parents only got wind of the school through their metavillain contacts.

And with only two guards to watch over it too! It's almost as if . . . as if . . .

Reine's head snapped up to look above the desk. A red light that hadn't been on was flashing subtly in a corner of the ceiling. She felt the butterflies in her stomach turn to stone. Scrambling, she ran her hands over the desk, searching for anything unusual. There was a passive infrared sensor hidden right at the spot where she had removed the map.

"*Shoot,*" she hissed before turning and running frantically towards the room's door. "Mom?" she half-whispered, half-shouted in the hallway. "Dad? We need to get out of here."

Hiding the map in one of her boots, Reine ran down the stairs, her shoes softly tapping against the carpet. She turned a corner. Nothing. Flattening her body against the wall, Reine ran a hand through her hair nervously. Where were they? Should she be searching in the dining room? How long did they have before Starlight got here?

"Mom, Dad?" No response. She tried again, "Where are you?"

Reine fell silent. She'd heard unfamiliar voices coming from the front entrance. With renewed vigor, she started tiptoeing towards the main hall. *Damn it! What if they've already been caught?* Reine drew closer and closer to the front door, straining her ears to hear what the intruders were saying. They were just around the corner of the hallway, but she knew she had to risk being found if it meant finding her parents.

"Did Pantheon send you?" a female voice demanded, sounding far off.

Reine jumped, and then realized it wasn't directed at her. Peeking her head out from behind the corner, she immediately retracted it for fear of getting caught. But it didn't matter. In a split second, Reine had seen enough: both her mom and her dad were in handcuffs.

CHAPTER 8:
THE LIFE OF A THIEF

THE PAST: 2 ½ YEARS AGO

The female voice that had spoken before started her interrogation again, but Reine wasn't listening. How could such a simple mission have gone so wrong? *Damn it!* She should have known to be more careful! Gritting her teeth, Reine shoved her ear against the wall. If she had gotten her parents into this mess, then she was going to get them out of it.

"Despicable lowlifes," Reine heard. "I guess Pantheon didn't send his minions after the map after all."

There was a pause and the sound of a door opening.

"Here. Take these thieves to the prison and reset the trap. I'm not giving up hope yet."

Another pause ensued, and this time, Reine's heart quickened.

"What? They don't have the map? Then who . . ."

A gloved hand appeared around the corner, scaring the living daylights out of Reine. She bit back a scream and turned to run.

"Stop that girl!" Starflight said.

In the distance, she could hear the hero shouting more instructions to her crew, but Reine had already bolted halfway up the stairs. She knew there was no way for her to rescue her parents now, especially with so many metaheroes guarding them. *Damn it!* she scolded herself again. As much as she hated to do it, Reine was going to have to escape by herself.

A blast of air passed over her head. She stumbled and ducked instinctively. *Was that a bullet?* she wondered. What else could move so fast? A second later, Starflight seemed to materialize in front of Reine as she reached the top of the stairs.

"Wha—" Reine started to say, almost falling backwards.

Starflight grabbed her by the front of her shirt. "Where is the map? Do you have it? Or is there another one of you miserable miscreants hiding somewhere in my house?"

Dazed, Reine shook her head slightly. She was still trying to process the hero's incredible speed. *How can anyone move so fast?*

Starflight slapped her in the face. "Do you like wasting my time? I'm giving you a chance to confess, you know."

Reine nodded slightly, not revealing the storm of emotions that was brewing inside. What if she knew she was lying? Did she even have a choice? Sweating, Reine ignored the urge to bend down and scratch her leg, where the map was sticking out of her boots. Thank goodness for long pants.

"No," Reine started to say, deciding on deceit, "I don't have a ma—"

Starflight cut her off. "Remember," she said warningly, "If you lie to me . . ." The hero grinned and raised a hand steaming with purple energy. "I'll do this."

She blasted the wall beside her with a small frown of exertion. Reine flinched, her face flushing from the sudden heat. She looked at the wall in horror. The projectile had cut through wood like chainsaw through paper; what would it do to her? Reine swallowed as she dragged her eyes from the smoking hole. Even more importantly . . . should she tell Starflight the truth?

Setting her shoulders, Reine met the metahero's gaze. There was no way she was going to give up so easily.

"I don't have it," she repeated with conviction. "The map is with my brother, and he has the power of invisibility. You'll never catch him."

Reine's head itched as the hero's Goethan pressed down on her, but she resisted the urge to scratch it. Any movement could arouse suspicion. After a moment of tense silence, Starflight frowned. She held her breath.

"Don't be so sure," the woman decided, leaning back. "Against my speed, he won't even make it to the door!"

She floated up into the air and spread her arms, infusing herself with Goethan. Reine bowed her head. She was trying to act resigned, but it felt terribly awkward. Thankfully, Starflight wasn't paying much attention to her anymore.

"And don't bother to leave the house," the hero added before flying off. "You'll never be able to outrun me."

WHOOSH!

As soon as the metahero had disappeared around the corner, Reine sank down to the floor, shaking. It had all seemed like a game to her before, she realized. But now . . . the consequences had gotten a whole lot more serious.

Reine pulled herself back up and decided to run for the back entrance. She probably wouldn't make it, but she had to try. Their "borrowed" car was parked in a nearby alley, and Reine had a set of keys, so she might be able to outpace Starflight if she were driving. Or . . . maybe not. Judging by the speed that Starflight had flown at, nothing short of a rocket could keep up with her.

Reine groaned silently. This whole thing was killing her brain. Why in the world had her parents chosen to steal from a maniac who could shoot purple energy beams of death?

Then she froze. She could hear footsteps heading her way from around the corner Starflight had flown through. Looking left and right, Reine tried to open a door in the hallway, but it was locked. Cold sweat broke out all over her body. She panicked and started running back towards the stairs. A transparent wall of bulletproof glass appeared in front of her.

"Stop right there!" a man shouted, his voice low and gravelly.

Reine looked back. Two purple-clad metaheroes were blocking her only way to freedom . . . and they were dragging her parents along with them.

"Come towards me slowly," the man continued, "and raise your hands up." Reine shot her mom a questioning gaze. Amy nodded slightly.

"Okay," Reine said to the man, complying.

She took her time walking towards the guy and mouthed a silent message to Amy. *Now what?*

Her mom frowned thoughtfully. *Where is Starflight?* she mouthed back.

Walking even slower, Reine hesitated. Who knew where the hero had gone? She decided to go with the safe answer. *Distracted.*

Amy smiled. Instantly, she phased her hands through the restraining metal cuffs, letting them fall to the floor. She then kicked her captor in the face. He reeled back, but didn't fall. Beside his wife, Oliver was also engaged in a battle with the woman guarding him. He grunted and used the element of surprise to bash the metahero on the head. His hands were still cuffed in front of him.

A lightning bolt shot past Reine, narrowly missing her head. She gulped. *Better stay down.* The bulletproof glass had shattered behind her. When Reine looked up again, the man who'd created the glass was lying facedown on the floor, having been knocked out by Amy.

Another bolt of lightning appeared, lighting up the corridor. Reine ducked instinctively, but it wasn't aimed at her.

"Behind you!" she shouted to Oliver.

Tendrils of electricity were reaching towards Oliver like hundreds of grasping fingers. They looked almost like a spiderweb, but one that would bring death quicker than a spider's fast-acting venom. Oliver frowned. With an intense look of concentration, he brought his cuffed hands together in front of his chest, and *breathed.* An almost invisible aura expanded out from a swirling center of green fog. Its mist-like, slow-reaching quality was a sharp contrast to the aggressive lightning bolts.

As Reine watched, the electricity repeatedly struck Oliver's green-tinged shield to no avail. It was simply absorbed with a ripple. He began to walk towards his assailant slowly, the aura curling around him.

The metahero desperately redoubled her efforts. She made a twisting gesture with her hands, and sparks emerged from under Oliver's skin. Reine winced; she figured the woman must be creating a lightning storm inside his body.

Oliver ignored the pain with an indifferent expression. Reine noticed that the mist around him had thinned out considerably. He was probably reabsorbing it to combat the attacks inside. He continued forward stoically.

Suddenly, the lightning stopped coming. Sparks fizzled out as the metahero finally collapsed to the floor, struck from behind by Amy. Oliver broke out of his trance and leaned against the wall behind him with a haggard expression. He was exhausted.

"Let's go," Amy urged, putting a comforting hand on her husband's shoulder. "Before Starflight comes back."

Reine nodded in agreement. With a burst of speed, she started sprinting across the hallway. Her leg muscles were well accustomed to quick dashes; living in an age where anyone could try to mug you made a habit out of that. Amy and Oliver followed a few meters behind her, having stayed to unlock his handcuffs before heading downstairs towards the back entrance.

"What should we do after we get out?" Reine called back to her parents. They were almost to the door.

Panting, Oliver gestured at Reine. "We're obviously not going to be able to outdrive Starflight, so I think that you and I should slip into an alleyway while your mom distracts that woman with the car. After we escape, she'll just phase through the door and meet us back at the apartment."

Amy nodded grimly. "Definitely. Now go quietly through the door before Starflight comes back—"

A gigantic purple beam of energy shot towards where Amy had been standing, leaving a smoldering hole in the wall. A second later, Starflight crashed through.

She roared, "Liar!"

"Nullify her power!" Amy shouted to Oliver as she phased through the metahero's attack.

He frowned, concentrating, but nothing happened. Starflight had already retreated to a safe distance. "Damn it," he muttered.

Starflight started retaliating with a barrage of energy beams. They landed everywhere, melting through furniture and metal alike.

"Ugh," Oliver grunted as he stepped in front of Reine to absorb some of the blasts. "She's strong."

More purple beams followed, but they were absorbed harmlessly by his green shield.

"Ugh," Oliver muttered again, this time more subdued. He was looking kind of pale. Seeing the feverish expression on his face, Reine quickly dragged Oliver into a nearby room and closed the door behind them. "Huh," he said, looking groggily at Reine. "Probably shouldn't have brought you with us." Then he passed out.

Reine stood up and peered nervously out into the hallway from her door's peephole while gripping a temporary power-blocker grenade in her left hand—she'd taken it out of her backpack. Reine was breathing hard. Originally meant to be used only as a last resort, she now had no choice but to ignite it. After all, how else was she supposed to take down Starflight? With her dad out of commission and no way of escaping, the metahero was going to have to go.

Please finish this quickly, Mom, she pleaded silently. *I don't know if I can do it.*

From the peephole, Reine could see Amy was still locked in deadly combat with Starflight. A whirling storm of fists and burning energy filled the hallway as the metahero whizzed around. It was all Amy could do to keep up.

Reine cheered her on silently, but she knew deep down how futile her mom's task was. Sure, Amy could phase, but she also had to keep Starflight's attention away from Reine and Oliver. That meant being corporeal most of the time, and being corporeal meant getting hurt.

Starflight backflipped into the air. Eyes narrowing, Amy immediately jumped forwards, hoping to use the metahero's moment of vulnerability to sneak in a strike. Reine's heart started beating faster. Was this the moment of truth?

"Die!" Amy shouted as she threw a kick at the exact spot where Starflight was going to land. "*Kiai!*"

Reine felt her grip on the grenade loosen. There was no way the metahero could—

Starflight stopped moving in midair. Reine could almost hear the shock her mom felt as she kicked nothing. Losing her balance, Amy tried to retract her leg and fall into a defensive position, but it was too late.

"Mom!" Reine shouted desperately. She lurched out of the room, pressed the ignite button on the power-blocking grenade, and threw it with all her might. It didn't matter anymore that Amy would be caught in the blast. If she didn't do anything, she wouldn't have a mom.

"Run!" Amy screamed back.

Reine dashed into the room again, hoping against hope, as the bomb bounced across the floor. *Explode!* she willed silently. *Please explode!*

Beep. Beep. Beeeee—

Starflight reoriented her body downwards with incredible speed. Pushing her hands out like she was doing a push-up, the metahero blasted Amy with a purple beam so huge that it incinerated her entire body. The light illuminated the crazed, wide-eyed grin of Starflight's glee.

The grenade exploded. Green mist spewed out and covered the world like a blanket until Reine could see nothing but the glowing afterimage of her mom's burning bones. Then there was only the glow, and her mom . . . was gone.

Reine blinked green mist out of her eyes, rubbing them with her hands. She frowned. *Why are they wet?* She rubbed them again, this time more gently. A droplet of water slid slowly into her mouth and filled it with the taste of salt.

Tears? she wondered. *Why am I crying?*

Puzzled, and filled with an unexplainable sense of dread, Reine tried to remember what had happened just a few minutes ago. Her memories of the past hours were kind of hazy, as if her brain was keeping them away from her . . . or protecting her from them. Then it hit her.

My mom is dead.

It all came flooding back like a tidal wave. Reine gasped. With a terrible calmness, she stood up and looked left. Oliver was still lying face up on the floor, feverish but breathing. She processed the information mechanically in her head. Even though she knew what she would find outside, Reine reached carefully for the doorknob.

My mom is dead.

She opened the door. A pissed-off looking Starflight was talking on a phone. Her violet costume looked comical without enough Goethan to give it an ethereal makeover, but Reine was too numb to see the humor. The hero was facing the opposite wall of the hallway.

"Those stupid lowlifes got away," Starlight spat angrily, oblivious to her presence. "They got some form of power-blocking grenade that destroys Goethan."

An indistinct voice replied on the other end; all Reine could hear was a crackle. She knew that she should be trying to decipher what the person was saying, but she couldn't bring herself to care.

My mom is dead.

Starflight frowned. "Don't worry about it," she said. "I can feel my brain producing more Goethan already—I'll be able to use my powers any minute now."

Reine strained her ears, but was foiled by the rustling cape on the metahero's costume.

"I know I should have called for backup!" Starflight continued as she paced around, her back facing Reine. "I admit it: keeping this mission a secret was a mistake."

Reine raised the tranquilizer gun she had taken from her father. *I wish I could kill her.*

"But that doesn't mean I need you now. I *can* still handle this on my own."

She inched closer and heard the question being spoken on the phone.

"Are you sure?" it asked.

Starflight began to turn around. "Definitely. You wouldn't be able to catch them anyways. Judging from the time I had been unconscious, there's no way they wouldn't have already escaped back to whatever hellhole they came from—"

Reine shot her in the side. One second. Two. The metahero's eyes rolled back and she collapsed onto the floor. Her phone fell with her, landing right in front of Reine.

My mom is still . . . dead.

"Hello? Starflight? What happened?" the voice on the phone asked.

Reine froze, cold sweat forming on her face. What should she do? Whoever was on the phone was bound to get suspicious if she herself answered, but they would send backup anyways if she didn't. Maybe she could get her dad to wake up and escape before they got here.

Darting a glance back through the open doorway, Reine saw Oliver knocked out cold on the carpeted floor.

She sighed, considering her plan of moving him. *Fat chance of that.*

Reine picked up the phone, cradling it as if it were a ticking time bomb.

"*Hello?*" she whispered, and then realized that didn't sound a bit like Starflight. She tried again. "Hello?"

The man on the other end immediately replied, "What happened? You sound a bit shaken. Are you hurt?"

Reine gulped. A golden warmth was spreading through her brain, infusing it with a sense of . . . power.

"I'm fine," she found herself speaking in Starflight's voice. "I got it all under control."

"What?" The man didn't sound convinced. "When? What happened?"

Reine scratched her head worriedly. She didn't even know how she was suddenly able to imitate the unconscious metahero's voice. She also didn't know how she would get out of this mess.

"Starflight?" The voice was asking again. "I'm sending in a strike force if you don't respond."

Reine's hands shook. If she didn't think of something soon, it would be too late to save herself and her father.

"Shut up, you imbecile." Inspiration struck. "I just managed to capture the two thieves I was telling you about."

There was silence on the other end.

Reine brushed the sweat off her face. "It turns out they were hiding in one of the rooms down the hallway. The grenade had knocked them out too."

The silence continued.

"You know," she gulped, "how the grenades destroy Goethan .. . and living things need Goethan to stay conscious . . ."

More silence.

Reine cursed. The guy must have seen through her deception. With a snarl, she was about to toss away the phone when—

"Hello?" the voice asked again, "Sorry, Starflight. I had bad reception."

Reine stared at the phone in disbelief, real anger finally boiling through.

"You useless, stupid . . . thing!" she yelled into the phone. "The point is that I found them, okay? I don't need you and your team's help to torture a couple of prisoners."

My mom is dead because of you.

The voice on the other end tried to protest, but Reine shushed him. "In fact," she continued, glad to have someone to vent her rage on, "you can join those villains in the cell if you arrive. I'll be happy to vaporize you along with them."

Fuming, Reine took a few deep breaths to calm herself down. The person on the other end went silent for a couple seconds, and then hung up. Reine almost collapsed, drained of Goethan. Everything needed Goethan to live, and too little could cause weakness or death.

"Amy?" she heard Oliver groan. "What happened?"

Reine rushed to her father's side, helping him get up. He had overtaxed himself—dangerously so. They needed to get out of here.

"Dad?" she said, and her heart broke at the thought of delivering the news. "Are you okay?"

Oliver ignored the question. "Amy? Where is she?"

Reine swallowed. She refused to look at the ashes that were beginning to disperse in the hallway behind her.

"She's dea—" she began to say, and then choked. The words were just too painful.

"Mom. Was. Killed," she tried again, spitting out the sentence like it was a poisonous dart. "Starflight murdered her—" Reine broke down crying. She couldn't take it anymore. Before, the threat of Starflight had stopped her from properly grieving. But now . . . the stress . . . the thought of never seeing her mother again . . . Starflight . . . the violence.

"Why?" she sobbed to her dad. "Why did she have to die?"

Oliver lunged past her and out of the room, saw the unconscious hero, then hesitated when Reine continued to bawl. He released his tensed shoulders in a long and reluctant sigh and came back to pull her into a tight hug. Reine's tears turned to dry sobs.

"It'll be okay." Her father said, for once at a loss for words. "Everything will be fine, you'll see."

She collapsed onto the ground. Nothing would ever be fine again. Her mom was dead, and she wasn't going to come back. No more daring heists or family time. No more joy and life. All her mother would ever feel now was darkness . . . and oblivion.

She started crying again.

"Maybe she's in a better place," Oliver suggested gently, sounding numb.

Reine wiped the tears from her eyes. Briefly, she entertained the notion that there might be some sort of life after death for her mother, that maybe one day they would be reunited. Reine ripped the idea into pieces. Better not to think about it. If the afterlife judged you by looking at what you did in life, then her mom would surely be condemned for committing the worst crime of all: being a metavillain.

"I just wish the government would give us the same rights as everyone else," Oliver was muttering. "It's not like all the meta-humans are bad. It was that one guy!" He turned to Reine, face wild. "They forced us into this lifestyle, you know. We had no choice but to become thieves; it was that or starve." Tears fell from his eyes. "The alternative was to be a metahero . . . and that . . . to kill my fellow peers who had done no wrong except for having a little extra Goethan . . . was inconceivable."

Reine nodded; she understood. "I'm not blaming you for anything," she replied as calmly as she could. She didn't know how she managed it. "Mom told me about the government and how they convinced the world that all the metahumans except for the heroes were dangerous. Of course you guys couldn't get a normal job." She hugged him back. "It's not your fault, Dad. It's the government's."

Oliver smiled bitterly. The silence that stretched out was like the shock after someone broke a piece of fine china. It made her wonder if something had cracked within both of them.

"Should we go?" She gestured at the back door.

Her father nodded, helping her get up. "Yes. Let's go."

They both wiped their eyes and withdrew into their own thoughts. As the night air greeted them, Reine closed the door behind her . . . but not before taking one last look at her mother's remains.

"Goodbye . . . Mom," she whispered. "Don't worry. I'm going to make things right."

CHAPTER 9:
EXPLOITATION

Reine sat in her dorm room and pored over the online course outlines they had been given. Pantheon tried his best to mimic natural lighting by using halogen bulbs, but underground was underground. Stone walls, no matter how smooth, still made her feel like she was living in a cavern.

"Damn it!" Reine muttered out loud. "You have to be a senior *and* valedictorian to lead your own assassination mission against a top metahero?"

Ever since she had arrived at school, Reine had been trying to find a way to seek revenge. It wasn't so easy, though. Most of the classes she could take dealt with basic scams, thievery, and power development. As a late newcomer, the only way Reine would ever get to enroll in a class on fighting metaheroes was if she scored extremely high on the exams. *And part of that exam . . . is everything from the four years I missed.*

Reine sighed. Not only did she need to find a way to fight Starflight, she also needed to accelerate through all her studies so that she could learn *how* to fight Starflight. This was shaping up to be an impossible task.

On the other side of their small room, Sky was reading a novel on her laptop; Reine could tell, because Sky was lying sideways across her bed with both of her legs against the wall, exposing the screen to Reine's side of the room. There was a little

85

bookshelf carved into the stone near her bed, and books with fraying edges lined the inside.

"Hey, Sky," Reine asked casually, "if you wanted to fight a top metahero, how would you do it?"

Remember, she told herself, *it's best if you don't drag her into it—so only reveal your true intentions if the situation absolutely demands it.*

Sky looked at her strangely. "You mean like . . . fighting tactics and stuff?" she asked. She closed her laptop and sat up to face her roommate.

Reine still didn't know whether to place her confidence in the girl yet, but at least she seemed helpful. They had met about a week ago, and Sky had been nothing but a treasure trove of information since.

"No . . . more like how you would plan or prepare for the fight," she suggested. "You know . . . like which courses you would take to maximize your odds, or how you would actually lure the hero into fighting you?"

Very smooth, Reine, very smooth.

Pursing her lips thoughtfully, Sky laughed. Reine hoped she didn't find her questions too unusual. She hated that she had to depend on someone she'd met only a week ago, especially since there was definitely something fishy about Sky's relationship with the rest of the students in the school. Maybe she was just unpopular—but that didn't explain why her classmates had glared at them when they tried to speak to each other.

Should I just ask her about it?

Reine scowled inwardly and decided not to push too much. She didn't want to offend her only ally. She made a note on her school-issued laptop to ask one of her classmates about the mystery. She was going to question someone else before, but there had been no other classes for her because of Mr. Nidek's outburst.

He was supposed to be my academic counselor, and we never even figured out my schedule.

"That's a really weird question, you know?" Sky said, bemused, and Reine winced. "But if I did want to fight someone like . . . let's say . . . Gravedigger, or Starflight, I would definitely opt for a mission."

Starflight?

Reine's heart skipped a beat. She only stiffened a little, but hearing the name still made her want to punch something.

"Missions? Like the ones you go on for part of your final exam?"

"Yeah," Sky replied. "Or the ones that your teachers sometimes assign you when they need something done."

Interesting . . . though the teachers here do seem a little unstable. Mr. Nidek, for one . . . Reine raised an eyebrow. Sky was always willing to help, and she never seemed to get frustrated. Just a day ago, she had given her a list of all the power categories— "Reality Manipulation," "Bodily Manipulation," "Illusionary Manipulation," "Atomic Manipulation," and "Miscellaneous"— and explained them in detail. She'd said something about how each one stood for a different type of power, but none were better than the others.

Reine paused thoughtfully. Sky seemed somehow *too* helpful, if that were possible. She shook her head. *Maybe I'm just over-reacting. It's not like this is bad for me; I need all the help I can get.*

"But they still need Pantheon's permission to do that," Sky was saying, "so it won't work. He only authorizes mission requests from students if they have two years of high school under their belt, and even then, only if there isn't much danger involved."

*Wait. So I can't—*Reine almost upended her chair when she stood up. She looked at Sky, who was casually slipping back into her novel.

"What was that about Pantheon?" she asked frantically, her heart sinking. She stopped herself and focused. "Never mind—I get it. Are missions the only option?"

Sky's face flooded with confusion. "Um . . . for what?"

"What do you think? For getting out of school, obviously! For fighting metaheroes!"

Sky closed her computer again and stared at her with wide eyes. Reine felt bad for shouting at her, but she needed to hear this. It didn't matter that she was willing to play the long game. Two years still felt like an eternity, and that was already the best-case scenario. For all she knew, Starflight could be out of her reach by then.

"I'm pretty sure . . . yes," her roommate confirmed.

Damn it!

It felt like she had spent all night memorizing a section in the biology textbook, only to find out her mom had assigned a different one. All her research . . . all her plans . . . all would be wasted if there was no way for her to actually fight the stupid metahero.

Without thinking, Reine banged her fists on the desk. There would be no enacting justice on Starflight this year. *Or the next.*

She refused to cry.

"Is something wrong?" Sky stood up, looking alarmed. Her voice came through slowly, as if she was on the opposite side of a thick bubble. "What happened?"

It was the first time all week that her overly helpful attitude annoyed Reine.

"None of your business," she snapped, then immediately felt guilty for doing so. *Try not to direct your anger at her, okay? She's helping you!* But Reine still felt an irrational burst of resentment.

"Sorry . . . sorry about that," she said quietly, and tried to focus on her roommate's green eyes. It was impossible to get mad at someone with such sparkly eyes. "Your answer wasn't what I was looking for."

Sky didn't respond; she just stood there awkwardly. A look of hurt passed over her face, and Reine slumped back down onto the bed. She had meant it as an apology, but some of her true feelings must have shown through. *Great job, Reine. Now you've ruined your only chance at getting an ally in this place.* Feeling terrible, Reine tried to think of something heartfelt to say. Maybe if she could figure out what her roommate was thinking . . .

Sky's face brightened. With an "aha!" expression, the budding metavillain turned to stare at Reine with a crafty smile.

What could she be up to now?

CHAPTER 10:
THE GOETHAN REACTOR

YEAR 2035

Sky was annoyed. Seriously annoyed. She had already tried every tactic in the book: giving Reine space, trying to be as helpful as possible, making a great first impression—okay, maybe not that one—but her roommate still got mad at her. It was like playing Jenga: every block she removed—representing every nice thing she did to earn Reine's favor—only brought their relationship closer to crashing down.

Sky pouted, straightening a few books on her tiny bookshelf installed in the side of the rock wall. She barely read the novels anymore—too many rereads—but it always calmed her to know that there was a piece of her world that she owned, and that she could control. Her dad had cajoled Pantheon into adding the bookshelf in for her when they first decided to move into the school. He was gone now, of course, but she wondered how he would deal with this situation with Reine.

Maybe you're just not good at making friends, a voice whispered in her head. *No one else likes you, either.* Sky paced around, frustrated. She couldn't accept that! She needed Reine's trust before she could betray her to prove Abby wrong about her . . . weakness. *Which isn't true!*

So what should I do?

Dejected, Sky mentally riffled through her list of friend-making tips again. There was nothing useful. She knew Reine was

91

still suspicious about the hostile reaction to their first conversation before that disaster with Mr. Nidek and Asher, but she was too scared to tell her the truth. What if Reine turned away from her too? Sky was painfully aware of her own place in the academy; she knew that being friends with her wasn't exactly the best step to anyone's social success.

And Reine seems to want something from this school, Sky thought. *Something related to fighting metaheroes.*

She stood still, plotting. *Fighting metaheroes . . .*

Sky turned to look at Reine, a crafty glint in her eye. What if she *could* get her to open up? *All I have to do is bring her to the simulation room . . . Yes. That might work. I'll just need an excuse . . .*

"Hey, Reine," she said, changing the topic. "You want me to show you around the school? Pantheon asked me to tell you about the Goethan donation program yesterday." That was, of course, not the full truth, but her roommate didn't need to know that.

"Sure," Reine replied with a guarded expression. "But I have to finish this research first, so—"

"You'll come?"

Sky knew that the girl was feeling guilty about her outburst earlier, and she decided to milk it for all its worth. She knew true friendship wasn't supposed to be like this—superficial and manipulative—but this was Pantheon's school. Metavillains were supposed to be ruthless, and if Reine fell for her ploy, then it was *her* fault for believing in Sky.

Reine gave her a pained look. "Sorry, but—"

Sky cut her off, going on the offensive. "It'll help you with your work by like . . . a 1,000 percent." Seeing the skepticism in her roommate's face, she raised her hands defensively. "I mean, I'm being serious here. One of the places I'm showing you is literally designed to help you achieve your goals."

Reine frowned, but didn't say anything. Sky knew she had won. "I guess I could use a break," Reine relented.

When Sky led her roommate to the center of the academy, Reine gasped in awe. The entire space was devoted to a gigantic, cylindrical machine trapped behind layers of glass. Misty Goethan entered from vents in the reflective ceiling and slowly drifted down, wrapping itself around the spinning generator until it turned into fine threads of electricity. Reine felt herself raise a hand to touch the glass. Excess Goethan passed through the walls before dispersing just out of reach.

"It's what powers the school," Sky explained. "The Goethan reactor converts Goethan straight into energy by . . . well . . . weaving it into that form. Pantheon perfected the design while he was starting up the school. He's kind of an expert at that stuff."

Reine raised an eyebrow. The initial shock of seeing the generator had worn off, leaving her with a slew of questions. Sky was surprised by how unimpressed she seemed. Her roommate wasn't easily fazed.

"What? Is he an engineer too?" Reine studied the complicated reactor again, trying to decipher how it worked. "Or does it have something to do with his power?"

Sky nodded absently. She led Reine through a door to the booth on the other side of the glass wall. "Pantheon's ability is under the category of 'Reality Manipulation,' so he can literally bend Goethan to his will. Some other metahumans can change the rules of reality too, but only with specific objects or other restrictions." She thought for a moment. "Like . . . you ever heard of Eajesuth?"

"Who?"

"The villain who could swim through the earth?" *And who also happens to be my dad*, Sky thought. *Why do I keep mentioning him? Pantheon's wrath, Sky,* she swore silently. *What if Reine asks someone else, and they tell her about his death?*

Reine shook her head. "No, but it sounds like his power would be under the category of 'Atomic Manipulation.' Since, you know, it has to do with elemental manipulation."

No, it doesn't.

Reine paused for a second, thinking, before continuing. "Or maybe even—"

"No, it doesn't!" Sky said, cutting her off. "Look, just stick with me on this, okay? Eajesuth's ability was Reality Manipulation."

Sky suddenly regretted choosing her dad as an example, but it was too late to change now. *I can't just say I know what his power was because I knew him.*

They fell into an awkward silence.

"Anyways," Sky continued quickly, getting back to their previous topic, "this is the Goethan donation center, where they accept Goethan from 7:00 p.m. to 9:00 p.m. Well . . . not really. Donating is actually a requirement, so you'll be getting an email with instructions whether you like it or not."

Wow, Sky reflected. *I sound like one of those advertisements with all the disclaimers at the end.*

Reine evidently thought the same thing; she didn't look very happy. "And how exactly am I supposed to get the stuff out of my body?" she asked.

"Oh," Sky said, grinning sheepishly. "Just arrive on time, and they'll siphon it directly from your brain. Like a leech, almost, but without the blood."

She didn't realize how weird the process would seem to someone new. There hadn't been recruits from the poorer sections of the city in a while—most students here were the children of well-known villains—so she underestimated how strange it must seem to treat Goethan so carelessly. A lot of people, especially if they grew up listening to government propaganda, even thought it was some sort of mythical or dangerous substance. *Imagine that,* Sky pondered.

"You're messing with me, right?" Reine said, running her hand through her hair nervously.

Sky crossed her arms and looked away. "It's not as bad as it sounds. Just think about it like part of your tuition, but with no added cost to you. Plus, your brain naturally replenishes its Goethan anyway, so you'll be fine."

There was no response. It was as if Reine hadn't heard her. *Ugh, I never expected her to be so squeamish.* Sky sighed, ready to debate with her if she had to. "I'm sorry, but if you want to stay in school—"

Sky looked back to her roommate and froze. *Wait. What in the world is she doing?*

"Reine?" Sky asked, eyes wide. "What—what are you . . . are you insane?"

While Sky had been looking the other way, her roommate had started walking forwards robotically. Her right arm unfurled as she stumbled towards a red button embedded in the wall.

"That's the emergency alarm!" Sky cried.

Reine frowned and beads of sweat formed on her forehead, but she didn't stop.

It's as if . . . she can't help herself, Sky realized. The answer struck her just as her roommate took another step, losing the battle for control. *Stupid mind control.*

Immediately, Sky looked around for the culprit. If someone was controlling Reine, then they must be close enough to be seen. *Level C . . . Level B . . . Level A . . . There!* High up on another floor, Asher and one of Abby's cronies were engaged in what looked like a heated debate. Sky's head swiveled. There was no one else, and since Asher's power was weather manipulation, it had to be his friend.

What now? Should I try to restrain Reine first, or stop that guy?

Sky judged the distance between them and prepared to tackle Reine. She stopped herself. What was she doing? Why was she helping Reine? Wasn't she supposed to be ruthless? Wasn't she supposed to hurt her roommate so badly that she never recovered? Here was her chance to do nothing and still reap the benefits, and she was blowing it.

I'm not going to let someone else do my job for me, she told to herself. The excuse sounded hollow, even to her. *I'm not! I—I just need more time to figure out a crueler punishment. That's it. There's plenty of time, and well . . . no way I'm letting Asher help me. Abby probably sent him to make sure Reine gets kicked out so I don't make my move and win the bet.*

Sky growled. "Asher's friend, or whoever you are!" she yelled as she ran towards her roommate. "Knock it off before I tell Pantheon!"

No one in the school liked snitches, but Sky was already so hated it didn't matter. What was one more offense? Unfortunately, they were too far away to hear her. Or maybe they just didn't care.

"Fight it!" she told her roommate, changing tactics. "Use the third level."

Reine seemed to be slowing down. She was getting really good at resisting mind control. Sky snuck a peek at Asher again, and saw him shove the mind-controller into the curved glass wall surrounding the Goethan reactor. *Is Asher yelling at that guy, encouraging him to try harder?* It would help if she could figure out who was attacking them, but the assailant was turned away from her.

Reine suddenly crumpled to the ground. Sky looked up. The person Asher was talking to had stormed off, leaving him looking red-faced and confused. From her angle, she could almost swear the bully was mouthing "sorry."

Hell, that's weird. Is he . . . apologizing for something? Sky couldn't be sure. After a moment of silence, Asher walked away too, and she gaped at his rapid departure. She didn't know *what* had just happened.

Is this payment for saving his life? Sky wondered. *I don't unders—*

"Let's call it a day." The words came out of Sky's mouth before she could stop them. Her roommate was already picking herself back up from the floor, with a bump beginning to take shape on her forehead. Sky felt overwhelmed by how fast things were moving.

You just said you want to deal the final blow yourself, a dark part of her said. *Now you're backing away again. She's weak and disoriented. You think you're strong enough to be a metavillain? Then take your chance.*

No! I mean . . . I need more time. That's all there is to it. I need more time.

"We can visit the simulation later," Sky continued, despite Reine's quick recovery. "You might have a concussion, and the infirmary can give you some ice for your forehead." She almost wanted her roommate to argue against her suggestions—to break the thin layer of doubt—but Reine didn't. She was too shaken.

Sky sighed. *It doesn't feel right to take advantage of her when she's hurt. I can't do it. I just can't.*

"Let's go," she finally decided, wrapping an arm around a weak-looking Reine, "before I change my mind."

CHAPTER 11:
THE SIMULATION ROOM

YEAR 2035

"Why do the mind-controllers always seem to pick on you?" Sky joked as she led Reine down one of the more popular tunnels. All the passageways that branched out from the center of the school were constantly swarmed with people, and the ones connected to *those* tunnels had a little less traffic. The stragglers that led to dead ends or caverns too complicated to repurpose, however, contained almost no students at all. Deep beneath the earth, the only thing keeping everyone grounded to reality was the presence of others, and untrodden stone floors, no matter how smooth and perfect, kept the students away. Those same students milled around them now, occasionally shooting Sky dirty looks. She lowered her head.

Another week had passed since the attempt to frame her roommate for pressing the emergency alarm, and they were using their free time during the weekend to visit the simulation room. Sky still didn't know if it was because Reine was thankful for her help, or if she had noticed Sky's obvious reluctance to discuss her rocky relationship with the rest of the school, but Reine hadn't started investigating Abby's challenge yet.

I can't risk one more week, though, Sky worried to herself. *Sooner or later, she's going to get suspicious.*

They passed the Goethan reactor again, reaching the other end to get to a tunnel. The generator acted as a travel hub for the school; they had to loop around it if they wanted to get any-where, and a holographic map was displayed above the machine and amid the descending Goethan to help guide their way. Thankfully, Reine had finally gotten used to the idea of selling her Goethan. She didn't have enough money to pay for tuition anyway, so the trade was perfect for her.

"I mean, seriously though, you should at least catch up on the third level," Sky continued when Reine didn't laugh. "We're not supposed to use our powers on each other, but some people still do it. We're teenagers. We do stupid things all the time."

Sky chuckled before continuing. "It's kind of ironic, actually, how mind-controllers can control everything except for their own temper." Her roommate's mouth twitched, so quick that Sky couldn't tell if it was a grimace or a smile, and it was gone after she blinked. *Hell. Why does she always clam up whenever I try to make a joke? It's like she doesn't understand humor.*

"Right?" Sky pressed.

Reine nodded, and Sky went to bang her forehead against the wall—or at least she wanted to. *The characters in my books never have this problem,* she grouched silently. *You don't see someone making a witty joke without some sort of reaction.*

The familiar sound of computers whirring filled the hallway. It sounded more like saws when paired with their stony sur-roundings, and she noticed Reine tensing up immediately. Sky frowned. Reine was so uptight that a mosquito in her room would seem like something suspicious . . . or even a spy.

Plus, the sounds are just for show, anyways. Pantheon likes to keep things mysterious.

She put a hand on Reine's shoulder, but she pulled away.

"It's part of the simulation technology designed by Pantheon and Maelstrom," Sky explained to put her friend at ease. "Only Pantheon, actually," she corrected herself. "He used Maelstrom's power to build it after killing her in battle."

Sky took a deep breath to clear her thoughts. This wasn't relevant. She needed to focus. The simulation room worked by combining all the data it could obtain to determine the best way to solve any given problem, so Sky needed Reine to enter her personal data—hopefully some secret weakness or past fear—into the machine. She could then move all of it into a realitydrive: an old invention of Pantheon's that allowed people to download information directly from his simulations and, most importantly, bring it back to the real world. The villain had since connected the simulations to his computer system, but the back door was still there in case it went offline. She couldn't just hack his database, though. Not only would the firewalls be impenetrable, it wouldn't have any info about Reine except for the entrance exam and onwards.

This is going to be so easy . . . not.

"Hey, Reine," she asked, "do you know what this place is?" She knew the question was rhetorical but hoped it would help get her friend talking.

"Isn't this the simulation room?"

"It's more than that. See the five different colored walls? Each of them represents a power category, like 'Bodily Manipulation' or 'Atomic Manipulation.' All you have to do is choose the one that you belong to, and it will lead you down the path you want to go."

Should I be doing this? Do I want to do this? Sky wished she knew which path *she* wanted to take.

She stepped forward anyway and pressed a button near the door. The room dimmed. She let the smile fade from her face when Reine turned to study the words appearing on each of the five walls: "Miscellaneous," "Atomic Manipulation," "Illusionary Manipulation," "Bodily Manipulation," and "Reality Manipulation." Sky didn't know how she was going to use the information she stole from Reine—she barely knew how to hurt someone. She'd have to figure it out later.

"What am I supposed to do now?" Reine asked. The young woman tentatively reached forwards to touch the wall closest to her, but yanked it back when her hand made a ripple. It was as if the walls were made of watery Jell-O—water that defied gravity.

It has to be emotional pain, Sky decided as Reine stared at her dry hand in confusion. *That's what the info is for. I'm not going to stab her, but Abby won't be satisfied until I make her cry blood. It's going to be rough. Reine feels both fragile and strong. It's weird. One thing's for sure, though: she's been through a lot.* Sky looked at Reine discreetly from the corner of her eye. *And I'm going to have to use her past against her.*

"'Reality Manipulation,' remember?" Sky explained gleefully, placing her own hand on the wall to show that it was safe. She leaned in and put an elbow on Reine's shoulder. "Don't worry, even though it ripples, it's not actual liquid," she confided. "I still think I'm going to get wet every time I go through the portal."

Sky turned to face Reine directly. "Now pick the power category you belong to. Did Pantheon tell you what your power is?"

"Yeah," Reine replied. Turning around, she inspected each of the walls carefully. Sky had a feeling her roommate already knew which one she was supposed to choose, but still didn't trust her own decision. It was like second-guessing on a test when the answer was clear. Why not check, just in case?

I felt like that too, when my dad died. It was as if all the things I thought I knew about the world had been stripped away. This must be really important to her. Whatever problem she's trying to solve . . . it might be my chance to understand all the weird questions she's been asking.

"Well. My power is the ability to create body-related illusions," Reine was saying, "so I guess it would fall under 'Illusionary Manipulation,' right?"

Reine paced around the room, dragging her fingers across the portals and making trails that immediately reformed into unblemished words. Sky frowned. *At least I don't have to feel guilty about doing this. I am helping her reach her goal, after all.*

"Yeah," Sky answered. "'Illusionary Manipulation' is basically any power that fools the senses." Then she paused and tried to sound casual. "Hey. Do you want me to go into the simulation with you? I could show you around."

Reine rubbed her head warily. "That would be really helpful," she admitted, "but I'm sure I could figure it out—"

"No, no, it's fine," Sky protested. "It'll be faster with my help, anyways."

Please?

Sky felt her heart melt a little when Reine looked at her gratefully. With some surprise, she realized that her plan was working. That only compounded her guilt, but her friend's gratitude was enough to stall it for now.

"Come on," she said, pulling Reine towards the wall labeled "Illusionary Manipulation." "Let's get you into the simulation."

The first thing Reine noticed when she entered the room was that, well, it wasn't a room. She stumbled as her feet sank into the spongy ground; it was like walking on a firm mattress. *I guess I shouldn't be surprised. We did just pass through a watery portal, after all.* But she was surprised . . . and not just a little.

"Where is the light coming from?" Reine asked Sky, squinting at the brightness infusing everything around them.

The two young women had appeared on a featureless plane of gray, blinding mist. The walls and ceiling—if there were even any—seemed to be made of the same material, but less dense. *Does the room stretch on forever?* Reine wondered.

"Beats me," her roommate replied. "All I know is that it works."

Sky tapped a rhythm into one of the clouds lingering beside her, and a gigantic textbox appeared in front of them. It had the word "Username" floating on top of it.

"Just let it scan your body," Sky explained.

Reine guessed it was like creating an online account. Walking forward, she waited until the edges of the textbox flashed green, and then readied herself for the next step. A few more textboxes appeared a couple of seconds later. They had varying captions like "Last Name" and "Permission to access school schedule?"

She hesitated. *Should I trust Sky on this? If she's just standing there, doesn't that mean she can see every one of my answers?* Reine ran a hand through her hair. *You've got to start with someone,* she told herself. *And she did save me from that mind-controller. If I trust her enough to not ask about her unpopularity, why not go another step?* Reine shook her head, conceding. *Fine.*

A keyboard had formed out of thin air while she was thinking. Though it was made of the same mist-like material that composed the rest of this world, she found it surprisingly solid. Her fingers didn't even sink into the keys as she entered her info.

I guess I'll switch to privacy mode when I'm typing in more personal information, she decided, coming to a compromise. *Trustworthy or not, I'm not letting Sky know about my parent's death yet . . . and definitely not my mission to kill Starflight.*

Glancing behind her at Sky, Reine got to work.

Sky yawned with boredom and forgot for a moment that she was supposed to be spying on Reine for personal information. Sure, the girl had some interesting tastes— *"Accelerated Advanced Thievery?" Wow*—but she'd switched on "privacy mode" right when it got to the questions about her past; deceptively thin black curtains had appeared, hiding Reine from view. How was

Sky supposed to be interested if Reine didn't let her see any of the juicy details?

Not that it matters, I guess, Sky shrugged. *I was hoping she would make this easier, but my other plan works too.*

Unable to stand still, Sky poked at the curtains. They were just tall enough to prevent her from seeing the floating textboxes, and she knew they would grow longer if she tried to lift them up or stick to the ground if she crawled underneath.

"Hey," she asked, making sure her tone was friendly, "you done yet?" She needed to know how long she had without seeming like she was rushing her. The last thing Sky wanted was for Reine to finish early.

Reine's voice drifted through the curtains, "Almost. Just give me, um, five more minutes; I still need to enter in some things."

Okay. A few more minutes . . . That seems to be my cue.

With a deft hand, Sky nonchalantly slipped a realitydrive—half sleek metal, and half condensed Goethan—out of her pocket and started the taxing process of submerging into her subconscious. She would have done it earlier, but staying in the fourth level for a long time wasn't something she could do yet. Sky sighed. Hopefully, Mr. Nidek would fulfill his promise of teaching her a simpler method to submerge soon . . . if Pantheon ever let him teach again.

And one minute is up.

Sky slid towards the far left of the simulation with her internal clock goading her on. Though it looked like there weren't any walls, the thicker parts of the mist actually formed barriers that were quite hard. She fingered the realitydrive; its Goethan half flickered as she rubbed it nervously. Sky was still waiting for the right moment to strike. She wanted to give Reine as much time as possible to enter her secrets.

The last second . . .

And her powers kicked in. The sound of loud breathing and heartbeats instantly engulfed her ears before dying down to a manageable volume, and it was only because of the privacy curtains that she didn't see every inch of Reine's bare skin turn almost alien with detail. Sky shuddered. Though the fourth level was far from the most overwhelming, it still felt kind of disturbing to invade a person's privacy without them knowing. Especially when it came to smell and touch . . .

Sky pinched herself, hard.

Just focus on the stupid mission already!

Making sure her senses were trained on Reine, Sky started to drum a syncopated rhythm into the seemingly spotless wall. This was a backdoor many of the older students had discovered during their senior year, and being the braggarts they were, had passed it down to the younger generation when they graduated.

The outline of a door appeared with a hiss, and mist drifted away slowly. She was left with a rectangular opening leading into darkness. As her eyes adjusted to the dim light, Sky tiptoed inside the room. There were several ports carved into the wall, and she plugged the Goethan end of her realitydrive into the one labeled "Export." She knew without looking that Reine hadn't finished yet. The privacy curtains muffled the sound of Reine's breathing, so if they rose, it would become louder: a miniscule difference for any other metahuman, but it was like comparing strawberries to bell peppers for Sky.

So all I gotta do is wait for two more minutes . . . Oh, Pantheon's wrath.

Sky's face sparked with alarm. Like a subtle joke from fate, the deafening sound of fingers on keys disappeared. That should have been okay, especially since her roommate couldn't be typing all the time, but . . .

"Hey, Sky," Reine asked. The black curtains surrounding her turned gray and then dissolved into mist. "Sorry for making you wait so long. What do we do next?"

Oh, I am so dead.

CHAPTER 12:
MAKING BAD CHOICES

YEAR 2035

Everything in the simulation acted as if it were part of an enormous computer: the preferred interface was a keyboard, mist formed into display screens, and the walls had lines of wire running through them. That was the source of Sky's problem. If she needed to, she could lie about the purpose of the room she was in and block the realitydrive with her body so Reine wouldn't see it. No sweat.

But not if the entire wall lights up! she thought.

As she watched with a growing look of horror, flashes of light started to pulse into the realitydrive as a way of mimicking the wires in a computer. This was something that the seniors had never mentioned before. How could she shut it down?

Sky gathered her thoughts in the blink of an eye. There were only a few precious seconds left before Reine noticed, so she had to make them count. The obvious solution was to walk out and close the door to the room, but that would take a suspicious amount of time. For one thing, she didn't know how to actually operate the simulation. The wall had dissolved when she had drummed a code into it, but that didn't tell her anything. Was she supposed to tap the same code into the empty entrance, hoping the wall would reform?

The lights seem to be contained in a trashcan-sized box around the area of the realitydrive, so I should be able to block it if I shift around a little, Sky thought. *They don't make any sounds, thankfully.*

She instinctively started entering the first level; it might become useful later.

Can I lie to her? Say that plugging in the realitydrive is a step that needs to be completed? However, as soon as Sky had proposed this to herself, she crossed it off the list; not only was Reine too naturally suspicious for the lie to work, but one slip from any of her asshat classmates on the topic would punch through the falsehood like it was made of paper.

Besides, I'm definitely not giving them any more leverage over me. Not even if Pantheon ordered it.

The next option was a bit more feasible—it also happened to be the safest—but Sky absolutely detested the idea. It felt so . . . cowardly. *How am I supposed to prove my worth as a metavillain if I'm not willing to take any risks?* Sky thought it through. *Unplugging the realitydrive and hiding it before it downloads all the information will make sure Reine doesn't get suspicious. However, it also means that it won't have enough time to process everything. It may even be corrupted by the sudden separation.* She paused. *So that's a "no" too then, I guess. Can't risk doing all this work for nothing.*

This left her with one last choice, and it was by far the most . . . exhausting. In fact, even with her powers, it would still take an enormous dose of luck for the plan to work. Success was virtually non-existent . . .

But I'm still going to choose it anyways.

Her decision made her want to rethink her life. Taking stock of the situation, Sky noticed that her first-level powers were still taking their sweet time to activate. That was annoying, but it wasn't like there was anything she could do about it. Sky pulled her lips up into a confident smile; she had read somewhere that acting confident made you feel more powerful, and Pantheon knows she needed all the reassurance she could get right now.

Because I know I can do this, right? What else was all that training for?

Sky took a deep breath. Many people insisted that her abilities were only good for scouting and spying, but she knew that they were wrong. If there was one thing reading books had taught her, it was that there were a billion ways to use her powers.

And her powers could do some pretty awesome things.

Reine flexed her fingers. They always felt a bit jumpy after typing for too long. *I wonder what I'm supposed to do next . . . Sky said something about entering another portal, right?* She turned towards her roommate, ready to continue.

And stopped.

Why is she in that dark room? Reine craned her neck to get a better look, but her surroundings were so bright she could barely see Sky in the darkness. All she could make out was a rectangular hole of blackness that contrasted sharply against the almost transparent mist. She squinted. *Is that a flash of light?* Sky's hand was suddenly there, angled just right to block Reine's view. She marked it off as coincidence; she hadn't noticed the panicked look that had been on her roommate's face. Absentmindedly shifting her position again to see what was behind Sky's back, she was foiled once more. Reine frowned. *What in the world?* She walked a few steps away, then quickly doubled back and scowled. Sky was somehow in her way again!

"Sky? Are you hiding something?"

"No . . ."

Reine waited, but her roommate didn't say anything else. She would almost have believed her if not for the fact that she was obviously doing *something* in that weird space.

Maybe it's like a rest area or something. I mean, people do get tired from standing around for so long, right?

"Come on, Sky," she started to prod, but then stopped when she realized how ridiculous her suspicion was.

Sky took advantage of that hesitation. "Let's go on to the next step," she cut in. "Do you think it's fun sitting around doing nothing?"

Reine immediately felt guilty, then confused. Sure, she might have made a few assumptions too quickly, but wasn't Sky the one who wanted to come into the simulation with her in the first place? Something wasn't adding up. Leaning one way, and then the other, Reine tried desperately to catch a glimpse of what she had seen before. If she could find out what Sky was trying to hide, maybe some answers would reveal themselves.

She started to walk towards the dark room.

"Now," Sky was saying, "the next step involves—what are you doing?" She almost dashed out of the space, blocking the doorway with her body. This time, Reine was sure she had seen some sort of flashing light. She ignored her roommate's question and directed all her concentration into catching a glimpse of that mysterious, pulsing glow.

Feinting left and then right, Reine rapidly approached the wall of churning mist behind Sky's back. Sky still managed to block any sight of whatever that light was, but that wouldn't matter if Reine got past her and into the room.

Reine wove around with a grim smile, slightly bemused by the whole situation. First she danced left, and then she rolled forwards before jumping up. *Nope.* Sky was already there, blocking the way. Reine gritted her teeth and tried to push past her, but her roommate drove her back with a kick.

She instinctively fell into a Krav Maga fighting stance—it was better for offense and street fighting than tournaments—and lashed out with a punch. Pantheon's school didn't really focus much on martial arts; did Sky even know how to fight?

To Reine's surprise, her roommate managed to deviate her attack with one arm while simultaneously striking for her chin at the same time. She dodged it easily. Sky's technique was pretty sloppy, but at least it had muscle behind it. Sky must have read her attack with her powers before she struck.

Reine found herself smiling widely. She hadn't had this much fun in ages.

Sky rubbed her sore arms, barely defending against another strike. Reine could hit hard! Pelvis and arms rotating, a well-balanced stance . . . she obviously had good martial arts training. *But from whom?* Sky twisted her body to block another pulse of the light behind her. It was hard, especially since she had to keep an eye on the realitydrive while simultaneously avoiding Reine's attacks. If it hadn't been for her powers, she would have failed at both tasks by now.

Hmmm . . . I'm guessing her parents are pretty rich; this level of skill must mean that she started training at a young age. They probably hired a tutor or something.

The thought made her pause. Who *was* Reine, actually? Some sort of rich metavillain's daughter who had fallen into hard times? She didn't know, but she hoped that the realitydrive would spill some details.

Sky glanced backwards. The realitydrive's sleek metal half had a golden stripe that displayed the percentage of data downloaded. With her eyes enhanced, she could easily make out the number 78 percent. *That's what . . . twelve—no, twenty-two till a hundred? Ugh. Just move faster!*

Sky grumbled and tried to *see* the pattern of the light streaming into the device. She had learned from Mr. Nidek that your brain's processing speed increased when submerged inside the subconscious, partly because Goethan naturally enhances every part of the body while in use. The concentration boost also allowed her to control her powers. Would she even be able to comprehend all the patterns and sensory information she was receiving if not for her heightened brain? Sky smiled, amused; the Goethan's enhancement—from both the first and fourth levels now—would at least explain why her thoughts wandered so much.

Focusing back on the task at hand, Sky started to predict what pattern the light would take. *Ummm . . . it seems to be—dodge a punch there, Sky—seems to be taking the form of a . . . ball?* She blinked and looked again. *Yup. Definitely a ball.* Thin spirals of light were congregating into a dot surrounding the realitydrive, making the ball grow larger and larger. It was obviously supposed to mimic one of those "loading screens"—that is, how much time was left before the download was complete—but why would Pantheon use something as boring as a ball for the loading animation? She knew him as well as anyone else; the guy had a flair for the dramatic. For example, if there were a door to a room, he would teleport inside even if someone else was holding the door open for him.

So what is that ball supposed to signify?

Her question was answered a second later. Instead of continuing to thicken the pulsing sphere of light, a curvy stalk sprouted from it. Sky cursed. It looked like a cartoon bomb.

And—judging by the sparks starting to form—the thing was about to explode.

Reine ignored the sweat on her face, throwing knee and elbow strikes without pause. Bruises were forming, but Sky's excellent defense skills meant no one had broken bones. She soon realized that her roommate outclassed her in every way except for skill; it was just a fact of life. If Goethan didn't give you such an amazing advantage, then metahumans wouldn't be on the top of the food chain.

Which was exactly why she was busy entering her own subconscious. After trying a few visualization techniques, Reine finally got to the last step. It had been hard at first—*Trying to become calm enough to touch the deepest recesses of the mind while being knocked around is not easy,* Reine noted—but she had gotten the hang of it. Not only were her fighting moves ingrained in her muscle memory, but Sky also didn't really attack so much as defend. Reine didn't even have to give away what she was doing, because she no longer needed to vocalize her submerging process in order to complete it.

It really is quite easy, isn't it?

Cycling Goethan through her hands—as each level could be accessed by focusing on a different body part—Reine entered the fourth level for the first time. Memories of her entrance exam immediately floated to the surface of her mind, but she tamped them down. There was no room for doubt here; she needed the enhancements to level the playing field.

Reine braced herself for the same explosive understanding of her body she had felt when fighting that mind-controller . . . but found something completely different. She could've punched herself. Of course, Goethan levels were unalike. Whereas the third level focused on defense and fortification of the body, the fourth level's specialty was to manipulate others.

Which is exactly what I need, anyway.

With new power pulsing through her body, Reine took an unsteady step backwards to take stock of her situation. She could already feel the strain of remaining in this state, and it was weak but persistent. She was sure it would only increase with time.

So calm down, she told herself. *Don't waste it by making hasty decisions.*

Reine jumped to dodge a half-hearted kick from Sky and flew backwards, landing on her back. She marveled at the volatility of her own body. It was hard to walk without leaping, and she might as well be flying when she jumped.

Maybe this wasn't such a good idea after all. She resolved to practice an hour every day, and abandoned her futile attempts for now. Reine probed around the edge of her senses. They felt . . . different. As if something extra had been added to them. She pursed her lips. It wasn't like they were much keener than normal, so what was she detecting?

She closed her eyes and tried to perceive Sky's form like she had done to herself during the test. If the third level allowed her to understand her body with her powers, then that must mean the fourth level did the same thing to other people, right?

Be on guard, Reine. She might still attack you while you're blind—wait, what is that?

Barely, just barely, a flicker of light teased her from the corner of her closed eye. She turned towards it instinctively and glimpsed the silhouette of a woman traced in gold before the image disappeared. Gritting her teeth, Reine tried again. A spark appeared this time, quickly expanding into a glowing network of veins, all of which were connected to three, swirling points. They were, Reine realized, the three spots Sky was focusing her Goethan on. Two were where her hands should be, and the last was located in her brain.

So she activated the first and fourth levels, huh? Figures.

Opening her eyes again, Reine froze. The darkness was gone . . . but the golden veins remained. They covered Sky like a tattoo, somehow remaining visible despite being inside her body.

Wow, Reine thought. *I must be looking at two planes of existence at once.*

116

She reached out almost instinctively. Sky wasn't even looking at her; instead, she was concentrating her attention on whatever was inside that room. She must have trusted her senses to alert her to any physical attacks Reine might throw at her.

That would be her undoing.

Reine splayed her hand and managed to force some Goethan out of her body. She sagged from the exertion. Goethan slowly coalesced in her palm, and Reine tried to send it at Sky, but it started to dissolve as soon as it left her skin. She had to focus on keeping it together.

Damn it. Just stop complaining, Reine. Do it the hard way!

Shaking her hand to dislodge more of the mist-like material, Reine pictured it worming itself into Sky's body. There really was no instruction manual for this kind of thing. As much as scientists like to categorize things, everyone's abilities acted too differently from each other's for there to be definitive rules. A person with an "Illusionary Manipulation" ability might only be able to weave illusions of ducks outside of its targets' bodies, while another could be able to create all sorts of mirages . . . but only inside its quarry's toes.

Reine was sincerely thankful that she didn't have such restricting rules on her powers. Even though she still didn't know if her illusions would work outside of herself, Pantheon had personally told her that her capabilities lay within anything related to human anatomy.

Well, what better time to find out then now?

Reine sent the Goethan flying towards Sky's body, and the golden mist zipped forwards like an eager puppy. She knew Sky could see it too, since the young woman was obviously submerged in the fourth level, but her head was turned, so Reine assumed she was distracted. The gamble paid off. Making no sound, the Goethan slammed into Sky's undefended back . . . and bounced off.

Damn it!

Reine scowled but wasn't deterred; it wasn't like Sky had noticed yet. Grabbing it sternly, she slammed the Goethan into Sky again, pushing past her natural defenses with a shove. She winced from the exertion; it was getting harder and harder to stay in this heightened state, especially since this was her first time. *This better not be doing any permanent damage,* she thought. *It kind of feels like my brain is being cooked.*

She pictured one of those eye diagrams she had seen at an optometrist's office when she was a kid, and Reine closed her own eyes to make it easier. Goethan slowly seeped into Sky's head and floated upward until it reached her eyes. She still hadn't noticed anything. *Of course. I should have known that her Goethan would repel mine. It's probably instinctive, though.* Reine frowned. *So why did it work this time?*

She guessed it had something to do with Sky not being in the third level; that was good to know. If she wasn't submerged in it now, then there would be nothing she could do against Reine's Goethan attacks.

She pulled up the eye diagram again and instructed the Goethan to form a wall of darkness over Sky's retinas. It refused to budge. Confused, she repeated her command, this time more forcefully.

Nope. Still not working. I guess the Goethan doesn't think light— or the lack of it—counts as a body-related illusion. Reine sighed, racking her brain for the biology worksheets she had slaved over with her mom. Wasn't there something about rods and . . . cones? She couldn't remember how they worked. Instead, Reine opted to use the one thing that she was sure could cause blindness: the "fake" severing of the optic nerves.

They connect the eyes to the brain, so an illusion of damage to that area should . . .

Yup.

Sky was not having a good day. First her carefully crafted plans had fallen apart, and now this—an animated bomb? Fuming, the girl glanced once more at that stupid realitydrive. Even with her enhanced eyes, repeatedly looking into a dark room and back at the light was extremely taxing. You would have thought that Pantheon would focus more on making his systems faster instead of flashier. It was still stuck at 96 percent.

She yelped, suddenly unable to see anything at all.

What in Pantheon's name? Her mind raced with fear and alarm.

She thought it was some sort of weird effect from straining her eyes too much, but that couldn't be the case. It must be Reine's fault, somehow.

How the hell did she manage to craft an illusion on her first try? Sky could only hope that the girl wouldn't have enough strength to attempt the same thing on her other senses. Not having sight was already making everything so much harder.

Like—how am I supposed to tell when the bomb is going to explode now? Listen to the light?

She growled, feeling trapped, her mind searching for a solution. *I could submerge into the third level, I guess, and burn away whatever illusion she's using, but I'm not even sure I have enough power to hold the two levels that I'm using anymore.* The telltale presence of Goethan weakness had already been hovering over her for the past few seconds. A little longer, and the risk for permanent damage would start becoming prevalent.

Oh, I'm so going to regret this.

Sky knew what she had to do. She let her mind slip from the first level and gasped at the sudden lack of feeling. She took a few seconds to steady herself. Using what was left of her Goethan, Sky could tell that Reine had regained control because she was sitting up again. It had taken her a few weeks to get used to her own Goethan-enhanced body, so she doubted her roommate could have mastered it too well . . .

Pantheon's wrath, Sky. Focus! You have about seven seconds before she notices.

Dimly, she felt Reine getting closer. The girl's movement was jerky and uncoordinated, but it had the power of her Goethan behind it.

Five, actually.

She fell into a wrestling stance.

Four now.

It was a bit late, but how did the move go again?

Three left, Sky. Three!

Why does it feel so weird to be doing this blind?

For Pantheon's sake, just get moving!

So she did.

Flowing forwards with one smooth motion, Sky threw herself onto Reine. It wasn't actually a wrestling move; in fact, it was little more than a glorified tackle, but it did the trick. Her target was trapped, face angled away from the realitydrive.

And Sky felt a billion sensations spread all across her body at once. She quickly dampened her already restricted fourth-level sense of touch to try to control them, but it was too late. A shudder passed through her body as it struggled to acclimate to all these changes.

She almost let Reine go.

Almost.

"Good training, right?" Sky wheezed innocently.

Reine just glared at her. She wasn't fooled. Pushing with all her strength, Sky could feel the taut lines of her muscles as the young woman made one last attempt to get out of her hold.

Sky's expression turned grim. *She may be more skilled, but she's weak after living by herself out in the city. They discriminate against* metahumans there—except for the heroes, of course—so she must have been scraping by on the streets.

Reine stopped moving, defeated.

Sky felt a surprising burst of sympathy for her roommate. What would it be like to have to scavenge for food, unable to get a job anywhere unless she disguised her identity? Sky knew she wouldn't have the strength to bear it.

She didn't even have the courage to stand up to Abby.

"Get off me," Reine said, "or I'll break your eyes for real."

It really wasn't a hard decision, but Sky pretended to think. She wanted to make sure the bomb animation surrounding the realitydrive was over before she agreed.

"Only if you give me back my sight first," she argued halfheartedly, buying more time.

"Fine."

They both became quiet for a few moments, and Sky found that she could see again. Shooting a quick glance back—the realitydrive was now a nondescript dot in a sea of gray—the girl grudgingly eased herself off her roommate.

"You know you're going to have to explain this whole thing to me later, right?" Reine said as she walked back towards the keyboard.

Sky hesitated. "It was just training," she maintained. "Come on, let's move on to the next step."

She pressed a button on the side of the keyboard, and then led her roommate through the portal that appeared right after. Sky remained behind her the whole time. She wanted to be able to catch her if she attempted to run back towards the dark room.

How is this even going to work? she thought suddenly. *Reine knows something is up, even if she can't prove it. How am I going to betray her if she doesn't even trust me in the first place?*

The answer was obvious: exposing whatever secret Reine had to the rest of the school. Sky hated to fall so low, but she would if she had to. The realitydrive twinkled mischievously behind her, and Sky felt guilt spread through her chest, twisting her eyes like lemons. She could always go get the realitydrive later . . . that wasn't the problem.

But should I?

Reine's face was stony. It wasn't purely because Sky had defeated her—no, that just meant she had to get a lot stronger—it was the fact that her roommate was hiding something important. Something that she thought was worth fighting for.

Reine now knew for certain that their friendship was too good to be true.

Stop being so emotional, she told herself, a lump forming in her throat. *It isn't like this is the first time someone has tried to trick you. You just met her!*

But she couldn't stop; Sky's actions hurt her in more ways than she could explain. Maybe it was an overreaction on her part, or even just a mistake, but Reine had met too many untrustworthy people to place her confidence in anyone anymore.

Sky could keep her lies; Reine was continuing alone.

"I'm going to be looking at the results of the simulation by myself," she explained, making her discomfort clear. The thrill of the fight had faded, and it left them both awkwardly hostile. "You can leave or wait. I don't really care."

Uncrossing her arms, Reine started walking towards the sign that had "Report" written on it. Sky's gaze followed her help-lessly. She looked like she wanted to say something, but couldn't find the right words. Reine didn't look back.

Good riddance, she thought, and pressed a button on the wall to activate the portal. It swallowed her whole.

CHAPTER 13:
HE REALLY LET HIMSELF GO

THE PAST: 1 ½ YEARS AGO

It was two in the morning when he came back, disoriented and red-eyed. Reine waited near the front door cautiously. She could smell the drink on his breath.

"Couldn't sleep?" Oliver asked, slamming the door behind him.

Reine's glare could have cooked meat.

"Just studying," she retorted. "Where in the world have you been? You promised you would be back by twelve!"

He ignored her and stumbled towards the cupboard. It was dirty and stained, despite Reine's best efforts at cleaning it. At least she still tried; Oliver did the *opposite*.

Arms crossed, she watched as he poured himself a glass of water. It didn't take a genius to tell that something inside him had died with Amy's passing. All he talked about nowadays were revenge, the "unjust government," or something his drinking buddies had said in the heat of the moment—and that was usually about revenge too.

Any moment now, and I bet he'll start spouting some political nonsense. What will it be this time? Another song?

"I inspired my friends with a great story today," Oliver slurred, confirming Reine's fears. "I think they might actually try my idea out."

She groaned. These conversations usually took the longest time, but he wouldn't let her sleep until she listened to every word. That was why she began to adopt the habit of going to bed *after* he had wandered home. Better to be tired than dragged out of bed because some delusional guy thought he held the world's greatest mysteries in his hand.

"Yeah, sure," she replied impatiently, "I'm listening."

I hope he doesn't take three hours again.

Walking over to the couch, Oliver took a sip of his water. He made no motion to sit down; the guy was far too energetic for that. Instead, he wordlessly pointed at Reine, and then at the couch.

"You want me to sit there?" she asked, and her heart sank. "How long is this going to take?"

Oliver just gestured again. "I'm sharing with you a revolutionary idea. The least you could do is sit down."

"But—"

"It's important, Reine!"

Okay, fine.

She yawned and complied with his orders. There was no arguing with him when he was drunk.

"So. As I was saying, me and my friend Sid were brainstorming a few ways we could spread revolutionary messages to the kids. You know what the government is like these days. They indoctrinate—"

"Yes, I get it! Go on." She knew he liked to get off topic, so Reine tried her best to steer the conversation. At least this way he might actually reach his main point instead of rambling on forever.

"Anyway, after we hung out a bit more, I decided to tell him about Amy's death. Sid bought me a drink. Then he made me repeat the story to everyone else in our group, because he knew someone who had gone through the same thing. They understood me, Reine. Some of them even suggested that we should kill Starflight ourselves."

He paused, as if checking to see she understood. She nodded testily.

This is bad.

"You told them about Amy?" Reine asked, more resigned than angry. "You know breaking into Starflight's house is a crime, right? What if they leak our secret?"

Oliver looked momentarily disoriented. "What? Oh—I didn't think of that . . ."

She wanted to pour his glass of water over his head. Maybe that would teach him to be more careful.

"Good point, but don't worry," he finally said. "My friends have too much on their heads to risk any backstabbing."

That's not exactly reassuring.

Reine sighed. His brain just couldn't comprehend that he was wrong, and the fact that he was only getting worse made her want to cry. After her mom's death—*don't think about it, Reine*—she sometimes felt like she was the only sane person left in the world. Oliver seemed to lean on her instead, and if she was being truthful to herself, even having to care for one person was wearing her down. Stealing trinkets or pickpocketing strangers was no easy matter when no one else was on the lookout, and even just talking with her dad exhausted her. Couldn't he tell that she might want to move on with her life?

"Alright then," she said. "As long as you don't kill us first."

"Why would I do that?"

Reine stared at him, and the face that looked back was completely clueless.

CHAPTER 14:
GETTING SOME ANSWERS

YEAR 2035

Reine felt like she was in a dream. The simulation blurred around her as the mist that had been everywhere slowly disappeared, leaving a blank canvas. She blinked. If the terrain had been uncomfortably bright before, it was now blinding.

Machinery whirred.

Reine checked her surroundings suspiciously. There was . . . nothing. Just an endless plain of radiant emptiness stretching on towards eternity. She raised an eyebrow. If this was the simulation "report" Sky had promised, then she might as well have stayed in her room. Reine didn't even know if she could trust Sky anymore.

It's probably just loading, she tried to rationalize. *Planning the assassination of Starflight can't be easy, right?*

Reine hoped it wouldn't take too long.

She took another look around and brushed away some sweat from her forehead. The beads glistened in the harsh light. Reine frowned. *Is it me, or is this place getting hotter?* It certainly seemed to be getting brighter. The glare emanating from every surface was now so blinding that she couldn't open her eyes without wincing.

Reine shrugged off her jacket.

I'm going to give this place five more minutes, and then I'm leaving if nothing happens.

Tapping her foot irritatedly, she then paced around for a little bit. The sounds of whirring computers were nagging at her brain. Reine couldn't help but feel that she was missing something.

Wait. Are those . . . fans?

Shielding her eyes with one hand, Reine looked up.

And then realization hit her like a stone.

"Oh, you've got to be kidding me."

Sky had mentioned before that the simulation mimicked a laptop. Reine just hadn't realized it would possess all the same problems.

Like a frog boiled alive, Reine was caught in an overheating computer.

The first thought that crossed her mind was: *Ah, damn it. I better find the exit.*

Then, something more reasonable surfaced: *Is it even possible for me to die here? I mean, this place isn't real, right?* Reine pinched herself just to be sure.

It hurt as much as it should have.

Yup. Definitely getting out of here.

Turning around to check for the portal's location, Reine ran towards it as if her life depended on it. And maybe it did. The portal looked just like the one she had used to get into the simulation: a smooth pane of watery Jell-O.

It wasn't open anymore.

She shivered despite the heat and pushed against it with her sweat-drenched hands, but they kept slipping. Even when she tried wrapping the hem of her shirt around them to soak up the moisture, the darn thing still refused to move!

"Hey," she shouted to whatever was controlling this place, "what kind of terrible simulation is this? I ask one question, and your entire computer collapses. Also, the portal isn't working anymore. What in the world is up with that?"

Nobody responded, so she tried asking again. Still nothing.

It's so hot!

Reine stumbled and racked her brain for ways to phrase her request. "Um . . . activate help system? No? How about consult protocol?"

To her surprise, it worked. Flickering like a lagging computer screen, the ghostly image of a nondescript orb slowly materialized beside her. Reine hesitated. The poor thing looked so broken down that she was afraid one touch would destroy it forever.

"D-0es the user wa-t to act1vate the con9ulting protocol? D0ing so w1ll use up a p0rt1on of the 2imu1ation's pro6essing p9wer," the orb said, its gap-like mouth moving jerkily.

Reine pursed her lips. She didn't want to accelerate the computer's overheating, but she also liked staying uncooked more than she valued Pantheon's simulation. Choosing "yes" with a nod, she turned around and shoved the now-hardened portal absentmindedly—you could never be too sure.

"P0rtal i2 n0t func1ioning. Co2pu1er sav1ng ene9gy," the orb explained.

Reine turned back to stare at it. "Could you set it so that the computer is not saving energy? I don't need to be in here for long; I just need to get out."

Literal gears turned in its head, and the little ball-shaped robot processed her question for a disturbingly long time. Reine was almost sure that it had broken when it finally spoke up.

"N0t any8ore. C0uld h2ve 10 se3onds ago, b2t was ta1king t9 you."

Damn it!

Almost crazed by the heat, Reine had to take a deep breath to calm down. *I need that orb thing to get out of here,* she reminded herself. *So I probably shouldn't break it. Probably.*

She drew on her ever-decreasing puddle of patience and asked one last question: "Do you know what is causing this computer malfunction, then? More importantly, do you know how to fix it?"

The ball seemed to glare at her.

"1t is us3r's fa0lt. Ki11ing Starfl1ght is t00 ha1d," it replied resentfully. "Us3r ne3ds to ch2nge the 2ettin6s." The orb paused, then asked, "W0uld us3r w1nt me 2 op3n optio1s?"

Reine had never said "yes" faster. With a sigh, the robot started to collapse inwards on itself.

"Wait. Why are you doing that—oh."

Before she even had time to contemplate whether killing her only adviser was a good thing, the little orb had already been replaced by a hovering sheet of text-filled paper. It flickered twice. *Shoot, that's not good. If even a function as simple as displaying a sheet of paper is breaking, how long before this simulation collapses?*

She tapped the floating image experimentally. It seemed to act like a touch screen computer, except without a physical keyboard—or a physical screen. Reine's hand went through the display several times before she got the hang of it.

Pressing on the screen brings up a keyboard. Does this mean that ctrl-F will work? I really don't want to read the entire thing . . .

One of the gigantic fans from the ceiling suddenly crashed to the ground like a meteor from space. Reine's heart almost burst from shock. As she watched, it flickered and started to disintegrate.

I swear . . . Is it hotter than before?

Shaking from the stress, Reine turned back to look at the fragile screen. A throbbing headache began to form in her head, and it was so scorchingly hot that her body couldn't even produce sweat anymore. She recognized it as the symptoms of heatstroke: vomiting and muscle cramps would come next.

And maybe even death.

I mean, seriously, why is this thing lagging so much? The robot said my request was hard to process, but nothing should slow the simulation down like this, right?

Reine slapped herself.

It's as if something is literally fighting to keep . . .

She immediately halted that thought, reprioritizing.

Concentrate!

Confused and dazed, Reine tried to pull her train of thought back on track. It was just so hard to think in the heat! Focusing on those tiny words on the screen was like watching ants swim across the ocean.

"Ctrl-F," she croaked, hoping the voice activation option was still on. "Find light controls."

[✓ Ding!]

The options page spasmed a little and zoomed in on the words selected. Reine would have let out a sigh of relief if her throat didn't hurt so much.

Light levels, she read. *Extremely high. Use slider to adjust brightness.*

Please let this work.

She complied and waited for the glare to die down. It didn't. In fact, she could have sworn it got brighter!

"What the hell is wrong with these controls?" she rasped at the options sheet. "Shouldn't turning down the light turn down the *damned* lights?"

The message on the screen read: [Light levels are a warning system used to show the user how much information the computer is processing. The brighter it is, the more the computer is managing. If the user wants to deactivate the warning system, please click this link to see 'overheating protocol.']

Legs trembling, Reine had to press her entire hand onto the screen a few times before it worked. She didn't even have the strength to be angry anymore.

[Does the user want to turn off lighting?" the screen asked. "It is not advised—error. It is advised in this situation because—]

"Yes!"

[Deactivation of overheating signal initiated.]

The lights in the room shut off. Reine slumped down onto the ground—not a good idea, considering that the floor was burning—and felt a blessed coolness finally settle over her skin. The fans seemed to quiet down too.

You can rest for a few seconds, Reine, she told herself. *But the job isn't done. The computer is still gradually overheating. Whatever time you bought by turning off the lights won't last very long.*

Indeed, she could already hear the whirling fans speeding up again. The only difference now was that the entire area was covered in darkness. Reine winced from the pain spreading across her body and got up by pure adrenaline. *I knew I should have drunk more tea this morning,* she thought. *Or coffee. And I hate coffee.*

Judging by the stifling heat, Reine could tell that whatever was making the computer act so weirdly was still in action, so that was the first mystery she was going to have to solve. The next step—if that didn't work—would be to stop the simulation from running her request in its code.

She suddenly wished she had Sky to help her.

Reine brushed a strand of hair away from her face and got cracking.

"Activate consulting protocol and options sheet."

[Acknowledged.]

Like before, a copy of the little orb materialized beside her. Then, the options sheet appeared a second later.

"What d0es the u2er wan1?"

Reine had deduced by now that the orb construct spoke so weirdly because it required an AI-like program to run it. This meant that it used up a lot of processing power—processing power that the computer couldn't spare.

The options sheet, on the other hand, was an interactive hologram with automated responses and settings. It could afford to use correct grammar and still be fine.

Or maybe the orb is just messing with me. Who knows?

She clicked on the options sheet to navigate to its shutdown protocol and waved for the orb to come closer.

"So, you mentioned that my request is too hard. What's so difficult about killing Starflight?"

"No1hing," the orb replied smugly. "Simula1ion has p1ann3d mu1h har2er thi4gs bef0re."

"Then what—"

It cut her off before she could protest.

"BUT! Sta3fl1ght has pro1ecti0ns. User s0e, co3puter cann0t ca1cu1ate fate fr0m just s0me 0f us2r's mea3ly data, co3puter also ne3ds a s3mple of G0ethan."

The orb stopped, as if waiting for her to put it together.

Reine raised her hands. "You mean this entire fiasco could have been avoided if I just gave you a sample of my Goethan?"

"No! Du3b us2r."

Reine could have sworn the little ball was playing with her.

"C0mputer wou1d ha2e jus1 tak3n us2r's Goethan if 1t ne3ded it. Us1r's defenses are t00 w3ak . . . to0 path9tic."

The corners of its gap-like mouth lifted.

"No, compu1er needs Starfl11ght's Goethan to w0rk. Us2r see, th1s simul1tion may ha2e be3n crea1ed by our master Pantheon, b0t he us2d Maelstrom's p0wer t0 d0 it af1er she d1ed. Th1s me2ns th1t the c0mp1ter's potential will al3ways be con2trained to wh1t Maelstrom h2d in l3fe: the 7th lev2l."

"What? You mean the seventh level of the subconscious?"

"Ex1ctly. Maelstrom m0y have be7n 3xtre1mely p0werf0l, b1t Starfl1ght is t00. Ma1be e7en m0re s0. Th1 p0int 1s th1t the c0mpu1er cann0t stea1 fr0m her d1rectly, it ne2ds an0ther s0urce. A s0urce it f0und in 0ne 0f Starfl11ght's bases."

The orb paused before continuing. "Us2r see, the g0vernm3nt that emp10ys St2rfl1ght and her g00ns als0 d0es r1se1rch on them. Th1s me2ns th3t th2y usua21y hav5 an ex1racted via1 of h4r Goethan on h2nd."

Reine gingerly touched her parched lips. She waved a hand for it to go on. "Okay, that sounds good. So what's the problem then?"

"We11 . . ." explained the orb, seemingly embarrassed, "the c0mp1ter . . . und2restimat3d the s2ength of the b2se's def0nse system. 1t 1s des1gned to b3 us3d for pla2ning stud3nt sche2ules aftera11, n0t infiltra1ion miss1ons! B3t s8ch is h1ndsight."

"That's an understatement."

The little ball let out a frustrated grinding of gears.

"Us2r d0es n0t under2and, d0es she? Th1s 1s not j0st a m1stake to j0ke about . . . Th1s m3ans the sim1lation m1ght h9ve tri99ed Starfl1ght's alarms."

Reine froze, and her fingers hovered over the icon that she knew now would shut down the attempt at stealing Goethan from her nemesis' base.

"Are you kidding me?" she laughed nervously. "You better be. Because if they trace it back—"

The orb suddenly materialized a robotic arm and hand out of its machine-like body, which it used to raise a finger to its lips to indicate "silence."

"Shhhh," it said. "We 4re **CONCENTRAT-102983. WAIT. Malfunctio- Error. Retry? RETRY?**"

"Um. Are you alright?"

"**Enter code: 12034194818495921934838128323234123 413451235235 NO WE ARE NO- Activating PA system . . . USER, SHUT US DOWN NOW!**"

The orb started compressing in on itself again as Reine slammed her hand down on the option screen.

"They're coming," it whispered, spreading its message through the PA system. "They're all coming."

CHAPTER 15:
ATTACK!

YEAR 2035

Sky wasn't prepared for when Reine barreled through the portal, looking as if she had just been subjected to the world's worst sunburn. She was even more surprised when the PA system blasted a message about a metahero attack throughout the school.

This shouldn't be possible, she thought in disbelief. Pantheon and his school board had hidden their location too well for an outside force to find it. Her dad had been part of it, and he knew his stuff.

"Reine," asked Sky resignedly, *"what the hell have you been doing in there?"*

The girl continued stumbling as if she hadn't heard her, and Sky felt a momentary hint of concern. *Maybe she can't hear me. I should get her to the infirmary before she collapses—*

"Attention all students! This is Virus, Pantheon's vice-principal speaking. Report to the north entrance now if you have been approved for combat. Remember to be extremely cautious; this is not a drill. Several high-level metaheroes—like Shady, Shadier, and Gravedigger—have been spotted near the disguised stone gate. Some may have already breached our defenses."

All thoughts of Reine's plight immediately flew out of Sky's mind. Gesturing for the girl to follow her, she rushed through a newly created portal. *I need to get to the armory before it shuts*

135

down, Sky told herself. Pantheon's procedures dictated that it would only be open during training and a short time before an attack in order to prevent misuse by the enemy.

"Reine, the infirmary is that way," she yelled behind her. "You're not approved for combat yet, so don't follow me to the armory. It's dangerous there."

It was the least she could do. Sky still felt guilty about their fight, but what was she supposed to say? Apologize? Doing that could mean betraying Reine again later, and her roommate wouldn't believe her anyway. Right?

Not waiting for an answer, Sky started to head towards the north cavern, where the armory was. She didn't—no, couldn't— listen to—

"Why didn't you tell me the simulation was supposed to be used for planning student schedules and not assassinations?" Reine wheezed, catching up with her. "I could've *died,* Sky."

Sky clenched her fists and turned to meet her roommate's glare. Why did people have to interrupt her in the least convenient times? "I thought both would work, okay?" she shot back, a little sharper than she intended. "And you're fine, aren't you? It's not like anything bad came of it—"

"*Nothing bad?* Look around you, Sky. You think a metahero attack is *nothing bad?*"

"What? I didn't mean—wait. You caused that?"

"You think me running out of that portal at the same time as the attack is a coincidence?"

Sky raised her hands up in an "okay, you're right" kind of way. "Yeah, now that I . . . Can we please not talk about this right now? I'm sorry, yes, but we kinda have bigger things to worry about." She started backing off, ignoring Reine's sudden coughing fit. By the time the girl was opening her mouth again to say something else, Sky was long gone.

I bet Pantheon is going to kill me any second now, Sky thought as she ran. *If what Reine says is true . . .*

She knew it was probably best to stay low for now.

Reine stumbled after Sky, every inch of her body trying to give in and sink down to the floor instead. But that wouldn't do. Part of this disaster was her fault, and she needed to be there to see the consequences, even if Pantheon blamed her.

Water. At least drink some water, Reine, she reminded herself. *And don't focus on your argument with Sky, please. See the bigger picture—what was that?*

Just a second ago, she could have sworn someone had been sticking little half-sphere-shaped objects on the corridor walls. *Didn't that person look awfully shady?* Her mind did a 180-degree flip from the thought. *No, of course not.*

"Don't look. Don't think." A small voice crept into her mind. *"There's nothing to see here. I'm nothing. Just you. No me."*

Okay, Reine responded.

Sky was still running down the hallway, and Reine knew it was hopeless to try to catch up to her. Instead, she stopped at a water fountain. The familiar hum of the Goethan reactor told her that she was near the center of the school, so she looked for one of those holographic maps that lined the tunnels branching out from the circular platforms around the reactor. It told her that the north entrance was, indeed, to the north.

Am I missing something? she thought as she dragged her fatigued muscles down into the last stretch of the hallway. A thought suddenly struck her. *Those half-spheres can't be bombs, can they? That would be awfully shady, and these beeping devices aren't shady at all—oh.*

Something clicked, and Reine remembered Virus's warning. *Shady and Shadier: two metaheroes known for pulling off arrests* before the criminal even knows they're there. *Always proceed with extreme caution, and if possible, avoid confrontations entirely.*

Beep, beep, beep, beep . . .

Damn it, too late now.

Closing her eyes as she ran, Reine braced for impact.

In all the books Sky read, the scout or the assassin always had to use some sort of sneaky weapon; a dagger . . . a suppressed sniper rifle . . . it didn't matter. As long as the weapon was concealed and deadly, it fit the category.

Sky didn't agree with that philosophy. She studied the weapons in the armory as others passed through and picked up theirs. There weren't that many people left; she had to choose hers now.

If my teachers are going to group my skill set into one profession, then Pantheon can smite them all. I need something with a bit more . . . firepower.

Holstering a standard pistol and taking a utility knife from the armory, Sky glowered at the weapons rebelliously. She would still use a spy's equipment, of course, but that didn't mean she couldn't also be a normal soldier. There were advantages to being able to kill more than one target at a time, especially in full-on battles like this one.

Sky navigated herself with increasing urgency to the semi-automatic weapon section. She didn't have much time left before the armory locked down. Sky chose a gun and took it off the rack. She had trained extensively with the M4 carbine the previous year—Pantheon dictated that you had to have at least one year of experience with a weapon before bringing it into battle—so she was glad that her teachers had reluctantly approved its usage. Sneaking and assassinations were all well and good, but sometimes area denial was just as important.

And it should make my first kill easier.

The realization shocked her: this was her first real battle, the first time she could prove herself as a fighter. What would it be like to take a life in the name of Pantheon? She didn't know, but it did fill her with a sense of pride . . . and a prickling unease.

What if I'm the one who's killed? I always felt kind of invincible, but what if? Sky brooded, knowing that this probably wasn't the best time to contemplate her mortality.

Not only that—but could I even kill a person?

She shivered. She had already made peace with stealing, but death was far more permanent. Once they had passed to the other side, not even the strongest metahumans could cross *that* barrier. Maybe this was why she had picked an assault rifle; it was far less personal than a stab to the back.

For once, Sky was glad she chose the coward's way out.

With surprise, Reine saw a dome of ice form around her right before the bombs detonated like tiny fireflies in the dead of night. She instinctively shielded her head and could only watch as cracks spread along the hallway walls, causing pieces of the roof to crash down and shatter.

Her shield of ice collapsed a second later.

She took a running leap towards the hallway's exit. Broken glass and rubble were everywhere. Reine desperately rolled out of the hallway as the entire thing collapsed, entombing any unlucky individuals still in it. She couldn't help but look back. It frightened her, how close she had come to death. Not because she was afraid of dying, but because doing so would rob her of her revenge.

Still, maybe there are other things worth living for. She paused, dazed. *Huh.*

"Hurry."

She stood up and looked around for the source of the voice. It sounded dead tired. Reine was alarmed—but then she relaxed upon spotting Isaac slumped against a nearby wall, his face scrunched up in an involuntary grimace. His expression was a telltale sign of Goethan weakness. He had been the one to create the ice dome.

"Shady and Shadier already left to ransack the other areas of the building," he told her slowly, "so the best thing we can do is head to the north entrance. The teachers will deal with them."

Reine nodded, portraying a confidence she did not feel.

She still didn't know what to make of Isaac. On one hand, he didn't seem like the backstabbers that were so common at this school—he had just saved her, after all—but he also wasn't the most trustworthy person. The guy would do *anything* to achieve academic success. She could tell that much from their classes.

"Thanks," Reine replied quickly, "I'll see you there."

He waved a hand for her to go first.

When I mean "anything," I really mean anything.

Tiny little earth figurines could really pack a punch. One of the small monsters leaped for her head, and Sky batted it away with the back of her hand. She immediately regretted the action. Their fluid movements didn't make them any less hard, and she might as well have punched a heavy brick. Sky retreated, spraying bullets at them with her assault rifle. Chips of dirt landed everywhere on the grassy field while some dissolved to dust before they could touch the ground. Her powers were fully concentrated on avoiding the figurines flying through the air, so she couldn't help the other students who were also getting battered.

One had already hit her in the stomach, and it *hurt*.

"Abby! Can you carve a path to Gravedigger? If we can get close enough to distract him, he'll have to pull his forces back to protect himself."

The girl, who had been fighting at her side on the clearing above the school, turned and stared at her doubtfully, but complied. This was no time for their little dispute. As Sky motioned for other students to join them, Abby rushed forward, vaporizing any creature that touched her skin. Her ash-like Goethan mixed with the dust from the disintegrating figurines until she had to stop to protect her face from the stinging bits of dirt.

Sky suddenly heard Asher's voice behind her. "Hey, uh, I just wanted to say I'm sorry about that prank my friend played on your roommate."

She looked behind her in disbelief. "You're apologizing *now*, Asher? Can't you pick a better time?"

He smiled uneasily and conjured a few rainclouds to melt the closest figurines into slush.

"Better late than never, right?"

Before she could reply, his voice turned serious again. "Wait. I—Gravedigger's doing something weird."

Pantheon blight him! Sky raged silently. Powerful metahumans like Starflight could utilize a far more dangerous ability when they accessed the seventh level. She had learned somewhere that Gravedigger's had something to do with reanimation—hence his name. He suddenly loomed in front of her.

His face's basically a slab of stone, but those eyes . . . Ah hell, those raving, righteous—

The broadly built hero *slammed* his sledgehammer fists into the ground. It was as if an earthquake had struck. Heroes and villains alike flew through the air like they were nothing more than pieces of paper, and Sky almost got impaled on a sharp rock when she landed. The chaos wasn't just because the earth had heaved; Gravedigger's Goethan was throwing them around like rag dolls.

"Abby," Sky said through gritted teeth, "keep pushing through. I'm pretty sure he doesn't have enough power to do that again."

Sky eased herself off the ground, groaning. She could see that most of the fallen students were getting up too. Some had collapsed into a heap, dead from head wounds or previous injuries, but most had survived.

I can't hesitate about killing anymore, she realized. *This is war.*

"Abby?" Sky asked again. "Why aren't you—ugh."

As if things could get any worse, the traitor was scrambling back into the school with some of her friends. Sky couldn't even blame them at this point; she wouldn't want to charge at someone who could kill her in a second either.

Focus, she reminded herself through a haze of pain. *New threat incoming.*

Gravedigger's attack hadn't just been about that one blast of power; it was only the foreshock before the earthquake. Sky's senses scrambled to take in the situation, and she realized that tendrils of sleek, dark light were already snaking across the uneven earth. And whatever they touched came *alive.*

"Help me!" she heard someone shriek as a wisp of dark power latched onto his shirt, making it choke him until he died gasping.

Even the metaheroes looked uneasy. Misshapen creatures made of every kind of material—steel, wood, and human flesh— were clawing their way through the metavillains. Their defenses wouldn't last for long. And to Sky's horror, whenever one of her classmates died, their body would rise and join Gravedigger's forces with a semblance of uncanny life.

It was a massacre.

Where the hell is Pantheon? Sky's mind screamed as panic began overtaking her.

Reine knew that putting this base in a hidden location far from Valmount City had been a bad idea. All the powerful metavillains lived there, and even they had to cross through several security checkpoints before Pantheon's automated computer system would direct them to his school. Reinforcements would take at least fifteen minutes to arrive.

And only five has passed.

Dodging another one of the bombs Shadier had littered across the floor, Reine cursed the useless teachers who were tracking down the handful of metaheroes that had successfully infiltrated the school. They might be good at teaching, but there was a reason they weren't committing crimes in the city. Most of them were barely good enough to fight off a metahero who could enter the fifth or sixth level.

At the edge of the schoolyard, she crouched down and took a few seconds to rest and collect her thoughts. *This is terrible! The heroes don't have any problem calling reinforcements because Sky— well, I gave them the coordinates. I really hope Pantheon and Virus manage to stop them from spreading the information to the other bases. If they don't shut down transmissions, we might have to deal with attacks not just from these metaheroes, but all the others too!*

She staggered out into the open yard—one step, and then a rampaging corpse with steel for fingers lashed out from behind her, its glinting thumb catching her eye.

Reine caught its decaying hand in hers and twisted. The bloated appendage seemed to squirm as the flesh separated from the bone. If she hadn't been so focused on not dying, Reine would have gladly puked her guts out.

She kicked, and then kicked again. Another kick broke its legs, and Reine knew a final swing would whack its head right off. But she didn't do it. *I don't trust that weird energy thing powering the corpse,* she thought, backing away. *Who knows what it might do if I destroy its body?* She left the mangled corpse to writhe on the ground.

Reine felt a burst of pride. She had just dealt her first blow to the enemy! *Only a million more to go.*

She geared herself up to enter the fourth level and joined in the fray.

CHAPTER 16:
PANTHEON'S REVENGE

YEAR 2035

In a distant corner of the school, two metahuman corpses lay smoking on the ground, neither hero nor villain anymore. Death didn't care about such things, so Pantheon wouldn't either. Good or evil, both would bow to him eventually.

He studied the former brothers with disdain. Shady and Shadier had been rampaging around the school and damaging his precious infrastructure while he worked to halt the transmissions that a *little girl* had caused. What a disaster. Eajesuth had built the tunnels before his unfortunate demise, and their destruction meant another piece of his legacy was *wasted*.

Pantheon spread his will throughout the underground facility, repairing parts that might cause further cave-ins. The ability had belonged to a metahero he'd killed minutes earlier—he still remembered the flavors of his Goethan. After a moment of hesitation, Pantheon also absorbed the wealth of dispersing Goethan from the dead brothers' brains. They had both been highly trained metaheroes with vast reserves of power, so now he would use them to fuel his efforts in fixing the cracked walls.

He smiled grimly. It seemed fitting—almost fated, really— that the destroyers of the school should also remake it.

"Principal." It was Virus, speaking to Pantheon through his phone again; he took it out of his suit pocket. The man had an annoying habit of hacking into electronic devices to contact him.

"Yes?"

"The situation at the north entrance is . . . not good. I think we're going to need your help."

Pantheon closed his eyes. His subconscious mind painted a golden picture of the unfolding conflict devastating his student population; that would not do. Even he couldn't bring them back once they were dead. He sighed, making a picture-perfect rendition of disappointment. He thought he had trained them better.

"Merely an inconvenience."

Taking a step forward, Pantheon concentrated . . . and reappeared in the middle of the schoolyard. It was chaos. The world seemed to explode with the golden silhouettes of petty metahumans, their Goethan looking tantalizingly close. He ignored them. They were nothing more than snacks on the battlefield, and there was a . . . downside to taking their lives, a long-term effect no one could know about. It was a problem he was working on. He would still have to compromise and take some, just like he would have to take Gravedigger's, but he would spare those who cowered from his power.

Gravedigger was the only one worth killing here.

Pantheon's eyes narrowed, and he started to stroll leisurely, closing his fist to snuff out only the lives of the heroes who dared oppose him. He spread his consciousness throughout the ground. Villains and heroes alike gaped as the cracks that had been formed by Gravedigger's attacks healed, and the deadly energy tendrils that'd taken so many lives were extinguished like candles. Pantheon had absorbed them like he would any other Goethan, but the metahero's power rebelled against his will and returned to Gravedigger.

An invisible beam of concentrated gamma rays—powerful enough to kill a hundred people—flew towards Pantheon, sent from a metahero who leaped in front of him; however, he had already dodged it before she even released her deadly attack.

With a casual flick of his fingers, the unlucky woman combusted as his Goethan overpowered hers, killing several others in the explosion.

"Focus your powers on Pantheon!" he heard the heroes scream into their government-issued intercoms. "I'll take a team to flank him from the right while you ambush the man with Gummyeater."

Pantheon staggered back. Explosive missiles made of various materials started detonating near his head and created a cloud of rotating . . . gummy bears?

The villain dismissed them with a thought. Why did these worthless flies insist on bothering him? It was as if they wanted to die. More and more attacks of every kind were thrown his way, to the point that even his heightened body could not avoid them anymore. He wished it hadn't come to this. Snapping necks or burning metahumans alive with Goethan meant nothing to him, not anymore, but consuming their Goethan . . . Unable to tolerate the barrage of missiles, Pantheon *pulled*.

And every hero except for Gravedigger slumped to the ground.

Sky knew something was *very* wrong when the dancing gummy bears started to gnaw on Pantheon's head. He was drawing all the attacks to himself, standing still yet somehow also dodging and absorbing all the attacks with no sign of fatigue. She grabbed Asher's shoulder and shook it.

"What should we do?" she asked him frantically. "Do you think he needs our help? He looks like he needs our help!"

"Stop it!" He pushed her away. "Maybe—"

Like the sound of a dying tree, a whisper of agony permeated the courtyard. She perked up her ears in alarm. The haze of gummy bears had disappeared from Pantheon's head, so maybe he was the cause. She still didn't know what that noise meant, though. Was Gravedigger—

"Look!" Sky cried out.

All the heroes except for the hulking one in the middle collapsed. Just like that. Sky had to blink a couple of times before her eyes accepted what they were seeing. There were no tears, no anger. The entire group had just . . . given up.

Sky tentatively put her fingers on one of the metahero's throat. *Hell. Still warm, but no pulse. What in the world did Pantheon do?*

Asher kneeled down next to her. "My parents warned me about this after I was held back a year. They didn't want me to get on his bad side again."

Even knowing they were enemies, she averted her eyes from the sea of corpses. There was something wrong about the way they were killed, as if their very souls had been ripped out of their bodies.

"Come on. Let's get to a safe distance before those two duke it out."

They checked another dead hero's pulse, just to be sure. Pantheon was striding towards Gravedigger again, this time with purpose, but the hero didn't seem to care. He stared blankly at his fallen friends.

"Let's go!" Sky urged.

We don't stand a chance against these metahumans, she realized as she began her escape with the rest of her surviving comrades. *If there's even one other Pantheon out there, fighting for the heroes . . .*

There was no doubt about it; Gravedigger would get to dig their graves after all.

Asher and Sky climbed up a grass-covered hill and retreated onto the school's roof along with the rest of the students. Pantheon had stopped about thirty meters away from the remaining hero; maybe he didn't like his chances at a close-range fight. Sky tapped her foot nervously on the cleverly disguised building. It wasn't the safest place to be—as the roof of the underground school was only a little higher than ground level—but no one wanted to miss the fight.

"Are you okay?" Sky asked Asher.

He didn't respond; his attention was focused on the throng of panicking and injured people around him. Her heart sank, and he glanced guiltily at her. *So that's why he picked that moment in battle to talk to me . . . Stupid social pressure.* Sky shook her head. Asher still didn't want to be seen associating with her. *If he won't speak to me after I saved his life, what do I have to do to be accepted again?*

"It's okay. I understand," she muttered, a hint of bitterness creeping into her voice, "No need to—"

As if a giant had dug a hole in the earth, the ground around Pantheon dissipated, then streamed upwards to create a tooth-filled mouth more than twenty meters tall. Sky heard the students around her inhale nervously.

Their principal had been standing still again.

Then he'd disappeared from view.

"Pantheon's wrath," someone breathed.

The earth monster had swallowed him whole, presumably bringing Pantheon back to whatever depths it came from. Why wasn't he breaking out yet? Why—

The villain reappeared behind Gravedigger's back. With her powers activated, Sky could see the hero's eyes widen as he realized his mistake. Constructs couldn't hold someone who could teleport. Grunting as Pantheon kneed him from behind, Gravedigger swung at him uselessly, the metavillain retaliating with a chop to the neck. The panic shown by so few who had the chance to cross fists with Pantheon turned to calm; Gravedigger's stony face suddenly hardened into determined steel. Even the villain himself couldn't move faster than a hero who had so much to live for: injustice had to be made right.

Gravedigger dodged, leaning backwards at an almost ninety-degree angle. It was such a stunning feat of speed for a hero his size that Pantheon hesitated, shocked for one crucial second. It was enough.

Exuding so much Goethan that it became visible, the villain *jumped* into the air. It was as if he had become a black hole; metal, grass, dirt, and stone all started floating up, drawn into the cyclone of Goethan whirling around his body. With her enhanced vision, Sky could make out his eyes even at her distance. They were glowing gold.

Then he landed.

And everything blew apart.

Stupid soil. Always getting into my clothes.

When Reine regained consciousness, she found herself among several other students who were struggling to get up. Pantheon had taken the brunt of the attack—that was for sure. The space around the area the students were in was studded with so many broken pieces of stone and metal that it could have been a porcupine's back.

She felt her well of gratitude for the villain swell. Gravedigger was gone; Pantheon must have let him escape in order to save his students.

"**What were you thinking?**" a voice growled behind her.

She knew without turning that it was Pantheon.

"**If Virus and I hadn't stopped those transmissions from passing the data to the other hero bases, this place would have been destroyed!**" He continued, "**And I had to go personally level that government research facility to the ground. It** still had the coordinates of our location, which you allowed them to discover. Do you know how risky that is?"

Reine leaned back uncomfortably. She had never seen the man so angry before. If her transgression was so bad that even Pantheon couldn't maintain his aloofness anymore, what could she do to fix it? *Stay calm, Reine. You've dealt with this kind of situation before.*

"Are we going to have to move the location of the base then . . . sir?" she asked, trying to direct the conversation away from her. "I mean, Gravedigger escaped, and he still has the location in his mind. He could be taking a squad to attack us right now, right?"

Sweat started forming on Reine's forehead. What on earth had prompted her to choose something that would incriminate her even further?

Pantheon frowned thoughtfully. **"Very astute, but don't worry. Gravedigger's last attack brought his Goethan down to dangerously low levels, so one of my staff was able to dull his memories on the subject."** His glare seemed to deepen. **"But it will not be as easy to fix the school's infrastructure or lack of students. Do you know how thin we are stretched right now? Enemies surround us on all sides. Heroes and villains alike will be looking to exploit our weakness.**

"No." He seemed to make a decision. **"You will not be getting off so easy. Either you complete a mission for the good of the school—an assassination, perhaps—or die trying. I will give you and the other people involved in this incursion until the end of the semester to train. If you do not kill one of my rivals—a villain named Tremor—by the start of the next school year, I will personally make sure you never find any success in the world again."** He looked her in the eye. **"Starting with expulsion."**

What?

"But," Reine sputtered, "you can't . . . it's not possible for me to defeat a villain as powerful as you with only a year of training." She stared and waited for him to see reason.

Pantheon turned away in disgust. "**And I thought you had the courage to take on Starflight . . . No matter. Tremor won't be as powerful as me, I can assure you that. He—no, it—is more *thing* than human, anyway. You can use that to your advantage.**"

Reine wilted. No one else could make her feel as ashamed as this man. She didn't know why, but even Starflight didn't have such an effect on her.

"I'll try my best."

"**Your best isn't enough,**" he responded. "**I thought it was, but you've obviously disproven that.**"

Shaking his head, the villain checked the time on his phone. Then he threw a small, rectangular object to her. Reine could have sworn his disappointment hurt more than the actual task he had sentenced her to.

"**Here. I found this in the simulation room you were using. Don't care what it's for—just stop with the irresponsibility. I still have to talk to that Sky girl.**"

He closed his eyes and teleported away in a shower of sparks. Reine felt tears build up, but she refused to cry. *Worse things had happened before,* she lied to herself. Lowering her head to avoid her classmates' hostile glances, she checked the object her principal had thrown her: half gold, half sleek metal. Reine's eyes widened in surprise.

It was a realitydrive.

CHAPTER 17:
WHEN EVERYTHING FALLS APART

YEAR 2035

The government may have taken away our freedom, but the choices you make are still your own.

That's what her father had told her, right before they said goodbye. Sky sniffed. If only she had listened to him. In an environment where everyone had to lie and cheat in order to survive, she had slowly begun to think that such tactics were the norm. And look where they had brought her.

Back to her room and crying in bed.

"Hey, Sky, did Pantheon tell you about the assassination too?"

Sky tried to wipe away her tears. Reine was speaking. Reine was a person who had gone through so much, yet still made it through—unlike her. Sky just exploited everyone she met. She buried herself in her blanket and let the shame fester.

Pantheon was right. She deserved to go on his impossible death mission.

"You know," Reine continued, "I was going to, um . . . ask you about this realitydrive our principal gave me, but if you don't want to talk, maybe some other time?"

Sky didn't respond. She couldn't trust herself to speak. Her dad had always told her that things only *looked* bad at first, but she just didn't see how they could get better. *Maybe I should have gone with Mom,* she thought to herself. *He doesn't deserve a daughter like me.* Her parents had divorced right after the Great Enhancement: a time that seemed so far away it might as well have not existed. She had grown up without ever knowing her mother, but she didn't really care. Why wonder about a person she'd never met? Her thoughts started drifting back to her dad's death. Those memories always surfaced when the future seemed bleak, and she felt too tired to fight them. As Reine sat down quietly on the edge of her bed—the slight sagging of the mattress gave it away—Sky let her thoughts consume her.

"Oww. Stop. It hurts!"

Sky struggled futilely and tried to pry Starflight's iron fingers off her neck. She knew that if she could just get to the ground— even if it meant falling twenty meters—her dad would catch her. He always did.

"Then start screaming, you little brat," Starflight snarled. "I swear, if your dad doesn't come out of whatever hole he's crawling through in the next thirty seconds, I'm going to gut you like a fish."

Looking around in disgust, the woman that held Sky glanced at her watch. She had been hovering for five minutes now, so Sky knew Starflight couldn't stay much longer before the risk of reinforcements arriving would force her to leave.

"Well?"

Her hands still gripping Starflight's arm, Sky shook her head in defiance. Her dad would save her. Starflight was no match for him.

"No," she croaked.

Her captor growled and slapped her across the face, but Sky endured the pain. She refused to scream; that would mean letting the woman win.

"You little—"

With such savageness that Sky recoiled, Starflight grabbed a large chunk of Sky's hair and pulled. Not hard enough to yank her head off, but close. She bit back a sob.

Dad? she thought, knowing he couldn't hear her. *It really hurts.*

A familiar hum buzzed through the air. The sound filled Sky with renewed hope, and she could almost hear the rage in its voice. When her father was angry, the earth spoke for him.

"Why are you doing this? I have spies among your lackeys, Starflight. If you don't release her now—"

The all-encompassing tremors from the earth subsided, diminished by some unknown force. Sky looked up at her captor. No one had ever stopped her dad from speaking before. For the first time, doubt began to creep into her mind.

Just how powerful is she?

"No threats, Eajesuth," Starflight growled. "No time. Give me what I want, and I'll let her go."

The ground began to rumble again, but it was much more subdued. "And what is that?"

"A fight, of course." Starflight laughed, tightening her grip on the girl's neck. "A proper one. If I see any indication that you're trying to escape, I'll kill her."

Sky started sobbing. This strange metahero made her feel like she was a little girl again, like she was helpless—no, even less than that. If her dad died trying to save her . . .

"How can I trust you?" The voice from the earth was strained. "You could go back on your word anytime, and I wouldn't be able to do a thing."

Starflight's smile faltered, her features contorting into a thoughtful frown. Sky looked at the woman with interest. She seemed so unreal—almost larger than life. Maybe this was all a dream.

"You can't," she finally decided with a sneer, "but if you beat me, you won't have to."

She set Sky down on a nearby roof and quickly flew back before launching herself towards the ground. Purple lasers scored the earth as the hero fired in seemingly random directions. Sky could almost see her father parting rocks like they were no stronger than tofu, methodically avoiding the woman's attacks.

She realized that she needed to get to the ground. Her dad couldn't swim up buildings, but he definitely had the power to get them both away if she could reach that fire escape ladder leading down . . . She walked to the edge of the rooftop. Kneeling and stretching her arm over the edge, Sky grabbed at a rung that was just a little bit farther down than she would have liked. She was already on her knees, so any more movement would pitch her over the side of the apartment complex.

It was the first time looking down scared her. Even her dad couldn't catch her without breaking all her bones if she fell more than thirty meters. Sky felt her eyes being drawn to the battle below, and her heart started beating faster. What was going on down there? She needed to know.

Sky recalled a set of instructions that every student had learned in the first year of Pantheon's middle school. There were three, and each one was devoted to training for one level of the subconscious. Freshman year of high school—which she was going into after summer break—was the only year in which you learned how to access the fourth level as well as entering the first four levels quickly.

She started submerging herself in the first level. It was hard to concentrate while shivering, but Sky waded through her fear and tried to feel for the Goethan in her brain. It was the easiest level to access because your Goethan needed to travel the shortest distance.

Think of something random to relax, she thought. *How about . . .*

In the remaining years of high school, students could work on the fifth, sixth, and seventh levels—depending on their Goethan capacity, of course. Most people would never reach the seventh. In fact, the lack of powerful villains was actually the reason why Pantheon and her father decided not to add more than eight years to their school. As far as they knew, Pantheon was the only one who had ever gone above the eighth level . . .

Got it!

Sky started circulating her Goethan around her head: the corresponding body part to the first level. It didn't take much effort before she entered her subconscious.

And *felt.*

Sky shivered as she blocked out the sensation of crumbling cement and freezing wind from her sense of touch. Then she tried to restrain smell and taste and let sight and hearing run rampant.

"Stop running, Eajesuth!" she heard Starflight bellow. "Fight me, or I'll go back and kill your daughter."

Sky's blood ran cold. The hero was coming! She knew she didn't have much time left, so she braced herself . . . and jumped.

It was a long fall.

Everything blurred around her as she tumbled through the air. Panicking, Sky was sure she had missed her mark. Where was the rung? She grabbed blindly around her.

"Ooph."

Her hands touched cold steel. The impact stung, and she scrambled to place her feet on another rung. She banged her knee against the wall and laughed. It was the sweetest pain she had ever felt. Even a punch to the chest would be better than falling to her death.

She started to climb down.

"Sky? Can I tell you something?"

She looked up absentmindedly, watching the shadows dance across Reine's face. The lights weren't on, so maybe her roommate didn't notice. That would be best. Maybe she could still convince her she was asleep.

"To tell you the truth," her roommate said, "I didn't think you were going to be anything other than a resource I could use when I first met you."

Sky pulled the blanket tighter around her. She had expected Reine's words, but they still kind of hurt. *What a sorry bunch we are,* she thought bitterly. *It's a wonder our "friendship" lasted this long.*

"But as we spent more time together—especially after you saved me from that mind-controller—you helped me realize that maybe the whole world isn't against me. That there are still people who can be trusted. You made me understand that there is more to life than revenge, Sky. Just by talking to me."

"What?" She couldn't help herself. What Reine just said was so far away from what she'd expected that she had to say something. "But . . . I . . ." She searched for words. "Didn't I do the *opposite* of that? You know what's on that realitydrive, Reine. You know about the bet and everything else."

Sky sat up with a groan. "I know what you're like. You wouldn't have agreed to give it to me unless you checked the contents first. Right?"

Sky turned to look at Reine, and her roommate shrugged.

"Yeah," she admitted, "I did check, and I also asked Asher about your situation. He seems to want to repay us for saving him during that class."

Reine strove ahead. "But that doesn't matter, Sky. He told me about your dad, so I can kind of understand why you did what you did. I . . . would have done the same thing." She paused. "Don't get me wrong. I'm still mad at you, of course. Really mad." They both laughed nervously. "But I don't want to end this year on a bad note. For what it's worth, you helped me a lot."

Reine walked over and gently edged her hand onto Sky's. She felt a tingle of happiness spread up her arm. Sky relaxed. It felt good for both of them to finally have all their secrets out in the open.

"Plus," Reine said, "I think you're . . . never mind."

Even through the darkness of the room, Sky could have sworn she was blushing. "I get it," she replied sympathetically. "Feels weird opening up, right?"

"Yeah. I guess so."

Reine lapsed into silence. She seemed to be debating something with herself, so Sky let her think. Finally, she buried her face in her hands.

"So . . . um," Reine began, and then idled, her tone changing. "You want to tell me about your dad? Asher only skimmed over the details, because he was in a hurry."

Sky had a feeling that wasn't what Reine had been about to say.

"Sure," She shrugged. "You want to know about . . . what he was like?"

"If you're fine with it—"

"Yeah, I'm fine."

"Okay then."

Sky leaned back and propped her back against the wall.

"Eajesuth," she started hesitantly, not sure how to explain an entire person with only a few words, "was one of those metavillains that, instead of looking for power, always thought things could go back to the way they were—you know?"

Reine nodded.

"That's why he helped build this school," she continued, "so future generations won't have to die before they can learn to control their Goethan. Hell, it was kind of his dream to stop all these wasteful battles between the villains and heroes." A wistful smile spread across her face. "It wasn't only for peace, either. My dad had been a politician before the Great Enhancement, so he knew Goethan could be used for more than just fighting. I mean, look at all the stuff Pantheon did! What if everyone had access to these technologies?"

Sky sighed and wondered what else she could tell Reine. It had been so long since she had even thought about her dad, and to be truthful, he'd always been more of a mentor than a father. Always busy. Always planning. She loved him, but his "Eajesuth side" was as real to her as his "dad side." Sky sighed again. *Better get straight to the point.*

Clenching her fists, the girl swallowed. "The reason all my classmates hate me is because I am the reason he died." She cut Reine off before she could interrupt. "You . . . won't understand this, but my dad was like a father to almost everyone in the school. He was one of the founders, after all, and someone they could trust to protect them from metahero attacks.

"In fact . . ." Sky paused, smiling fondly at the memory. "He would bring in new recruits personally while Pantheon negotiated with the other villains. Most of them were from labs or prisons—this was way back when the government still conducted experiments on children—so they practically grew up in this school!"

She exhaled and lay back down. A rueful look came over her face. "Sometimes I wish he had just left me there. You ever get that feeling? Maybe Starflight wouldn't have hurt him."

"Did you say Starflight?"

Sky turned to look at Reine. Her normally beige skin suddenly flushed red, showing an angry side she had only seen once before.

"Yeah . . . why?"

"It doesn't . . . well I guess it does matter, but not right now. You're telling me that Starflight killed your parents too?"

Sky shrugged. "My mom left when I was two, so maybe? As for my dad . . . wait. Did you say 'too?'"

It was Reine's turn to shrug. "I don't want to talk about it yet," she replied evasively. "Sorry about interrupting. Why don't you continue?"

So Sky did.

Sky was back on top of the apartment roof again. Starflight had noticed her escaping, and had taken a second of her time to undo all of Sky's work, dragging her back up. However, Sky's father was faring better than the metahero. With his dexterity and speed in the ground, even Starflight couldn't hope to keep up with him. And she was getting frustrated.

"Eajesuth!" the hero screeched, "I'm warning you!"

Instead of trying a new attack like she expected, Starflight flew back towards Sky instead. She panicked and tried to dodge the hero with a choked scream but was dragged up into the air by her neck. Starflight's free hand started to burn. Sky's eyes widened as a concentrated laser about a third of her neck's width formed in Starflight's curled fist. The metahero held it threateningly over the girl's head.

Sky kicked at her stomach. *Where's my dad? Why is he still hiding?*

"Enough!"

She looked down. Starflight had brought them to what must have been a tantalizingly close distance for her father. Either this evil woman was extremely confident, or she truly thought Eajesuth wouldn't try to save his daughter.

Will he?

Sky suddenly felt much younger than thirteen.

"Oh well, *little girl,*" Starflight growled maliciously after a few seconds of waiting, "I guess your daddy doesn't think you're worth it after all."

She began to inch the laser closer and closer to Sky's neck, and the girl shrank back. She could feel the blade-sharp heat emanating from the hero's hand. Sky forced defiance into her eyes. If this was going to be her last moment, then she wasn't going to make it easy for the hero.

"Please stop. I'm begging you."

Sky glanced down with shock, and her heart almost exploded with relief. Starflight's face slowly curled into a smile. She guessed the hero never had any doubts about whether her dad would rise from the cracked earth.

"If I surrender, will you let her go?"

Sky blinked in surprise. What was her dad saying? For a moment, she almost thought the man hunched over in a bow wasn't someone she knew at all. Where was the boldness, the warmth in his voice? But no—she had known him too long to make a mistake like that. Short and slim: that was him.

"You think I'm stupid?" Starflight responded with a crazy lilt. "I want to see you dead, Eajesuth! Not in custody! Even I know I'm not allowed to kill you if you come peacefully, so attack now, or watch your daughter die."

The hero raked her energy-filled palm down from Sky's neck to the middle of her back. The girl's muscles spasmed as a burning pain greater than any she had felt before branded itself into her body. She gasped for breath. Her body was literally burning.

"Be thankful it's just a laser," the metahero told her. "I cauterized your wound for free."

She turned back to the trembling villain and took a moment to toss Sky back to the top of the apartment. At this point, all the girl could remember was the pain and the coldness of the cement beneath her. She was afraid to move, afraid to find out the extent of her injury. For the first time in her life, she felt like she might actually die. Sky choked back tears. No one was going to save her—not even her dad.

She started crawling towards the side of the building. Why not? It distracted her from the pain, and she wanted to see what was going on.

Sky stopped. The shifting of the building was making her sick, and the only reason she hadn't vomited yet was because of the burning . . . *What am I doing again?* Sky concentrated, but she couldn't think through the haze of pain.

She could hear her heartbeat . . . and it was . . . getting slower . . . getting . . .

"Get away from my daughter, you monster!" her father bellowed.

Like a missile, something crashed down a few meters away from Sky. Even with her cape and purple outfit in tatters, the object was unmistakably Starflight. The girl whimpered. As the hero started to stand back up, she struggled to move . . . to escape.

Then the building came alive.

And Starflight vanished.

Sky blinked, frozen with shock. She didn't know how to describe it. The cement had split as if it were opening a gaping mouth and dragged the woman down with tentacle-like cables. One second the entire building was writhing, and the next it turned still, leaving only her memory as evidence.

Sky let out barely a whisper, asking, "Dad?"

It couldn't be anyone else—but how? She had only ever seen him use his Goethan to travel through the earth, and controlling an entire building was . . . different. *More.*

Shhhhhh . . .

The sound surrounded her, giving her enough comfort that she didn't scream when the building pulled her in—this time gently. She felt the familiar sensation of rocks parting and earth

163

moving as she sank down deep into the ground, propelled by her dad's power.

"Where . . . where are we going?" Sky murmured to him. She couldn't see him, but his presence was all around her. It felt like being in a little cabin in the middle of a storm. Sky curled up in response. She was safe, even while everything around her fell apart.

And that was enough for now.

When they reached the school, a smooth, stone wall disintegrated into crushed granite, and the marble ground softened as she tumbled onto the floor of a classroom. The desks moved themselves out of the way. Sky panicked momentarily when she felt her dad's presence leave, but relaxed when he returned with Pantheon. The metavillain dealt with her most serious wounds as Eajesuth's disembodied voice recounted the events to him. His face was drawn into a serious frown, more troubled than he should have been. Hadn't things turned out pretty well?

Sky frowned.

And why couldn't she see her father?

"**Do you truly think your sacrifice is worth it?**" Pantheon asked bitterly. "**Damn it, Eajesuth, I need you to help with the school.**"

He seemed to be much more emotional than usual, as if something could actually worry *him*. Sky loved her dad, but this guy was on a whole other level.

"Is it because of what Starflight did to me?" she asked curiously.

"**What?**" He actually seemed confused. "**No. You should be fine. Scarring won't kill anyone.**"

"Then what is it?"

It was her dad who finally answered. His voice filled the room with the peace of an underground stream, directly contradicting the message he was about to deliver.

"Sky . . . I'm dying."

"What?" She laughed and her voice broke. What else was there to do?

"Using the eighth level always has a cost," he explained soothingly, "and it just happens to be steeper for me than others. Once I become one with the elements, I can never go back."

The words seemed to resonate in Sky's head, making her dizzy and confused. Pantheon had to catch her as she almost fell. She didn't even turn her head when a semblance of her father, made of dust and wind, hugged her gently from behind.

"How long do we have?" she whispered, "I can't . . . I can't believe—"

Sky buried her face in his shirt and started shaking uncontrollably. Even when Pantheon stepped forward, as if impatient to talk to her dad before he faded away, one look from Eajesuth made him stop. He had enough respect for her father to allow them this one moment.

"Only a few hours left," he replied, smiling sadly, "but that doesn't mean anything, Sky. Just think about it. I'll always be here for you, even when I'm gone."

She swallowed.

"In fact, you'll never feel lonely again. I'm one with the earth, so whenever you take a step, I'll be right there supporting you."

He hugged her tightly, and Sky felt a little better.

"Now listen. I have to talk to Principal Pantheon for a bit, so why don't you hurry to the nurse's office and get checked up. You know where it is, right?"

She nodded. She knew he wanted to talk to Pantheon in private, but it wasn't like she was going to fight him on it. Sky was too tired to care. As she walked off, she slowed down enough to hear the villain say something before leaving.

"I hope you understand the consequences of your actions, Eajesuth." He seemed to be back to his emotionless self. **"Can one girl truly replace your invaluable assistance? Of course**

not. She might as well have killed you, and yet you still love her."

Sky's entire body went tense, but she continued out of the room as if she hadn't heard his words. They followed her like a pack of hounds and drove away any comfort her dad had given her. Only when she was far out of earshot, did she let the tears fall.

"Are you okay, Sky?" the nurse asked when Sky arrived at the infirmary.

There weren't many students at the school yet because it was summer break, so everyone—students and staff included—knew each other on a first-name basis. Sky just showed her the wound, and the woman didn't bother with small talk. She hurried Sky into her office.

"My gods. What happened to you?" she said, snapping on a pair of gloves. "Come here, quickly." Then, closing her eyes, the nurse stood still. Sky could feel power emanating from her hands, and the woman gently peeled what was left of her bloody shirt from the wound.

"I'm just going to do a checkup on you, alright?"

Sky nodded. It felt strangely invasive, but knowing it was good for her helped. After a few minutes of probing, the nurse released her control of the fourth level. She told Sky to lie down.

"The scar tissue looks pretty deep," she explained, "so you might have some permanent damage in that area. However, it's too early to know for sure. Why don't you come back in a few days?"

Sky nodded again. Blankly. Even the prospect of being crippled paled in comparison to her father's impending death. Wasn't there supposed to be a way for her to save him? That's what all the stories she read said. Someone important gets cursed, and the hero has a day or two to find the cure.

Sky rubbed her burn wound. She was beginning to realize that real life was so much more complicated than generic stories.

"Stop it!" Shaking her head, the nurse swatted the girl's hand away from the injury. "You shouldn't touch it," she scolded. "Pantheon did something to your Goethan to numb the pain for a few hours, but it still needs to heal. That reminds me—here's some ointment and medicine for you. Just follow the instructions on the back." She passed Sky the medications and gave her a warning glare. "I'm being serious here. If you keep messing with the wound, I'm probably going to have to bandage it."

Sky did her best to look chastised and tucked the medicine into her pocket. She tried to go back to where she had last seen her father and Pantheon talking, but the nurse held her by the shoulders and escorted her to her room.

"Now lie down or relax. You'll thank me later when Pantheon's pain-numbing wears off," she told her as she walked out of the room. "And remember to apply the burn salve!"

Sky yawned in response.

It took another five minutes before she managed to get the nurse out of her room. When she finally heard the door close gently behind her, Sky pulled the pillow over her face. The nurse had left behind a darkness that pressed on her mind with the weight of an anvil, pushing out all the bleak and depressing thoughts she had accumulated during the day. It made her want to turn on the lights, but she was too tired to get up. Too tired to even cry.

Shhhhhhh . . .

An underground breeze from the corridor blew through her room's window and bled the warmth out of her body. Sky shivered. She felt like she was being drained dry. Pulling the blanket closer, the girl tried to fall asleep, but dark thoughts kept creeping into her mind.

Things will look better in the morning, she told herself. *Don't think about that. Count sheep or something. Wait . . . does that even work?*

"Baby? Are you awake?"

Sky rubbed her eyes blearily. She must had eventually fallen asleep because, well . . . someone woke her up.

"I can feel my consciousness unraveling, and I don't want to leave before I say a proper goodbye," the voice explained. "How are you feeling? I heard the nurse say you were pretty tired."

She blinked as her memories came rushing back. "Dad?"

The man grinned. He was composed of rock this time.

"Are you okay now?" she asked hopefully, sitting up.

Eajesuth shook his head.

"I'm sorry, Sky, but it's like I told you before. I'm just here to say goodbye." His smile was pained. "Don't worry. I'm sure you'll be fine. The school will protect you."

She felt tears start to well up in her eyes again. "But you won't! You—you don't deserve to die!" She stood up and hugged him tightly, ignoring the sharp edges of the rocks that composed his body. "Can't Pantheon do anything?"

Her dad just hugged her back.

It was enough.

For now.

CHAPTER 18:
TRUE THIEVES DON'T GET CAUGHT

YEAR 2035

Reine lithely dodged to the side of the mannequin as it turned slowly, following an easily discernible pattern. Real humans wouldn't be nearly as predictable, of course, but that's what reading body language was for.

She snatched the watch—a rarity—out of its pocket. This was already her third time completing the challenge, and no one else in her class had mastered it yet. For a school that was so centered on committing crime, it sure didn't make basic pickpocketing a priority.

Everyone's probably too busy fighting heroes, she thought. *Pantheon seemed pretty worried the last time I talked to him.*

Accelerated Advanced Thievery was one of the only classes where villains in training weren't allowed to use their powers to solve every problem. It made for a refreshing change. The exercise she was doing right now was a basic warm-up to develop her behavior reading and reaction speed—or at least that's what Ms. Oderman, the teacher, had said. Why couldn't the woman just understand that Reine was ready to move on to more complicated stuff?

"Alright class," Ms. Oderman finally yelled, "that's enough for today. We still need to cover the end-of-year exams, and if you don't want to fail, you'll listen."

That was another thing Reine found weird. This was the fifth class she had been to today, and every one of them had briefed the villains on what their missions—a.k.a., end-of-year exams— would be on. It was as if the entire point of school was to pass these tests instead of retaining the information they learned.

She shrugged internally. Maybe that's just how real school was. She knew her parents always made sure she honed every skill to perfection, but it must be harder to do that when there were hundreds of students, right?

"So pay attention," the woman continued to say. "I don't want to have to repeat myself, even if the information *is* inside our database. We're going to be doing an assessment in the simulation room to show you how much you still need to work on."

She turned to glare at a student typing something on her school-issued laptop. "Computers away. I already told you the information is online, so no need to take notes."

Reine's classmate reluctantly shoved it back into her bag.

Ten boring minutes later, the class finally got around to the part that Reine was looking forward to. Ms. Oderman had explained the goal—sneaking in and out of a metahero's mansion with a valuable object—and she was excited to finally see how much she had to catch up on.

The previous classes hadn't been easy for her. She still couldn't access her subconscious easily because her mind was constantly flitting around, unable to become calm unless she was threatened by real danger. It was kind of ironic, actually. Fear and anger distracted her, but she couldn't find the will to concentrate unless they were there.

Reine ran her hand through her hair nervously. Her turn would come soon, right after Isaac's. They were allowed to use Goethan, but since everyone else had more experience than her, she didn't gain much confidence from the fact. At least Ms. Sinclair had taught her a few tricks. The mission results, including the simulated ones, were like a social status thing in the school.

She stood up to enter the simulation portal. Reine didn't really care if someone else did better than her, but she didn't want to get last place. That meant rejection from people who could help her defeat Starflight—and maybe even expulsion. Who knew what Pantheon would do if she put that last straw on the camel's back?

The watery feeling of the portal washed over her, and Reine took a deep breath. Even though the teacher would be supervising her from the classroom this time, she couldn't help but feel a hint of apprehensiveness from her previous experience.

You can do this, she told herself. *It's not like there's going to be a sarcastic robot this time. Or a system failure.*

She swatted the thoughts away. Thankfully, the inside of the simulation was completely different from a featureless room. Instead, Reine appeared on a bustling street full of people. The target was clear: a massive, meticulously designed modern mansion stood in front of her, dwarfing all the other slightly transparent buildings and their decorations. She navigated awkwardly around the throng of people. Reine was used to operating at night, so she had never encountered a crowd so big before.

Still, they should provide good cover if I ever need to make a run for it.

She pushed past another featureless person and finally arrived at the front door of the mansion. She would have tried to find another entrance, but it wasn't like she could scale the building with so many people watching her. Not to mention that Ms.

Oderman said she only had fifteen minutes. There just wasn't enough time to take the risk.

But . . .

If this was truly a test of skill, then it would be unreasonable to assume that a person could navigate through an entire house while dodging security cameras, guards, and traps without any knowledge of the floor plan. Finding a valuable object under these conditions would depend more on luck than skill, as even the most practiced villains couldn't use tools when they had none.

Reine backed away from the door. She had a hunch that the test wasn't as straightforward as it seemed. The door solution was too obvious. She headed left and came up to a fence twice as tall as her. There was a flashing light peeking through the cracks of the wall.

She grinned. The only thing they had been given was an electronic code—one that she assumed would be used for the door. However, maybe it would work for something else too. Reine ran her hand through her hair nervously. They were allowed to use their powers, but were supposed to assume that everyone would view the action as illegal. Even being noticed by a pedestrian would make the rest panic and attack, so it wasn't the best choice. She took another look at the fence.

Yup. I'm not scaling that thing without handholds.

She sighed, feeling resigned.

Two precious minutes later, Reine, fueled by her anxiousness of the ticking clock, entered the first and fourth levels. She was immediately greeted by all the customary perks; the world became clearer as her brain started to work overtime, and she could now access her Goethan.

Reine projected an illusion of a still body from herself and walked around, examining it carefully. She needed to make sure that the illusion she created was a perfect replication of her external body. It hadn't been too hard, especially since all she'd had to do was "copy and paste," but a lack of Goethan here or there could have disastrous results. The principle was that she would be invisible to everyone as long as no one touched her image and disrupted the illusion. Reine frowned, wishing she had more time. Her projection was stiffer than a soldier, and she had no idea if the simulation people would find it suspicious.

Oh well.

Reine tensed her legs and *jumped.* Her Goethan-enhanced leap propelled her hands just high enough that they could grab onto the wall and pull her over. She winced. It hadn't been noticeable before, but glass shards lined the fence like icing on cake, and her hands were cut in a dozen places. She ignored the pain. Careful to land on the pavement that occupied half of the yard, Reine shied away from the grass. She was invisible to security cameras, since the first level allowed her to affect nonliving objects; the imprint of her shoe on grass was not.

Nine minutes and counting.

Reine slid over to a flashing control panel with practiced grace. As she had suspected, the test makers had left the little gift for students to exploit if they were smart enough to find it. She started deactivating the traps but ignored the security cameras; they posed no threat to her in her invisible state. The guards would probably get suspicious if their camera feed was turned off, anyway.

Eight minutes and counting.

Feeling a surge of adrenaline, Reine waited until one of the security cameras rotated to face the other way, then opened the side door and quickly went inside. She closed it behind her, of course; its well-oiled hinge made no sound. The young woman raised an eyebrow. The room she had entered was filled to the brim with all sorts of treasures, from golden statues to diamond necklaces. She was sure it was bought by government money that was earned from capturing or killing villains, so Reine felt no remorse as she scooped up a handful of jewelry. *Huh,* she thought, bemused. *I'm pretty sure Ms. Oderman didn't mean "consider the ethics" when she told us to treat this test like the real thing.* She chuckled and prepared to leave. Then stopped.

What did she say we were supposed to steal again? Reine searched her memories. From what she could remember, the woman had been incredibly vague, mentioning that the object they were looking for was valuable and nothing else. Her mind went back to the ten-minute lecture she'd given to her class.

"Even though you can obviously steal more than one item from the metahero's mansion—and you're welcome to do so for the real test—we're only going to count the most valuable object you steal for the purposes of this simulation. Remember: the more expensive it is, the more points you get."

Seriously?

Cursing under her breath, Reine checked the golden clock hanging on the wall. She had only six minutes left before the portal would close, leaving her with five minutes to find a suitable prize and one minute to get the hell out. The young woman slipped a simulated platinum bracelet into her pocket. There were bigger prizes to hunt, but it never hurt to have a backup. She tiptoed into the open hallway. She had memorized the basic floor plan while deactivating the traps, so she knew to head left and up. That was where the laboratory was located, and the path didn't have security cameras monitoring the doorways.

I really hope there aren't any traps unconnected to the main grid, Reine thought as she climbed the stairs. *Like that sensor in Starflight's house. Ugh. I can't believe I fell for that.*

She had considered checking the study first before heading to the lab, but just thinking about it brought back nightmarish memories. *Better to brave the unknown then confront the past.* Adrenaline surged through her veins, and she analyzed the situation. Two guards stood in front of the laboratory entrance, their bulk blocking the electronic keypad required to open the sliding door; this was both good and bad. On one hand, it meant that whatever was in there had to be worth stealing. On the other, there was no way for her to get in the room . . . even if she managed to slip between the guards without being touched. They would notice the keys being pressed down, and if not, definitely hear the door open.

Reine took a moment to renew her connection with the projection that was still standing outside the mansion's walls. Submerging herself in two levels at once was becoming more taxing by the minute, and she knew that if she even relaxed her concentration for a second, the invisibility would break.

I only have three minutes left . . . think, Reine. Think!

She decided to try the age-old technique of distraction. She gave in to the urge to detach herself from her subconscious and breathed out slowly. The horde of simulated people outside would notice if anything out of the ordinary occurred, Reine knew, so she waited for her illusion to disappear and draw their attention. The guards' heads turned sharply as muffled cries of "Did she just vanish?" and "That girl was standing there a second ago!" came from beyond the mansion walls. Reine hid herself inside a nearby bedroom. She had felt a pressure on her mind lift, confirming that she was no longer invisible or submerged in any levels.

The young woman peeked out from behind the room's door. One of the guards had left to check on the situation, but the other was still guarding the entrance to the lab.

"Damn it," she muttered, looking around the bedroom for a weapon. Reine didn't have any qualms about hitting someone with a lethal weapon—at least not in a simulation—so she dislodged a decorative dagger from its stand on the wall. She briefly considered turning it invisible to make the sneaking part easier, but there was no time. Not to mention that her powers only extended to creating illusions related to the human body. What was she going to do . . . make the dagger look like an extra hand? The only reason she was even able to make herself invisible was because she had been projecting her image into another space.

Focus.

She exited the bedroom and made her way back to the laboratory door, where the solitary guard still stood.

Reentering the fourth level, Reine transferred her Goethan to her hands. The fourth level allowed her to trick humans with illusions, so she made the guard's gun look like a beating heart and dashed forwards with her knife. The man dropped it with a shudder. She couldn't blame him; not only must it have been a heart-stopping transformation, but the heart she made . . . wasn't very heart-like.

You really need to practice, she reprimanded herself.

She dodged behind him with her Goethan-enhanced reflexes, wincing as she drove the knife into the guard's neck. It penetrated right at the base of the skull and severed the brain stem. She wiggled the blade around to compensate for any errors.

"It'll be over soon," she whispered, more for her own benefit than the dying guard's. She lay him on the floor gently so his body wouldn't make a thud. "And there's no need to struggle. With your spinal cord disconnected, it's literally impossible for you to move."

The man glared at her. He didn't seem too impressed with her knowledge of biology. She left him to fade away into lines of code—*I wonder if the other guard will notice*—and calmly typed the password Ms. Oderman had given them into the keypad. The two halves of the sliding door opened like an entrance to another world, revealing dangerous-looking instruments scattered around the lab. There were drills with impossibly thin needles and unusually large scalpels, but Reine reminded herself that they couldn't hurt her unless there was someone to use them. She abandoned caution and used her remaining minute to scour the room for anything that looked remotely valuable. She didn't close the door because opening it again would take too long, and she kept herself submerged in the fourth level because it would help her focus.

There!

Like it was a beacon, Reine felt her eyes being drawn to a thick, leather-bound book placed in the center of the room. She couldn't understand why. Though a novelty, this kind of thing couldn't be that rare inside such a rich metahero's house, right? She started to walk towards it, picking up a glowing potion labeled "Reality Enhancement" as the book title came into view. The swirling lines of code swimming inside the flask should have entranced her, but all she could think about was the textbook.

An Advanced Guide to Goethan Usage? Isn't that a government-issued read for all metaheroes?

Reine almost left it where it was. It wasn't anything special, after all. The school had a few copies, but her class wasn't allowed to access them until they met certain academic requirements.

Still . . .

She knew all the jewels and riches in the simulation were fake, but perhaps the book was different. It did feel . . . more real, as though it were less superficial than the world around it. If she took it with her, Ms. Oderman might let her keep it. There were no rules against taking extra objects—just that only the most valuable one would be scored. Reine tucked the book under her arm and patted the vial of golden liquid in her pocket. It would have to do. Ms. Oderman was a believer in science, right?

And I still have that bracelet too.

Then there was a percussive bang, and a bullet struck her right above the belly button.

CHAPTER 19:
REVOLVING REALITY

YEAR 2035

Reine lost control of the fourth level as more shots fired, gun tips poking through the open lab entrance. She knew she should have closed the door. For a second, everything was a blur of wood as she collapsed behind one of the desks dotting the room; then she felt a horrible burning sensation begin to creep from the middle of her stomach. The pain from banging her head on the floor was like a mosquito bite next to a tiger mauling, and it was only the fear of getting shot again that made her get up and look.

She was surrounded on all sides by guards holding guns, barring her way to the portal. If Reine didn't get there in the next minute, she would fail the test. The young woman gave a pained smile to the guards. They were evidently aiming to arrest rather than kill.

"Mind if I sit down for a second?" she asked, already hunching over. "Don't worry, I won't tell your boss. He's not here today, right?"

Every one of the guards was wearing a stereotypical "security guard" uniform, meticulously ironed and almost *too* perfect. One of them glanced at his captain warily. The captain waved her hand and said, "Let her sit. We have to wait for Mr. Duksy to come document this capture anyway."

Reine scowled. She wanted to ask if they knew how ridiculous their boss's name was, but resisted the temptation. It would only endanger her plan. Instead, she sat down heavily, shifting her left hand so it touched the vial in her pocket. None of the guards noticed a thing.

Pop!

With one swift movement, Reine whipped the potion out of her pocket and chugged it down. It tasted like a fresh outlook on the world, and she shuddered as reality unraveled.

The captain leveled her gun at Reine's head. "Shoot her. Now!"

Bits of lead leaped from all sides. Time seemed to slow. No—it *was* slowing. As she whirled around in panic, the young woman realized that the world was . . . different. Everything around her had become a mass of Goethan and numbers, as if the simulation were concocted from reality-changing Goethan that brought the computer code to life.

She looked down and noticed the glowing, rectangular anomaly in her pocket. It seemed to be made of the same material as her cloth and skin. A pale, shining fire that signified her roots in reality.

It's the book, she realized. *I guess it is real after all.*

Jerking her head away from the mesmerizing glow, Reine hunched down. Where were the bullets? She should be peppered with holes by now. She stood back up as the guards raised their guns again.

BOOM! CRACK! BOOM!

This time, she paid attention to the little specks of code when they sped towards her. It was almost comical how slow they were, but still fast enough that Reine couldn't dodge them. She winced. The first one was already touching her skin, and then it . . . vanished?

Reine blinked, not quite believing her eyes. Was she burning up the bullets?

She ignored the guards' flabbergasted expressions, and started running towards the lab's front wall, then shoved her hands against it like she was going to do a push-up. The metal-like material crumbled inwards with a satisfying crunch. The barrier couldn't withstand her burning flesh; her realness was literally destroying the simulation.

I hope the bracelet in my pocket is alright. I wouldn't want to return empty-handed.

She grinned. Such paltry concerns were beyond her now. She looked down; even the bullet wound in her stomach—almost certainly deadly in real life—had been healed. The prospect of getting to the portal suddenly didn't seem too hard at all. She felt like a god: immortal.

"On my order," the captain said, "attack!"

Her subordinates threw themselves at Reine as soon as they realized their guns had no effect on her. Reine punched a guard through the chest while blocking an incoming baton with her other arm. It seared right through it and its holder's neck at the same time. Another man backed away as his partner jumped on top of her. She felt hands pulling her into a chokehold, and then they were gone—nothing but hot air. She barreled through the walls of the mansion. They brought down the rest of the building in an explosion of dust.

"Stop her!"

As if they were a collective hive mind, the pedestrians that had seemed so nice before snarled like a pack of freaking monkeys and grabbed at her uselessly. She didn't stop. The only thing blocked was her vision, and even that was remedied by a few annoyed swats.

Reine left a trail of destruction in her wake.

"Five!" Huge numbers began to count down in the sky. Ms. Oderman's voice echoed in her eardrums. "Four."

She swore that her shoes were leaving holes in the ground. She was moving so fast it didn't matter.

"Three!"

Is it me, or is this potion wearing off?

"Two!"

"Oh, shut up."

"One!"

Tensing all her muscles, Reine leaped into the closing portal just as the countdown hit zero. She emerged on the other side a second later and crashed arms-first into the student waiting for her turn to enter. Her vision instantly returned to normal; the reality enhancement potion didn't work in the real world.

"Muirne!" Ms. Oderman shouted, looking aggrieved. "What did I say about not standing too close to the portal?"

The girl backed away and let Reine pick herself up. She for one was glad there was somebody there to cushion the blow. As Muirne entered the simulation, Ms. Oderman began to type on her laptop, giving Reine some time to rest. The young woman leaned against the table. The feeling of invincibility that came with the reality enhancement potion was wearing off, and she couldn't help but feel a hint of regret.

Could I have defeated Starflight if I had that in real life?

Ms. Oderman waved her over. "Let's see," she said. "The portal was supposed to recover and score any simulated items you might have brought through it, but . . ." She frowned. "You didn't get anything? I gave you fifteen minutes!"

Reine patted her pockets instinctively, then set her hands down, darting a glance at Ms. Oderman to see if she'd noticed. Of course the platinum bracelet wouldn't be there. Anything created by the simulation stayed in the simulation. Even for this test, the things they stole would just be assigned a point-score before returning to their original position. She raised her eyes to the ceiling. *The platinum bracelet must have been destroyed by the potion's effects. When it enhanced the reality around me, I guess it spread to my clothes as well as my body.*

"Um." Reine racked her brain for an excuse. She held up the book she had found in the lab. "Does this count?"

"A textbook?" Ms. Oderman's eyes widened. Hurrying over to Reine, the teacher squinted at the title through her glasses. "*An Advanced Guide to Goethan Usage* . . . what made you pick this out of all the other choices?"

Reine ran a hand through her hair. She was painfully aware of how crazy her explanation would sound. *It just . . . felt right? I based my entire test result on a hunch?* She had no idea what to say.

"It wasn't really my choice, you know," she said defensively, "I had to take the reality enhancement potion."

"You know . . . that one in the lab . . ." she added before shutting up. *Stop digging yourself deeper into your hole, Reine. It's not like you weren't the one who wanted to take the risk in the first place.* She braced herself for admonishment, but Ms. Oderman nodded her head knowingly. It had somehow been the right thing to say.

"Well . . ." she started, "I would normally give you a score of ten out of fifteen since you actually brought back an item—half of my class didn't—but . . ." She sighed. "We're not grading on a curve for the final exams, so we can't do that for this test either. I swear. Kids these days don't even use their brains!"

She started typing on her computer again. "I guess . . . you deserve an eight out of fifteen. A book we already own isn't all that valuable."

Reine looked down glumly. She knew she deserved the mediocre score, but it still hurt her pride. Wasn't stealing supposed to be the one class she was good at?

Then she noticed the wry frown on Ms. Oderman's face. "However, as it was placed purposefully in the hardest area to get to test your ability at thievery, I believe this book is more than a mere leather-bound textbook." She scratched her head, as if even *she* couldn't believe what she was about to say. "It's an indication of your readiness to move on to the next class."

Whoa!

Reine stood, trying to smile to show her gratitude, but failing miserably. She had never been good in situations like these. What was she supposed to do? Thank the teacher profusely in a way she was sure would seem insincere?

"What do you mean?" she asked.

Questions. Questions were good.

"Well . . . I suppose you could move up a level in our thievery courses, but that's only if you want to do it as a career. I would suggest filling it with some other class. Maybe a free period?"

Reine crossed her arms. She . . . didn't want to be a thief. None of her parents' cunning had mattered when they fought against a top metahero, for one, and it's not like she was going to steal Starflight to death. She wanted power—physical power she could use to bash the hero's face in.

"Is there any chance I could take a more advanced class on Goethan usage along with Mr. Nidek's basics?"

Ms. Oderman adjusted her glasses. "Let me see . . ."

Mr. Nidek had been cleared by Pantheon to teach again, probably because the guy didn't care too much about attempted murder. No actual harm done, right? Reine suspected it was to spite Asher. Pantheon couldn't punish him for almost getting killed, but that didn't mean he thought Asher deserved to be let off the hook completely.

"Well, the school rules certainly aren't against it. You'll just have to take another half semester course when Mr. Nidek starts teaching the more advanced stuff."

Reine nodded, and Ms. Oderman waved for her to leave. She stopped at the doorway, and then turned and said, "Oh, I forgot to ask. When should I start?"

"How about now?"

CHAPTER 20:
THE CLASSIC TRAINING MONTAGE

YEAR 2035

Reine trudged out of her Principles of Goethan class, tucking the textbook she had stolen from the simulation into the crook of her elbow. It had been an exhausting lesson. Mr. Nidek hadn't been joking when he told them they weren't ready yet for the more advanced techniques. She could barely understand anything, let alone put her knowledge to use.

The young woman weaved around a sea of students. Everyone acted surprisingly normal, considering they were all ruthless metavillains. She guessed a school with too much infighting wouldn't be very effective. Even if its inhabitants weren't the most moral of individuals, they knew enough to obey the rules set by Pantheon.

But they will still bend them if they can, she reminded herself. *Never be too trusting, or you'll repeat your mistake with Sky.*

Reine scowled at the memory.

Because this class now replaced the Accelerated Advanced Thievery course as the last class of the day, she could do whatever she wanted with the rest of her time before curfew at 12:00 a.m.—which was probably studying, judging by the amount of progress she still needed to make. She reluctantly headed towards Sky. Asking for help was going to be a must, but she still didn't trust her roommate fully.

Well, there are no other options. She has more experience and stamina in using Goethan than you, so you're going to have to do it.

Reine was comforted by the thought that the villains in the school had been gradually talking to Sky again. Seeing Reine interact with her must have made it seem more normal, and people had occasionally said hi or exchanged a few pleasantries before acting hesitant. They weren't close to forgiving either of them for leading the metaheroes to their school, but Pantheon's punishment had sated their appetite for revenge. Abby hadn't pushed it either. She knew Pantheon's mission to kill Tremor was basically a death sentence, so why bother?

And she is *sorry about tricking you, you know. I guess that now this whole "hurt Reine as badly as possible" thing is over, I should give her another chance.*

Still brooding, Reine almost didn't notice when someone creeped up behind her. Practice remaining vigilant and living on edge paid off. The back of her neck prickled, so she turned around.

"How did you do on your test?" Isaac demanded, way too intensely. "And I didn't see you for the rest of class. Where were you?"

He stood in front of her, blocking the way back to her room. Reine had never liked his type. She bet he had been interrogating all the other students to search out his competition. And he was blond like his father. On Mr. Nidek, the color paired well with his friendly suit and bow tie, but with Isaac, his coldly cocky demeanor made him seem *way* too much like Starflight.

"It's none of your business," she shot back, taking a page from Sky's book, "but if you really want to know . . . I was a bit sick from my period."

It was satisfying to see his face turn red. Reine didn't know Isaac could be embarrassed.

"Alright then," he said, looking like he was the one who wanted to get away now. Then he left.

The young woman sighed. She knew he would eventually find out that she had moved up a level—the results were public, after all—but it would hopefully take him at least another week before he confronted her again.

C'mon. You still have a lot of work to do. She returned to her room to study.

Sky stood on the edge of the bed and her face turned red with exertion. She was trying to access the fifth level before Reine did, but the process was as unfamiliar to her as it was to her roommate. The trick was to force your way through. Unlike the relaxation and searching you do to access the previous levels, submerging yourself in the fifth required an iron will. They had already mastered the first four levels in the last few weeks, able to puzzle out Reine's new textbook with Sky's experience and the girl's knowledge. Sky was amazed at how fast they had progressed. Her roommate had such a drive to learn and develop her skills that even a procrastinator like Sky had been caught up in the excitement of revenge. After all, they both hated Starflight. Sky just needed a spark to fuel it.

"You got anything yet?" she asked, collapsing back onto the bed.

Reine put a finger to her lips. That was an agreed upon sign that meant "shut up and let me focus!"

Sky smiled. Idly, she tried to enter the second level. It didn't work, of course. Though the scar stretching all the way from her neck to her back had healed a long time ago, the damage was permanent.

"I got it!" Reine yelled.

Sky was about to tell her to be less loud when a golden glow filled the room, so bright that she forgot what she was going to say. She let out a couple of surprised curses.

"Sorry."

The Goethan receded, drawn into Reine's lungs. Lungs were the body part that corresponded with the fifth level, just like the heart for the third, or the hands with the fourth.

"How do you feel?" Sky asked eagerly. Her roommate should be at least four times stronger than someone's passive strength boost from using Goethan.

"Like the first time I accessed my subconscious," Reine replied and took a step forward. "I can—whoa!"

Losing her balance, she tripped, falling backwards. The fifth level acted as a full-body enhancer. Reine might be stronger, faster, and smarter than ever before, but her movements would also be more volatile.

And that's why we have a backup plan.

Sky snapped with both of her middle fingers against their respective thumbs, entering the first and fourth levels a second later. It was a neat trick they had learned from the textbook Reine stole. By associating a level with an action—snapping your fingers, for example—your brain could get used to the idea of the shortcut through repeated practice. The process required perfecting the long way first, though, which explained why Mr. Nidek wanted to put it off until later in the semester.

Feel that wind pattern on the left. She's going to fall . . .

Sliding forwards, Sky caught Reine before her head could hit stone.

There.

"Good catch," Reine said, and Sky blushed. Reine instinctively reached out to steady herself against the wall, "I'm go—"

Her arm shot out in a blur, breaking a hole in the perfectly smooth rock. Sky barely stopped herself from dropping her roommate as Reine cursed and clutched at her hand in pain.

"What the hell?" someone said. Their voice came through the cracked stone.

"Reine!" Sky admonished.

"My bad."

"Tell that to our neighbors."

Sky rolled her eyes as panicked shouting from the students neighboring them rose up through the corridors. She knew how it must have looked. With the recent attack on the school, who knew what form an enemy could take?

"Anyway . . . let's do it again."

"Here?"

"Sure, why not?"

"Reine . . ."

"C'mon, I'll be more careful."

Over the course of the next few weeks, Sky and Reine secured their use of the fifth level, pairing them with physical triggers like they had done for the other levels. Reine settled on a raise of her left eyebrow because she thought it was intimidating, and Sky decided to use whistling on a whim. Or at least she tried to; it ended up being completely silent.

So is it still a whistle? Hmmm . . .

Unfortunately, they had no luck with the sixth level, so the two friends shifted their focus on to appeasing Pantheon. Avoiding death during their upcoming mission was a great motivator. They found that classes were so much easier now that they could use the fifth level to help them memorize facts and comprehend problems. To Isaac's jealousy, Reine and Sky quickly rose to become some of the highest scorers in the entire grade, second only to him. He noticed them taking higher-level material from the teacher's folders, and would have turned them in if not for the fact that he occasionally liberated the odd booklet himself.

The two girls were so successful that Isaac couldn't help but be afraid for his dream of becoming valedictorian in senior year. How else would he prove everyone wrong and step outside of his father's shadow? How else would he show that his powers were so much more than the weak ones they thought he had inherited from his father?

In some ways, they were so similar. That was the worst part. Isaac knew they saw Mr. Nidek in him whenever he manipulated water—but couldn't they understand that his powers were different from condensing liquid from air? And it wasn't just his strength. Not only did he have more Goethan than most, he also had the drive to learn. The drive to succeed.

He sneered and wished he hadn't saved Reine's life.

Something needed to be done. The girls needed to be stopped. Sure, they were likely going to die by the end of the year, but was he really going to trust some unknown mission from Pantheon to do the job?

No, that would be stupid. And if anyone could ever say anything nice about Isaac, it would be that he was no fool.

CHAPTER 21:
DON'T JOIN CULTS

THE PAST: 1¾ YEARS AGO

Reine built up her courage, stepping into the dim lighting of the bar in which her father liked to squander his life away in. It was already two in the morning, and she was worried about him. What if he had gotten into a fight, or had too much to drink?

The sound of glass breaking greeted her as she snuck past the bouncer while he was distracted. No problem at all—just a shadow pressed against the wall, and she was gone. No one stopped her when she found the room her dad was lounging in.

"Dad? I uh, need you at home. There's a problem with the sink," Reine lied firmly, trying to save him face among his friends. She might as well have not bothered. They were so drunk that they didn't even hear her.

"Sooo . . . what's our plan for . . . killing . . . what's her name again . . . Starflight?"

Her ears perked up at the mention of the metahero, and Reine turned to look at the speaker. He was a bald-headed man wearing sunglasses.

He's probably blind. There's no way anyone could see in this lighting with those glasses on.

"Blowing that . . . building up . . . ammm I right?" another responded. He mimed an explosion with his hands, and his friends laughed. Reine swore never to drink in that moment. She didn't want to end up like them, foolishly slurring her words.

"Dad. I really think it's time to go—"

"Those are the troublemakers, hero. The ones who refused to leave my bar."

Reine's head darted around, and then she scuttled under a table in the corner. The voice had come from a woman, presumably the bartender, standing next to a pink-haired man. She didn't like the look of him. His hands were balled up, his face alight with tension. He was obviously expecting a fight.

"Come on now," the metahero said in a light tone that did not match his composure, "let's get this show moving. It's not like we're some jobless metavillains, right?" He chuckled nervously, but no one else seemed to find his joke funny. Reine gritted her teeth as the eagle-shaped pin displayed proudly on his shoulder flashed into view. She didn't trust her dad—or any of his friends, for that matter—to handle themselves in a fight, especially after a night of drinking.

Damn it, even if they did, they'd be stupid enough to come back tomorrow . . . right into the waiting handcuffs of this pink-haired guy's hero friends. She glanced at the bartender. Would the woman need to be taken care of too? If they managed to kill the metahero, could they bribe her into silence?

Let's focus on one thing at a time, Reine.

She took a deep breath, letting her shoulders sag as she fought back a yawn. She felt tired . . . weary. It was late, but more than that, it was as if worries beyond her own were constantly weighing her down. Her mother's death had forced her to stop her studies and take up stealing, and now Oliver couldn't even take care of himself. Her weakness only lasted a moment. She crept out from under the table. Hopefully, there would be better times for her to relax.

A girl can hope. Damn it.

Reine stood up and made her way behind the metahero's exposed back. He was still arguing with her dad and his friends, so he must not be that powerful. Any metahuman worth his salt wouldn't bat an eye at the prospect of fighting ten or more people at once.

"I'm warning you," he said, "I don't have too much jurisdiction to deal with humans, but the police are only a block away." The man stared at them for a moment longer, and the drunken group finally got up to leave. Maybe they had some sense after all.

"Well who says we're all human, backstabber?" one of her dad's friends barked.

Or maybe not.

"What?" The metahero tensed. "Are you implying something, scum? Get out of here now before I—"

Unable to bear the growing tension, Reine grabbed a glass plate off a nearby counter and broke it over the metahero's head. It shattered, sprinkling shards of glass all over the floor. She stepped back as he crashed onto the ground. Maybe the pain from the cuts would teach him a lesson about killing others of his kind.

"Who—who's there?" It was the same guy who had called the metahero out.

Reine stepped forwards when she realized they couldn't see her face, hidden as she was in the shadows. Then a hand latched onto her ankle.

The metahero had regained consciousness and was looking up at her with fury in his eyes. Reine grabbed another plate off the counter.

CRASH!

That should do the trick, she thought.

He fell back to the floor, this time knocked out for good.

"Reine?" Oliver said, eyes wide. "What are you doing here? I thought . . . it's not safe."

She bit back a sharp retort. It was about time her dad recognized her. Didn't she just save them? How dare he try to protect her when he couldn't even stay sober and sensible for a week? Reine almost gave up pretenses and dragged him home, but she was nice enough to repeat her previous statement.

"Let's go," she said with exaggerated slowness. "I need your help with the sink." She glared at the door, and he finally stumbled off his seat, ignoring his friends' attempts to get him to stay. They could deal with the metahero for all she cared. If he turned the tables on them, all the better. She would make sure her dad never went near the place again anyway.

"Hey child," a woman's voice called.

A stone wall rose up in front of Reine and she recoiled. It fitted perfectly into the open doorway. She scowled at the barrier. Just her luck—there were no windows, since the room was in the middle of the bar. *Do they really care so much about him leaving?*

"Why don't you join our group?" the voice asked. "Your father has been putting out some pretty radical ideas, but it seems you're the real knife in the family. We can always use someone ruthless . . . someone who has a personal score to settle with Starflight herself."

She added, "I'm Aahna, by the way."

Reine turned around. The villain who'd spoken looked bored, her features arranged in an arrogant smile and not flushed with patches of drunken red. Reine would have to be careful around her. The metavillain was probably using this sorry group to take responsibility for whatever idea she had planted in their brains—or maybe not. But when you lived in a world where your very existence could be a crime, you could never be too sure.

Who knows? Reine thought wearily.

She looked down, hiding her face so they couldn't see the frustrated tears that had appeared in her eyes. She hated crying in front of people. It made her feel like she was a kid again, and she couldn't be a kid—not anymore. She had to be capable of dealing with all the adult crap life tossed her way, and she had to grow up before it buried her. *Why can't people just leave me alone, huh?* she wanted to say. *Is that too much to ask? A moment where my alcoholic father isn't getting himself into trouble. A moment where my mom is still alive. Why do I even bother with all this?*

"Fine," Reine spat. There was nothing else she could do. "But we better deal with this hero first. Who's the memory-wiper here?"

The group—no, *her* group now—looked at each other and shrugged. Reine sighed. Tossing the sheathed knife she'd tied to the side of her boot to the nearest man, she mimed slitting her throat. There was no way she could stomach killing someone.

"We're going to have to fix this."

CHAPTER 22:
SABOTAGE IS FOR THE GUYS

YEAR 2035

Reine and Sky chatted while they waited for the first students to show up at the reactor for Goethan donation. It was their turn to sign people in, and they had to keep a list of the villains who didn't arrive on time for reference. Pointed reminders could range from warnings to suspension.

"So you're coming with me to see that old movie tonight?" Reine asked, leaning back into her chair. "It's the only one we're going to see all year, you know. Pantheon's been feeling pretty laidback since he managed to get his hands on that large stash of weapons from a rival villain." She raised an eyebrow at her friend, and Sky felt indecision build up inside her.

"I don't know. The students . . . They don't really like me, and tomorrow is the last day of school. What if we aren't ready?"

It was an unspoken worry that they both shared—almost taboo, really. Pantheon hadn't talked to them since the attack led by Gravedigger, but he had made his point clear. Either they killed Tremor over the summer, or they didn't return for a second year.

Hell, it's simple, Sky thought. *Simply impossible.*

Reine patted her on the back. She was working on her friendly gestures after Sky mentioned her constant scowling was a bit intimidating. "C'mon, don't be like that. The exams are over, and we did great! It's not like preparing for one extra day is going to make a difference."

Sky was about to respond, but she stopped when the first student arrived. It was Asher, running towards them with a flustered red face. She unconsciously curled her fingers. He seemed to have changed since they saved his life for provoking Mr. Nidek, but she didn't see him enough to be sure.

"Hey, Sky and . . . uh, Reine," he said, waving to them. "Am I late? I saw Isaac doing something inside the Goethan extraction center, and his time slot is after mine, so I thought I might have misread the time."

Sky checked the Goethan-powered clock embedded inside her desk. "Nope. You're fine—"

"Wait," Reine cut in. "Did you say you saw Isaac in the room below us?"

"Yeah," Asher replied, a little confused. "The structures around the reactor are all glass, so—"

"I know," Reine interrupted. "My point is: it's not his turn yet, so why—and how—did he get in there?"

There was a collective silence. Sky was already getting out of her chair to check. "Let's go. We can ask him when we find him."

Reine nodded grimly, and shoved all thoughts of the movie out of her mind. She couldn't, however, get rid of the hollow disappointment she felt inside her chest. She had really expected Sky to say yes. *Well, it can't be helped.* Reine knew firsthand what Isaac could be like, and she wouldn't put it past him to sabotage their future with a cold and unregretful hand.

"We should take the fire stairs," she told Sky and Asher. "He'll be monitoring the main ones."

Asher hurried over as Reine disconnected the fire alarm from the emergency exit and then headed down the stairwell with Sky by his side. He didn't seem too bothered by the fact that they were breaking the rules—you were only supposed to open the fire exit if there was one—likely because he was used to being punished by the teachers. They hadn't forgiven him for all the past annoyances he had caused, even if he did seem to have gotten nicer.

Asher rubbed his nose. A brush with death taught you a lot, and he knew now that he didn't want to be remembered as an egotistical jerk. Who knew when death would catch up to him? It would suck if the last thing someone remembered him for was his petty comments about a wrong pronunciation.

A hissing sound filled the bottom of the stairwell, and Asher frowned.

"Wait." He paused. "Do you hear that—"

An explosion rocked the school, blasting the door to the Goethan extraction room open. Asher gaped. He could only watch, stunned, as the rectangular piece of reinforced metal flew off its hinges and tumbled towards him. There was no time to react—no time to think. He was about to be pulverized by a door.

"Pantheon's wra—"

Raising her left eyebrow, Reine was suddenly there, her body crackling with Goethan. As Sky yelled at him to get out of the way, Reine drew back her hand . . . and punched right through the projectile. Asher blinked. Shards of metal flew around him, but they all missed. Sky had grabbed the closest ones out of the air before they could hit him.

"Thanks," he gasped, almost faint with shock.

Reine's hand was bleeding, and Sky was holding half a dozen pieces of jagged metal, but they both seemed fine. Asher had no idea how they had done it. Mr. Nidek had taught them how to enter their subconscious quickly, but not at *that* speed! They must have practiced at least a thousand times, he figured.

"C'mon," Sky said, steadying Asher as he swayed dangerously close to a burning table leg. "We have to get out of here before someone comes to check. Isaac caused that explosion, so he won't be anywhere near. What if a teacher finds us? We're in enough trouble already."

Reine nodded and cleared some debris away from the stairs before letting go control of the fifth level. Her body sagged with exhaustion.

"You're right," Reine replied. "If we can get back up to the sign-in counter, then maybe—"

"No one will be going anywhere."

Asher jumped at the voice and stumbled around in time to see the last embers of Goethan fade away. Pantheon had arrived. His suit jacket broadened his already broad shoulders, but it was his rage that pushed against the walls of the room. The emotion was almost tangible. Pantheon didn't get angry often, but when he did, he got *furious*.

"Reine and Sky . . . I should have known letting freshmen study sophomore-level material was a mistake. I felt the Goethan expenditure all the way from my office." He glared at them. **"Did you cause the explosion with your reckless practicing? The fifth level is volatile—perhaps too hard to control for beginners. It would be easy for someone careless enough to tip off an entire army of metaheroes to break the delicate machinery in the reactor."**

The three students exchanged looks, but only Reine was brave enough to speak up. She knew she'd used up any leniency Pantheon had left when she caused the death of his students, and Sky wasn't much better off. Asher, however . . . She considered throwing him under the bus. He could take it. *Mr. Nidek attacked him after only being verbally provoked, so Pantheon can't blame Asher for that fight without implying that it's okay for teachers to hurt students.* Hesitating, she decided against it. He *had* stopped his friend from controlling her, and he might not go along with her accusations anyway. "We went down to the room because Asher thought he saw Isaac there," Reine told Pantheon. "And why would we want to set off an explosion so close to where we were? Whoever did it is probably on the other side of the school already."

Pantheon shrugged. "**I know you two are confident in your abilities, and this isn't the first time you've created a potentially dangerous situation for the school. Quite a coincidence, really.**" His eyes narrowed. "**It almost makes me question whether you are actually unlucky . . . or just working for someone else.**"

Asher turned pale and started fidgeting, and then realized it made him look guilty. An idea was beginning to form in his mind.

"But you have no proof!" Sky was protesting. "It was Isaa—"

"**No. _You_ have no proof. Since you were the only ones around, the suspicion will fall on you, unless you can prove otherwise.**"

The villain checked his phone and sighed. "**Seems my time is up. I need to fix this mess before the entire reactor malfunctions, so unless you find the culprit by tomorrow, I will have you all expelled immediately. No more chances.**"

"Wait!"

All eyes turned to Asher, and he gulped. _Did he just say that?_ Reine thought, shocked by the sudden outburst. Almost unwillingly, Asher looked Pantheon straight in the eye.

"I was the one who blew the reactor up," he said.

Sky gasped, but Reine shushed her. She and Pantheon were both evaluating his claim with an appraising eye.

"**Really,**" the villain said, a hint of sarcasm in his voice. "**You would risk detonating a bomb when you have no ability to survive it?**"

Asher glanced at Sky. "I knew they could protect me from any explosion, and it wasn't like I made this mess on purpose. You see, they asked me to fix something inside the room, so imagine how scared I was when I messed it up. I made up that tale about Isaac to avoid the blame."

"We did?" Sky asked, before Reine could prod her again. "I mean . . . of course we did."

"**Hmmmm . . .**" Pantheon's face set into a thoughtful frown. Asher knew that he wanted to believe him. After all, how could he send Sky and Reine to defeat Tremor if he expelled them first?

"**Alright,**" the man admitted grudgingly. "**No need for my students to panic. Better to blame it on an accident than an act of sabotage.**" He turned his burning gaze upon Asher. "**But that doesn't mean you're exempt from punishment. Since it was an accident . . . how about you do something to pay me back for the damage you caused?**"

Pantheon's frown shifted into a smile. "**Help the girls succeed on their mission, and we'll call it even.**"

CHAPTER 23:
THE SANDBUG MAN'S PEST

YEAR 2035

Summer had arrived with its brutal heat and skin-cracking dryness. Well, the season actually began a few weeks ago, but living underground didn't let anyone experience the change in climate. The trio decided on bringing three backpacks, a bottle of water each, two changes of clothes, and *a lot* of cash for food and lodging. Tremor's headquarters and his subordinates were located in the city after all, so no one was going to be bringing camping gear.

Reine patted the multiple wallets she had hidden among her backpack's compartments. It felt satisfying to be using all the money she had stolen from the heroes as part of final exams. Though they had about two months of summer break before school started, she hoped to be done with Pantheon's mission in only a few days. It was an unrealistic dream, she knew, but Reine was the kind of person who liked to finish everything well before the due date.

"So, you know a good place for dinner?" Sky asked, looking around the derelict streets with distaste. "Wow. Half of the road was still here last time I visited. Is it me, or is this entire city falling apart?"

Asher made a face and stepped gingerly around the sewage water flowing through the street. He didn't seem to mind the heat, and Reine wasn't bothered either, but Sky looked uncomfortable and a little unsteady in her sweaty cloth and cap. She'd spent half of her life underground.

He must have grown up in one of the rich neighborhoods, Reine realized. *Didn't Sky say his parents are powerful metavillains?*

"What exactly are we doing here, anyway?" Asher complained, a hint of nasalness coming back to his voice. Reine thought it made him sound like a child. "Will someone please explain to me what our plan is?"

She bit back a sharp retort at his obvious disdain of the broken-down buildings surrounding them. He was right, after all. Even if she didn't appreciate him criticizing the place where she grew up, Reine had to admit her home was only getting worse.

Plus, we owe him one for lying to Pantheon. I guess I'll let it slide this time . . .

"We're trying to find a metahuman called The Eye," Reine explained patiently. "He's the only one who can tell us where Tremor's headquarters is located, but it shouldn't be too hard. No one would dare hurt the man. Both metavillains and metaheroes alike get information from him, so he doesn't try hard to stay hidden."

Sky jumped in, saying, "Pantheon also gave us a few contacts to try. He told us that one of them might know where the guy's doing business, and they're supposed to be relatively cheap."

Asher still looked skeptical. He avoided some suspicious-looking mud, then took a drink out of his water bottle. "I don't know . . . If this metahuman is so powerful, how come he hasn't ratted Pantheon out yet? You would think the metaheroes would have already recruited him or something."

Reine laughed. "Pantheon scares him too much. Plus, The Eye has friends in high places. Think of it this way, Asher. No side wants to offend the other, especially since this guy has dirt on all of them. He's too useful to be killed, so they can't even raise a finger against him without the risk of his other clients retaliating."

Asher opened his mouth to make another point but stopped when Reine saw a familiar sandwich place. It had a badly fitted steel plate for a roof and was missing a door. Walking more briskly now, the trio entered the ramshackle little hut. The menu was protected by plastic and plastered onto the wall for everyone to see, and the shopkeeper was snoring on the only rocking chair with his jacket pulled tight.

"Wow," Asher exclaimed with a critical eye. Reine had told him that her parents used to take her here after a big heist. "I hope they're doing better now that you're earning money from the school. Your parents must have been really poor."

Reine decided not to correct him. "Yeah," she responded darkly, "they're doing great."

They heard a loud creak, and the man in the chair stretched, yawning. The shopkeeper looked older than she remembered. He couldn't have been more than forty-five, but his back was bent and there were spots of gray in his hair.

"Not much business?" Reine asked when he shook himself awake. She realized she didn't remember his name. Maybe she never knew it.

The man grumbled, "Everything's fine, missy. You and your friends are the only ones dumb enough to be out at this hour. It's still hot, but the sun's going down, and no one's going to risk their lives for a sandwich." He cocked his head suspiciously. "You seem awfully familiar. Do I know you?"

Asher and Sky traded glances, and Sky raised an eyebrow at her when the shopkeeper continued to glare. Reine shrugged, glancing down at herself. She was wearing a new but normal T-shirt that the school had provided—Pantheon thought school uniforms were an invitation for the enemy to recognize you—and her hair had grown a little longer. Nothing too drastic, right?

"My word . . . Reine, is that you?" the man asked.

She turned to face him, and he seemed to take a step back. "We all thought you were dead, but—but look at you now! You seem . . . well."

"Thanks." She hesitated, and then lied. "A nice family took me in."

"Who . . . okay, listen. I know it might be too soon, and I'm—I'm hesitant to ask, but . . . is it true . . . about your father?"

Reine nodded slightly. Grimacing, the shopkeeper looked down at his shoes. She wanted to say something, to express her grief as well, but it was like her old life had caught up to her in an overwhelming wave of familiarity. Starflight had changed everything when she murdered Reine's parents. It was a lot to take in, and yet . . . *I don't know. It feels different, somehow.*

She surveyed herself again: clean clothes, lean muscles instead of a tired hunch. Reine realized she was standing confidently with no fear of being noticed, assured in her power as a meta-villain. People on the streets generally tried to draw as little attention to themselves as possible. Even the shopkeeper didn't seem entirely comfortable in his own hut. No wonder he hadn't recognized her.

Her old world hadn't changed—she had. Reine felt a bundle of emotions unwrap in her eyes. She put some money onto the counter in advance, just like her mom, and experienced a sense of déjà vu.

Can you picture it, Reine? A world where everyone was normal, where anyone could cross a street without being mugged? Her mother's voice echoed in her mind, and Reine blinked to keep the memories away. She felt . . . hopeful. Hopeful and sad. Maybe she *was* progressing fast enough to meet Starflight head-on. Or maybe she just wanted to curl up in a corner and cry; she immediately stopped *that* train of thought. There would be time to grieve when Starflight was dead. Sky tapped her shoulder.

"So," Sky asked, staring up at the menu with a perplexed expression. "What is this 'Valmount Delicacy?'"

They had been eating for a good ten minutes or so before the first high-pitched scream broke through the windy silence of the street; it sounded like a young boy. Reine ignored it, steeling herself from the temptation to go investigate. This was a common occurrence in her part of the city, and she knew from personal experience that it might already be too late. The shopkeeper certainly wasn't reacting. He just looked cautious, occasionally poking his head outside to monitor the nearby alleyways in case the conflict got too close to his hut. His hand inched towards a club studded with twisted nails.

"What was that?" Asher whispered as the screams died down. "Sounds pretty close to me. If we go check now, the—"

Reine interrupted him quickly and the shopkeeper backed her up with a serious glare. "No point. I know it sounds harsh, but if we stop to help every kid from getting raped or robbed, we'll never get out of this place." She stared at him, daring him to argue, but Asher didn't take the bait. He turned to Sky for help instead.

"Let's go, Sky," Asher said. "We're wasting time here by talking, and I'm not leaving him to die. Are you coming?"

Not waiting for an answer, he hurried out of the shop, pulling on his jacket as he ran. Sky hesitated for a moment, then followed suit. Reine sighed.

"You found yourself some pretty noble friends, eh?" said the shopkeeper. "That's not necessarily a bad thing for *you*, but I say let the others be noble. You don't have to go with them." He crossed his arms and leaned back into the wall.

She scowled, turning away to look at their receding shadows. *At least I tried,* she began to reason. *No—oh, who am I kidding?* She was not the same person as the helpless little girl who couldn't help if she wanted to. She was not—well, not *entirely*—the

207

malnourished and neglected child of a drunken father who had to grow up to take over his responsibilities. She was strong enough to look after herself now, and maybe that meant she should extend the favor.

"Reine?"

"I'm going after them."

The shopkeeper threw up his hands in exasperation. "Teenagers . . . fine. Go on then, and try to keep the fighting *away* from my shop."

Exhibiting more caution than the others had when they rushed to find the alleyway where the screams originated, Reine entered the fifth level and listened for the sounds of a scuffle. There were plenty north of her position. It sounded like multiple knives scratching on stone, but she couldn't be sure without Sky's enhanced senses.

"Hey," she whispered, knowing that her friend could hear her, "go around and take the back end of the alley. I'll block their way from the front." She used the speed gained from her Goethan to peek her head into each alleyway. She found the right one a second later and . . . did a double take.

What in the world is that?

A bug with long, translucent legs and a tick-like body was standing over a young boy about twelve years old. One of its claws had impaled itself into his arm, stopping him from using his gun. As Sky and Asher arrived at the other end of the pathway, Reine saw the boy take the weapon up with his other hand and fire.

The bug squealed, and she noticed a golden, pulsing mass at the center of its see-through chest. *The heart.* She focused. If the boy had a gun, then he was either important, unusually wealthy, or working for the government. Only federal employees—metaheroes included—had the right to own one, but it was possible to buy them on the black market. Either way, it would make for an interesting conversation.

Only if we manage to save him first, of course.

Pointing her index finger at the bug and concentrating, Reine entered the much-neglected second level. She hoped the bug wasn't very smart. The more intelligent a creature was, the harder it was to affect them with this level.

"Asher! Ready your lightning. I'm about to get the monster off the kid." She felt the warmth of the Goethan concentrated in her neck and willed it to weave an illusion of frightened movement, pheromones, and heat that only the bug could detect, then placed it about six meters away. Simultaneously, she weaved another one of cold, unmoving flesh, and flung it onto the boy.

The effect was immediate. Raising its legs towards what it thought was its prey's new position, the bug jumped forwards with its squirming mouth open . . . but tasted lightning instead.

"Got you!" Asher shouted triumphantly as he made his Goethan-powered electricity arc through the bug's translucent body. "This is—*gah!*"

He flung his arms wide in panic and managed to deflect the creature with a gust of wind just as it pounced at him. The monster's heart was pulsing harder; it seemed to be trying to counteract Asher's Goethan with its own. Sky finished the job. Slipping through the insect's flailing legs in a pattern Reine couldn't even set her eyes on, she slid her knife through its transparent skin like it was made of butter. It was as if someone had opened up a zipper. Gooey fluid started flowing out, and Sky looked like she wanted to puke.

"Ah. Pantheon damn it," she spat.

The bug's heart dispersed into a cloud of Goethan. Its inner glow faded as the rest of the golden mist drifted into the murky air and dissolved away. The body collapsed, the thin legs snapping. It seemed somehow *less* without Goethan—more so than the usual corpse—as if it had been Goethan first and flesh second.

Reine looked at Sky with envy. At least her friend could dodge the bug guts flying everywhere; she herself was splattered!

"Here," Asher said. He held out a hand to the boy, who recoiled in fear, crouched on the ground. Reine knew what he was feeling, and what he must be thinking: Who were these people? Metaheroes or metavillains, and would one be better than the other? She didn't really know, either. After all, she had to admit that just like the government, she would try to unearth whatever secrets he might have.

"We're just passing by," Sky said, discreetly kicking the gun out of his reach. "No need to panic. We'll be gone in a minute—"

Reine stopped her. "Wait." She picked up the gun and tucked it into her backpack. "I want to ask him some questions first, and he needs medical attention anyway." She faced the bleeding boy. "Do you have anywhere you can stay? A safe place . . . maybe where you got that gun?"

The kid glared at her, but she didn't back down. Eventually, he let out a pained gasp, and clutched the spot where the bug had impaled his arm.

"Second building on Checker's Street," he whispered. "Tell him it's Kace." Then the boy, presumably Kace, lapsed into unconsciousness.

CHAPTER 24:
MEETING . . . SOMEONE

YEAR 2035

Since he wasn't going to move himself, Sky had to hoist the boy up and carry him to the address he gave them; Asher didn't work out, and Reine had bug goo all over her body, so it was up to her.

Thank Pantheon he's light, she thought. Puberty hadn't hit him with a growth spurt yet.

They had bandaged Kace's arm to stop the bleeding, but they still had to bring him to a place where he could rest and recover. Sky was no doctor, and even she knew the wound would fester without treatment.

"Sky," she could hear Reine whisper from about a kilometer away. "I found the building. It's the only two-story apartment with no graffiti on it. Turn left, keep going, then turn right." Sky adjusted her arms, supporting the boy's weight. They had sent Reine on a scouting mission to find the place first, since she was familiar with the area. The gun seemed to burn in her backpack—Reine had given it to her in case she got caught.

But what if the metaheroes find us first?

It might be her imagination, but she could have sworn . . . "Pantheon's wrath," she cursed.

A man with a disgusted look on his face was walking out of the alley where they had killed the bug. That wasn't the problem; it wasn't even the fact that carrying a young boy in her arms might seem suspicious. It was the pin on his chest. The shape of an

211

eagle stood out starkly against the violet of his uniform, and his eyes were speckled with gold.

Sky suddenly wished her vision wasn't so sharp.

"Stop!" the metahero shouted. "I'm law enforcement. Did any of you see the person who killed the sandbug? There's been several of those monsters, but this is the first time I've found one dead." He looked them over with a frown, and Sky just knew he thought they were guilty.

Asher spoke without thinking. "Wait. There's more than one?"

The man's eyes narrowed. "It's been all over the news. You're not from around here, are you?"

Sky felt extremely awkward holding an unconscious boy near the dead sandbug. It didn't take too much thinking to connect the dots. She moved to set him down, but realized the action would only draw more attention. The hero started walking briskly towards them.

"Um. He's just . . ." Sky tried to make an excuse, and then realized it was hopeless. Asher had bug guts all over him, and blood was soaking through the makeshift bandage they had created with the boy's torn-up jacket. What else could possibly make the situation clearer? They needed to use the element of surprise now—while they still had it.

"Asher," she said, trying to keep her tone light, "can you shock him real quick? Thanks." She kept her eyes on the uniformed hero as she unceremoniously dumped Kace onto a soft-looking patch of dirt in the middle of the sidewalk. She made sure to choose one without palm trees taking up space, and then signaled for Asher to hurry up with a frantic hand wave.

Nodding grimly, he focused and stomped his foot. Golden mist formed a thin haze around him, and then coalesced around his hands. The fourth level: perfect for affecting humans. She just hoped the metahero wouldn't kill them first.

"You're under—" the man had time to say before he erected a sloppy energy field that redirected the bolt of lightning into a lamppost. He recovered almost instantly, and Sky could feel him starting to prepare an attack. She entered the third level just as he planted a force field in her brain, crushing the neurons inside—or at least he tried to. Manipulating the Goethan inside her body, Sky struggled against the attack. Her will to live persevered.

My body, my rules.

She kept her mind submerged in the third level and unsheathed a knife that was hidden in her sleeve.

"Sky!" Asher shouted. "He's calling for help, and I—I can't get to him!"

Asher was bombarding the metahero with all the weather powers he had, but neither the hail nor the raging wind was getting through the man's shield. He had formed an impenetrable cocoon of blue energy around himself.

Should we run? Hell, how long will reinforcements take to arrive? Sky did a quick mental calculation. He seemed to be fumbling with his phone: a rare, government-issued device that required two nine-digit passwords to use. She hoped what she learned in class was right. If this didn't work . . .

"Keep it up!" she told Asher. "We have to distract, maybe even overwhelm him."

The guy was already sweating, his pores visible to her now submerged mind. The fourth level also allowed her to see through the blue energy, and the sight gave her hope. He was typing slowly with one finger while holding the other trembling hand up to maintain the force field.

Sky yelped as she entered the fifth level—*Goethan weakness sucks*—and plunged her knife into the blue energy.

It sparked . . . then broke. She blinked in surprise. The tip of the knife had dulled as the metal melted into sparks of red-hot ash, and the blade itself snapped, separating from the hilt. She dropped it, her hand shaking like rubber. Without thinking, Sky slammed her other fist into the churning shield. It burned, but not too badly. The Goethan coursing through her body negated the force field's disintegrating effects.

What if . . .

Sky allocated to the third level all the power she was using to stay submerged in the fifth and fourth. Weakness and dulled senses almost overwhelmed her, but she pushed through, relying on the new strength that coursed through her veins. She mentally steeled herself and used the last of her willpower to *shove* the Goethan out of her skin.

Sky threw herself onto the hero's force field. It was as if someone had hosed down a raging fire with a tsunami. For a second, all she could see was golden fire and ocean blue, and then pain infused her veins, replacing the comforting power emanating from her Goethan. The metahero grunted. The phone slipped out of his hand, and he fell to one knee.

The force field flickered out.

"Pantheon's wrath . . ." Sky gasped.

Clawing at the ground, she tried to prevent the man from picking the phone back up, but he kicked her arm away, and she vomited all over his shoes. He recoiled, disgusted. The hero took out a gun, aiming it at her chest . . . then flew backwards when Asher blasted him with a final bolt of lightning. Smoke rose out of his skin like his soul was leaving his body.

Too close.

Sky coughed out the rest of her dinner.

"Seriously, Sky?" Asher teased with an unsteady smile, hoisting her up. His eyes, however, were serious. "Do you think we need to hide? He managed to call them, right?"

She gave him the tiniest of shakes. "We're—we're fine." Sky shuddered with the effort of standing, "but we—ugh—still need to move. The metaheroes might come to investigate, and half the neighborhood probably heard the fight. Not to mention those bugs."

Reine said to find the apartment.

"You're carrying Kace, by the way," she added. "I don't care if you work out or not. I feel like I'm about to die."

He rolled his eyes.

Too close.

Reine was almost dead with worry when her friends arrived at the apartment, but she didn't show it, of course. She examined the building instead. It was an utterly unremarkable and featureless two-story flat, as if whoever designed it had wanted it to melt into the background of an already gray and ivy-covered neighborhood. She turned back to greet them.

"What took you so long?" Reine said, and then she saw the state they were in. "What happened? Did another bug come along or something?"

Sky steadied herself against the wall, and Asher set Kace down with a relieved sigh. He didn't seem too rattled, but she was covered with burns, scrapes, and tattered clothing. They were all splattered with bug goo too. Reine hoped whoever lived here would let them in.

"Had to fight a metahero," Sky managed, too tired to say anything else. She gestured towards their appearance for explanation, and Reine nodded. Taking the boy from Asher and slinging him over her shoulder, she rang the electronic doorbell of the building. It was cracked and barely flickering, so she raised an eyebrow when a loud, clear chime rang through its interior. *I hope the right person picks up. There's probably more than one person living here.*

"Who is this?" the intercom spat. "No need to be secretive. There's no one in the building but my . . . family and me."

It was a man's voice, but they couldn't tell much else because the quality was so bad. There was so much interference it sounded like fireworks going off each time he spoke. They all exchanged hesitant frowns, waiting for someone to speak up.

Sky was the first to comment. "Hell, that doesn't sound suspicious at all."

"Not helpful, Sky."

The machine continued to sputter, "Louder! Are you here to do . . . business? If not, don't come begging for scraps. We have a low tolerance for beggars, and I'm not afraid to pump you full of lead."

Seriously?

Whether it was because of all the stress she had been put through, or the fact that they had done so much to rescue his . . . son, servant, or whatever, Reine suddenly felt freezing rage smother her words.

"We found a boy named Kace with a gun," she warned. "We're both armed. Don't even think about shooting. Open the door right now, or I'll let the police deal with your corpses."

A forced laugh. Even through the distortion, she could feel his discomfort.

"Stupid girl. Do you have any idea what—"

Almost casually, Reine smashed her left fist into the intercom's fragile plastic exterior.

CRACK!

"Stop that—"

CRACK!

Silence followed, and Reine expected bullets to come flying from the window above at any moment, but there was nothing except the creak of a door opening. She glanced at her fingers, inhaling slowly. She was surprised to see blood coming out of a cut. It stung.

C'mon Reine. Just step inside.

She peeked through the darkness but couldn't make out anything dangerous. That wasn't necessarily a good thing.

"Um. We going?" Asher asked.

Reine looked back for support, and Sky gave her a thumbs-up. It fueled her determination. Walking into the dark building, she left the door open as Sky and Asher followed suit. The hinges didn't creak.

A surprisingly well-kept place, she thought wryly. *Except for the suspiciously distorted intercom, of course.*

The lights turned on with a click, revealing a threadbare room with a flight of wooden stairs tucked into the back. She whirled around in the direction of the sound. A man was standing there, his potbelly slumped in a gesture of resignation.

"Wha'd you want?" he asked as his eyes flickered to the boy in Reine's arms. "Knew I should never have gotten into this business. One moment they're asking for information, then they're kidnapping your son." He raised his arms up to show that he was weaponless, and Reine noticed that he had an eye with numbers across it tattooed on one hand. She cocked her head.

"I should warn y'all though," he continued, "if you hurt even one hair on my family's head, there'll be hell to pay. The metaheroes for one—"

"What a liar," Asher interrupted, looking at his companions. "Seriously. Look at this place! Do you guys really believe him?"

Reine ignored Asher, keeping her gaze on the man. The pieces were all coming together, daring her to make a bold statement. If it didn't work . . . well, was embarrassment so bad?

"Mr. . . . Eye," she said, disregarding her friends' shocked faces. "That's who you are, right?"

His mouth maintained its downward arc, but his eyes widened. He replied dryly, "What gave it away?"

"We didn't abduct your son. We saved him from this giant . . . bug thing. And as for what we want . . ."

The Eye sighed. "Let's talk upstairs."

This is a pretty neat place, Asher thought as he almost tripped on the last step. It had looked kind of broken down at first, but the second floor revealed a couple of cozy—if not large—rooms. He absentmindedly tapped the cement walls while Reine and The Eye argued about the cost of his service. She wanted Tremor's location, but the guy was not making it easy.

I wonder if it has anything to do with the fact that we broke his intercom and covered his carpet with goo? Reine wondered.

She slammed her fist on the table, shaking the furniture. Asher shook his head. She intimidated him a little, but he couldn't help but feel that technique wouldn't work on someone who faced down heroes and villains alike. Still, The Eye—he had told them to call him Trevon—*had* been willing to sell them everything else. With a little cash, the trio was able to buy new clothes, showers, and a meal.

"I'm telling you. This will be totally anonymous. It's not like we're going to tell Tremor you gave us his location!" Reine was saying.

Trevon shook his head. "No deal. There's only so many people who can locate his base, and the only way to guarantee his silence is to kill him—which, no offense, I'm not sure you'll be able to do."

Asher walked over and stared pointedly at Kace. He was still recovering on the sofa.

"Does your son really mean that little to you? We saved him, remember? It's only fair for you to return the favor."

Reine winced at his brashness, but Trevon didn't seem too offended. He just ignored his words, pulling the same card as when he denied Reine's offer of money. *The man's too rich to care. He doesn't need our dollars when he has the entire government funding him.*

Sky jumped in as the silence turned awkward. "We're thankful that you're letting us stay here, Trevon. That's more than enough repayment."

"Mmhmm," The Eye grumbled.

"But is there really nothing we can do to earn your trust? I'm sure that we can give you more than just money, you know. We're pretty resourceful."

The man raised an eyebrow, and Asher felt a stab of jealousy at how effortless he made the motion seem. Why could everybody do that but him?

"I do have a problem you can solve," The Eye mused. "I sent Kace first, but he, well, obviously failed, so maybe your team will fare better."

The trio exchanged looks. This was their chance!

"We'll do anything," Reine said coldly, and Trevon smiled.

"Have you ever heard of the . . . Sandbug Man?"

CHAPTER 25:
THE SANDBUG MAN HIMSELF

YEAR 2035

It turned out that The Eye's section of the city was infested with dangerous "sandbugs," which had been created by a former entomologist determined to dominate the neighborhood. The guy had obviously never read a book. No one liked the type of person who refused to make allies with anyone except for mindless monsters bent on stabbing and hunting humans. Hell, even Starflight didn't try to kill everyone she met.

Not to mention that world domination is so cliché.

Sky flattened herself against the wooden wall of the Sandbug Man's "safe house." It was squeezed between two taller apartment buildings and stuck out like a sore thumb even with its equally—if not more—tumbledown appearance and moss-overgrown pool. The Eye had found it for them in an instant. He refused to tell them the specifics, but his powers worked by "distinguishing Goethan signatures at any distance" or something. She was just glad he had done most of the work.

Taking out a keg of gasoline, Sky started pouring the liquid near the sides of the house. Sneaking around had been surprisingly easy. The scientist must have thought that his "secret base" would fall under suspicion if he placed a bunch of bug guards around it.

Or he's just lazy. Honestly, Sky, I swear you're giving him too much credit.

They had seen him through his window yesterday, using his Goethan powers to create another of those monstrosities. He didn't seem to be quite sane. Yes, he looked normal enough with his average build and longish, charcoal-colored hair, but his eyes were propped up by dark circles and he acted . . . intense, as if every move were a struggle he refused to lose. Sky was sure that even Kace could have finished the job if he hadn't been cornered by a sandbug first.

Speaking of which . . . what is he doing here?

Reine liked simple plans, and simple plans liked her. It was always a gift when a heist didn't involve complicated escape plans that required her to jump into a sewer. All she had to do was complete her part, and the rest would build on itself.

Except for the fact that someone always messes up.

Eyes sharp, Reine took in her surroundings. The wooden cottage with a modest yard in the back had one door and two rooms, each paired with their respective window. She was only in charge of the door; the other two liabilities were taken care of by her friends.

We should strike soon. Even if he doesn't notice the gasoline smell until he opens the window blinds, there's still a chance he might try to release one of his creatures. Her mind wandered as she kept watch of the door. *I wonder how he gets them out of his house. Maybe he brings them out to the city when they're still small and leaves them there to grow.*

Reine prepared to go into the cottage. She steeled her nerves. Though she was kind of desensitized to killing, she still didn't like to perform the act. It helped to imagine murder as a small step in a staircase that led to her ultimate goal: ending Starflight. Guilt fled before need.

And that was when she noticed the boy running towards the house with a pistol in his hands.

"Kace," she whispered fiercely, "what in the world are you doing here? Leave. Now."

Even to her ears, his footsteps were unbearably loud, made more prominent by the silence of the night. It was approaching midnight, and though Reine doubted the scientist could hear them through his house's walls, she still didn't feel entirely comfortable watching a kid ruin all their plans.

"Kace!" she repeated as he ignored her and ran straight for the door, "stop!"

Sky was set to light the gasoline in a few minutes. If she didn't go in and kill the mad entomologist beforehand . . .

"Sky," Reine whispered, hoping her friend was listening through the fourth level. "Change of plans. Don't set the gasoline on fire until I tell yo—"

It was as if the first thunder of a storm crashed right next to her ear. Reine thought for a second that it was Sky's fault, but then Kace was swinging open a ruined door, and she realized he had shot open the lock.

"What the heck is happening?" she heard Asher shout, all caution forgotten. He and Sky both came running over, just in time to see Kace flashing them an apologetic but unwavering glance before he barreled into the testing room of the insane metahuman's house. Reine groaned.

"Asher. You stay outside with the lighter. Sky and I will deal with him."

Asher looked a bit disgruntled but nodded his head. Reine was glad he trusted her.

"Be careful," Asher said. "Who knows what kind of stuff he has cooking up in there?"

As if proving his words, growls both primal and human erupted throughout the neighborhood. It sounded more like chittering, actually. Reine could just imagine mandibles scraping against each other.

"Alright, let's go."

There's probably a secret underground laboratory around here somewhere. This mad scientist sure likes doing things by the book.

Unsure of where the cacophony of bug sounds was coming from, Sky peeked cautiously into the house. Neither the Sandbug Man—*Yeah, that's a good name*—nor Kace were anywhere to be seen. The living room was filled with the same array of giant glass dishes and strange liquids they had seen yesterday while scoping out the house, but she couldn't see the source of the screeching.

Reine checked the bedroom

"Sky!" Reine called. "Hurry. There's, uh, a trapdoor here."

I knew it!

Sky burst into the room. It looked normal, well furnished, and might as well have been a dorm room in Pantheon's academy—except for the hole in the ground.

"Oh. It's just a storm cellar," Sky remarked, feeling slightly disappointed.

"What did you think it was?"

"I don't know . . . but I don't like it. This guy's boring," she complained.

Reine raised an eyebrow and suddenly giggled as the screeching from the cellar died down into a low buzz. She put a finger to her lips, still shaking slightly with laughter. Sky looked at her, perplexed, and decided to roll with it. Human voices drifted through the open trapdoor, but Reine couldn't make out the words. Sky's eyes widened.

"Kace's trapped! We have to get down there. Now."

Reine set her jaw. Gazing into the murky darkness, she jumped first as a panicked shout rang out through the damp air.

Reine landed and rolled to break the fall. She heard Sky hit the ground next to her, raising her head to see Kace holding the entomologist at gunpoint. The boy was breathing hard, and she soon realized it wasn't just because of exertion.

They were surrounded by monsters.

Bugs of different variety, all enlarged and twisted to become deadly predators, waited tensely in a half-circle around the two. The cages that had held them were empty, and there were at least ten that Reine could see. Among them, five were the same breed as the ones they'd encountered in the alleyway. She noticed all the monsters had their own pulsing, Goethan heart inside see-through flesh.

"I knew it," the man spat, his face scarlet at the sight of two more assailants, "the government is finally sending hit men after me. And oh . . . to think . . ." He stopped, his tone becoming more melodramatic so quickly that Reine knew it had to be fake. "To think that all I wanted in my life . . . was to spread a little happiness . . . to share my passion for insects . . ."

Kace paused, confused. He lowered his gun before Reine could stop him.

"We're not from the government," he argued, "and your bugs are hurting the neighborhoo—"

Like a flyswatter, a beady-eyed praying mantis smacked Kace into the wall. A loud, percussive sound wiped away his agonized groan, and the Sandbug Man roared in pain at the same time. Reine had to give Kace credit; the boy had managed to get off a shot before he was knocked unconscious.

"Sky," she directed, "focus on killing that guy. I'll protect Kace."

Reine understood why he had hesitated. There was just something about killing people who believed they were unconditionally right; it made you assume that you could change their mind and avoid bloodshed. Of course, it had been a trick in this case, but it was hard to tell in the heat of the moment.

Ah, the innocence of youth.

"My army will eat you alive!"

The scientist's frustrated cry sparked her into action. They might be distracted right now, but Sky couldn't hold the insects off forever. Reine entered the fourth and second levels. Her vision immediately allowed her to see the Goethan lines running through Kace's body, and she started weaving an illusion. The boy was no metahuman. Everyone had Goethan, but only the people who had an ability—such as Starflight's lasers—could ever hope to utilize their natural power.

Though he does have an unusually high amount of it . . .

Tucking the thought away for later, Reine flung her web of Goethan onto Kace. It helped that he wasn't actively resisting, so the illusion fit like a glove.

Wow. That's . . . realistic.

Fake blood started pooling at her feet, and she had to look away to convince herself that the boy wasn't actually dead. The dumb insects would definitely be fooled. Readying another illusion—this time only through the fourth level—she used a good chunk of her Goethan to create a replica of herself. It was still hard for her to make something so complicated, so Reine had to take a breath before projecting her image into a dark corner of the room, rendering herself invisible.

"Stop her!" she heard the entomologist screech as he directed his army of bugs to stop the replica she had created.

They just crashed into each other, blindly obeying their master's orders. Only humans were affected by the fourth level, so the bugs couldn't even see the mirage, let alone catch it.

I need to . . . damn it.

He had caught on way before she expected. Directing half of his bugs to keep Sky busy, the Sandbug Man gave the signal—a clicking of his tongue—for the spider-like sandbugs to start searching for vibrations instead of trusting their eyes.

Reine backpedaled, and then dropped both of her illusions. They were useless now. She entered the fifth level with the raise of an eyebrow and managed to smash in the face of one of her assailants before they were upon her, scratching and cutting with the ferocity of a hailstorm.

Kace woke up to find himself in a pool of blood. He panicked, flailing around and dislodging the illusion while he ran his hands over his body, trying to find the source of his wounds. He gave up when a sharp pain stabbed him in the head. It left him shivering on the floor. It was the head injury, he remembered, the one he'd gotten when . . . a mantis had flung him against the wall.

I don't want to die!

It all came crashing back: the battle, his stupid decision. Kace whimpered as he saw the weapon still gripped in his hand. Why had he thought it would be a good idea to come here again? He had no powers, no plan, and not even an inkling of his enemy's true strength.

It's your ego acting up, stupid, Kace thought as he blinked tears out of his eyes. *You couldn't stand the thought of failing at your mission before you even had the chance to try.* He felt his throat close, and the boy had to stop himself from wallowing in self-pity before he fell unconscious again. *They'll get you out of here,* he reassured himself. The people who had saved him before had dealt with one sandbug, right? The Reine woman would definitely have a plan, so he had nothing to worry about.

Right?

No! his mind roared back. *You messed it up, moron. Who would have accounted for a stupid kid alerting everyone in the neighborhood with his toy?*

The thought filled him with discomfort, and it was enough to get him on his feet. He shook off the receding pain. The gun felt familiar in his hands, solid, and he knew that all he needed was one shot to end this. People—the small number he had the chance to meet, anyway—had always told him he was a crack shot. Kace didn't know if it was true, but he wasn't going to give up either way.

He adjusted the bandage against his dark skin. His arm was hurting again, and Kace winced as he remembered the bug's claw piercing his skin. He hoped it wouldn't affect his aim.

Only two bullets left, Kace reminded himself. His father had told him to count the ammunition spent. *Miss one, and you won't get the chance to fire another.* He had seen how viciously the predators had gone after Reine when they realized they had been duped. He wouldn't—no, he couldn't—fail if he wanted to live.

Okay. Breathing out, Kace aimed the Glock G29 with two slightly shaking hands. The gun seemed to pulse nervously, but he ignored the feeling and placed one leg in front of the other. Concentration was key.

"Get him!" the entomologist screamed.

The command jarred the boy, but Kace continued to let the world fade away, making his only sensory input come from the image of his target seen through the notch of his gun. He moved a little to the left where no bugs were blocking the scientist. He didn't even flinch when a mantis closed the distance between them with a vicious lunge.

BOOM!

Time froze, and the milliseconds that passed seemed to stretch into hours. He could almost see the bullet fly—but that was of course, impossible. *Right?*

The thought was wiped away when his target's head exploded.

CHAPTER 26:
CULTS SUCK

THE PAST: 1 YEAR AGO

Reine dragged her feet as they approached the hotel. It was five stories tall and, most importantly, without cracks or broken windows. Even though she'd tried her best to convince Oliver to never go back, he had refused to abandon his friends because they "needed him."

"I'm the one making the plans," he explained. "The others contribute ideas, but I make them real."

She highly doubted that—the arrogant woman who had convinced her to join their group probably gave him an inflated sense of self-worth—but it wasn't like Reine was going to let him head off alone. If her father was determined to continue down this path of lunacy, then she would have to do the same.

"It's a nice place you've got there," she said in an effort to please her dad. Oliver had never been here either, but she let him take the credit.

"It was Aahna's idea," he replied proudly. "She knew we couldn't go back to the bar after that, um, altercation, so she rented a room in this hotel. How awesome is that?"

Not so good, considering that it means she's getting serious, Reine thought bitterly. *If this Aahna woman is willing to pay for these meetings, she must have some sort of goal in mind.*

"Great," Reine grumbled.

Oliver pulled her into a hug, ending any further conversation. The building they were approaching had a small fountain and a few, well-groomed flower beds. Not too out of place, considering the amount of time they had to walk to get here. This was one of the richest sections of the city.

Huh. If Aahna is some rich philanthropist who chooses to spend her time with depressed men, then I'm a girl with a mother.

"Stop there!" a voice yelled.

They both tensed, but Reine relaxed when she realized it was only a security guard. Their unwashed appearance must have been very out of place in a world where everyone could afford decent clothing and daily showers. *No worries. Last time I checked the government hasn't made dirtiness a crime yet.* She chuckled at her own joke, but it was an empty laugh.

"We're with Aahna," Oliver said authoritatively, and a little of his old self leaked back into his voice. "You can check with, ah, the resident of Suite 42 if you need confirmation."

The guard looked skeptical, but he let them past.

Reine instinctively thought about stealing something from the hotel, but thought better of it. *Not the best idea to steal from a place that you're going to come back to, is it?*

She stepped through the rotating doors and touched the moving glass with a finger. The inside of the building was the cleanest thing Reine had ever seen; there was no other way to describe it. Somehow, the staff members of this place made everything seem new and polished. Maybe it was the gilded chandelier, or the woman waving to them—wait.

It's her.

"Aahna!" Oliver exclaimed. Reine scowled. It was the metahuman who had raised the stone wall last time they met. She was wearing a simple but elegant low-cut dress laced with deep indigo and a cooler gray. Reine crossed her arms. Aahna looked, well . . . amazing, and it only made her feel more out of place.

"Hey child," she said, using the same greeting as in the pub, "and our esteemed Oliver, of course. Why don't you get a drink at the bar before joining us in the suite? I have an important proposal to put out to the group." She pointed to a counter with multicolored glasses arranged on a shelf.

Not good. She's buttering us up for something.

But her father seemed entirely taken by the idea, even walking over to check the drinks out before declining politely. The stuff here was way too expensive for them.

He wants to believe her, Reine realized. *His brain can't handle the idea that she might be scamming them.* That just made the whole fiasco more dangerous. She didn't know how far he would go to keep the illusion going.

"Alright then," Aahna said as Oliver returned. "Just follow me."

After riding an escalator—an actual, real-life escalator—up to the second floor, they walked down a carpeted corridor and into an airy room with people milling about. Someone had removed the bed, and the windows that made up an entire wall looked pretty cool to Reine. Her father didn't seem too surprised by the glamor. Maybe hotels were common in the old days?

"Hey!" a man said cheerfully, crushing Oliver's hand in his. "We're about to start. Why don't you guys have a seat?"

Her dad patted him on the back, "So formal today, huh? Guess we're doing something important."

His friend chuckled. "Always, but if you ask me—" he leaned in, "—it's time for the big plan."

Oliver's playful demeanor vanished. It was the first time Reine had seen him serious the entire day.

"Starflight."

"Yup," his friend said, and his smile turned as dark as Oliver's voice. "Let's get going, shall we?"

They took their seats, and Reine sat a little straighter when curtains were drawn across the windows, plunging the room into darkness. Aahna opened up her projector a moment later. The bright light on the screen was the only thing they could see, and Reine had to admit it was an effective way to catch someone's attention.

"Alrighty," she said, stepping into the light. The projector showed a picture of Starflight with an ugly smile across her face. As always, the hero looked larger than life, almost comical. If Reine hadn't met her before, she would have thought the picture was altered.

"We all have lost loved ones before—it's not as uncommon as you think. Did you know that metahumans have three times the mortality rate of a lesser human?" Aahna spat out the last three words like they were poison. "That is *not* right. From a scientific perspective, shouldn't we be the ones living longer?"

Reine began to feel uncomfortable. Was she promoting the idea that humans were somehow worse than their counterparts? For the first time, she considered the fact that every person in this room was a metahuman. It was unlikely, but not impossible.

"Dad. Is she being metaist?"

Oliver reacted like he had been hit. "What? Oh, you mean Aahna. Of course not—I mean, you've got to understand. What she says kind of makes sense."

It was her turn to falter. *My dad? A metaist?*

"Perhaps they didn't die by the hands of this woman," Aahna was announcing passionately, "but they did by what she represents. The metaheroes. Government lackeys that have renounced their people for money."

Reine continued to whisper to her father. "I'm a human too, you know. Does that mean I'm worthless?" She had long since written off the voice-changing incident at Starflight's base as luck, especially since no other power had manifested itself in her. She was hurt that her dad would even consider such a thing.

"She only hints at it," Oliver said defensively, "and that's not the point—" He was retreating into himself again. "I still love you regardless of your worth."

Ouch.

Reine fell silent, and no amount of prodding would get her to speak again for the rest of the meeting. Not even when they announced their plan to kill Starflight.

At least their goal aligns with mine, she thought. *But that doesn't make a difference. Once the job is done, they'll never hear a word from me again.*

CHAPTER 27:
SURPRISES AREN'T ALWAYS GOOD

YEAR 2035

"You did good work," Trevon told Asher grudgingly, "but I hope we never meet again."

Asher nodded, unsure what to say. Kace was standing beside his father, and he waved to them as they left. Asher waved back. He knew he should feel resentful towards the boy for risking their lives, but the kid's competence and bravery had moved him. Impulsiveness could be a virtue, after all, and Kace sure had a lot of it.

"Can't say the same," he told The Eye. The man just shrugged.

Leaving him to his grumbling, Asher checked the map he'd given them. Trevon had used his powers again yesterday, forming a sheet of countless golden dots that shone with varying degrees of brightness. Then, as if noticing something else no one could see, he had marked an "x" on the map Asher was holding now.

"You'll find him on the top floor," Trevon had told them. "Try not to say it was me when he tortures you to death."

Well, that's optimistic, Asher silently retorted.

He split up with Reine and Sky and went to find the bike store marked on the map. It was supposed to be pretty expensive, but none of them wanted to walk all the way to the other side of the city after such an exhausting night. They needed the rest, and he was the only one who wasn't half dead from fighting the Sandbug Man.

I wonder if they have coffee around here. And tea. The girls like tea.

Sky sat with Reine in the room of her friend's old apartment. Dust coated everything. She hadn't been paying rent for the past year, of course, but since no one else had moved in, Sky didn't feel any qualms about Reine breaking into the building. Lockpicking was infinitely easier when there was a skeleton key hidden under the doormat.

"It's . . . a nice place," Sky said.

Reine was lying on the couch, head propped up against the armrest and legs crossed. She closed her eyes, as if breathing in memories. Dust settled on her face, and she wrinkled her nose.

"No. It's terrible."

Sky redid the bandages on her left hand. Blood was still soaking through from a cut made by a particularly vicious cockroach, so she disinfected it again with some antiseptic. The pain felt like tiny barbs ripping into her hand.

"Don't say that," Sky protested. "I'm not even kidding. Your home has a sense of . . . history."

Reine shifted her head but didn't respond. Sky could have sworn she saw her friend smile a little. It was still there when she sighed wistfully.

"Sky? I know we should be sleeping or something, but can I ask you a question?"

"Ask away. You know I never sleep."

Reine grinned, but it felt forced. Her eyes were still closed. "What would you do if you had to pit your father's life against other innocent ones, Sky? Even if saving your dad also came with . . . amazing rewards."

Sky settled back against the couch's side. The most obvious answer was to save the innocents, of course; many lives over one was the first moral concept taught in Pantheon's academy. *You should always prioritize saving as much as you can instead of letting your emotions cloud your judgement . . . yada yada yada . . . and so on.* She paused in her reflections, turning them back on herself. *But I still won't do it, will I? That's just not . . . me.*

"I'll save my dad," she replied carefully. "But only because I'm not strong enough to do otherwise. Maybe someone else better than me can make the sacrifice." Sky realized it was true as she said it. Not only did Eajesuth mean too much to her, but also, watching him die once was already painful enough. She couldn't bear the thought of letting him go a second time when she had the power to stop his death.

Reine exhaled. She looked satisfied, as if a great weight had been slightly lessened.

"Sky." Her friend's voice trembled, and she was surprised by the rawness of it. "Remember when you told me the story of your parents? Do you still want to listen to mine?"

Sky nodded before realizing that Reine's eyes were closed, but her friend seemed to get it.

"Well . . . It all started on the night of the heist . . ."

Hours burned away as Reine's retelling rekindled the flames of time. Sometimes they were barely more than coals, and sometimes they raged higher than bonfires. Sky put her hand over her friend's. It tingled with a surprising warmth, and, well, she didn't understand why, but . . .

Thud.

"I'm back!" Asher yelled cheerfully, "with bikes and— holy Pantheon!"

He closed the door behind him and almost tripped over his own feet as Reine and Sky lunged forward at the sudden noise.

The room was very cramped, leaving little space between their shocked gazes.

Probably thought I was a metahero. I should have knocked before I came in. Asher scratched his head ruefully. *Next time.*

"So, anyway," he continued as if they hadn't scared each other half to death, "it was really hard hauling—wait, you guys. Are you having an allergic react—oh, you've been cryi—I mean . . ."

Asher stopped as Sky burst out laughing and Reine scowled playfully. They seemed happier, lighter somehow. He didn't think too much of it. If he had learned one thing about how not to be annoying, it was not to pry into other people's businesses. He studied the empty beer bottle under the sofa and pretended not to notice when they let go of each other's hands.

"Thanks, Asher," Sky said, mirth still lingering in her voice. She started to pick up her backpack but stopped when she remembered something. "Oh yeah. Do you need some rest? And how much money do we have left? Is it enough for getting back to the academy?"

He shook his head. "I slept at The Eye's house. Um, I'm pretty sure we only have a few dollars left, but it's fine. We don't need too much to get back to the school, right? And you guys can always come stay with my parents for the rest of the break. They were pretty mad after the 'accident,' but I'm sure they'll be fine with it once they hear we assassinated Tremor."

"*If* we assassinate Tremor," Reine corrected.

He tilted his head at her as if saying "*Now?*," but she didn't back down, so Asher let the words hang in the air. They were all becoming more sober to the reality of the situation. Forget about getting back to school; if they failed, there wouldn't even be a piece of them left to apologize for their incompetence—for anything.

"Alright then," he decided. "Let's go before someone steals our bikes."

Tremor's base was surprisingly ordinary looking. In fact, it was essentially a large office building—special only because most of the still-standing skyscrapers had gone into disrepair. Reine remembered the day she had gone to that hotel with her dad. Places like these were extremely uncommon—virtually non-existent in the poorer sections of the city—so the villain was wise to build it somewhere richer. Its shiny new look blended in better with the other displays of wealth, and she had to admit she would never have suspected it to be anything other than a boring bank.

Still, how on earth has he kept this place a secret? Reine wondered. *People are bound to become suspicious if they do enough business with a fake finance company.*

Reine put aside her thoughts. She knew when to concentrate, and now was not the time to get distracted—not when their mission's final goal was within reach.

"Okay. So—" she started to say.

Suddenly, a familiar, purple-caped figure landed right in front of the "bank" entrance. The concrete cracked. Her breath caught, and Reine could have sworn her heart missed a beat, but she quickly schooled her features. Who knew what Starflight could detect?

"Guys," Sky whispered, "she's literally a few feet away from us."

Reine shushed her. It wouldn't seem weird for a group of teenagers to be surprised at the appearance of a famous metahero, but it would be if she heard them talking about escape plans. Starflight's eyes darted over to them.

Asher chimed in quickly. "Yeah. Starflight is soooo cool."

They turned away from the metahero so she couldn't see their faces. Reine thanked Asher's quick thinking; Starflight couldn't resist a compliment. With an indulgent nod, she entered the building. The trio immediately burst into frantic conversation.

"What in the world is she doing here?"

"I doubt it's about borrowing money. This could be good."

"What? Are you even hearing yourself? There's no way we're taking on both Tremor and Starflight."

"But just think about it. What if she's trying to take him out?"

They lapsed into silence. On one hand, it would be safer to leave and come back later. On the other, Reine really wanted to know what the metahero was doing here. If they could bring back some valuable information, maybe they could skip killing Tremor altogether!

"What do you think, Reine?"

She shoved the doors open. "We're going to follow her."

Starflight captured the attention of every single person in the room as she entered, so the trio was able to follow her into the building without much scrutiny. It was an unimpressive reception area—first impressions often decided whether customers came back—and Sky was surprised at the lack of security.

The couple of people milling around could be spies, I guess. But . . . oh.

Two people dressed in black three-piece suits blinked into existence, looking disgruntled at Starflight's flashy entrance. They had been completely invisible, and she shuddered to think what would have happened if they had snuck in without knowing.

"Greetings," one of them whispered uselessly. The fact that there were barely any people in the room, coupled with its echoey construction, made his words quiet but clear. "Please do not immerse yourself in your subconscious during your stay. For safety reasons, of course." The woman harrumphed, but complied. Sky felt a presence in the room go away.

I swear, Sky thought. *That hero is unfairly powerful. She probably stays submerged in the levels when she's sleeping!*

"Talk in the bathroom," Reine muttered to them and tugged at Asher's hoodie when he looked reluctant. Starflight had already gone up through an elevator so they had to be careful not to draw anyone's attention. Exiting the building and then coming back in would seem too suspicious.

Creak . . .

The bathroom door seemed to make fun of them as they pulled it shut. They let out relieved sighs. Sky doubted anyone would put security cameras in the bathroom. *Would they?*

Asher broke the tense silence. "So. Since we can count Starflight assassinating Tremor out, we just need a plan to get past those ninja guards. Any ideas, anybody?"

"Nope," Sky admitted. "They're obviously trained to detect metahuman Goethan signatures. Even if Reine turns us invisible, they'll still be able to feel our Goethan." She shrugged, and Asher scratched his head, pacing around the bathroom.

Reine brightened. "But what if I project our signatures elsewhere too? No idea if it will work, but the technique worked fine when I used it in the Sandbug Man's house. It'll just seem like we're still in the bathroom no matter where we go."

"Hmm . . . Seems dangerous to count on no one checking on us."

Or even using the bathroom, for that matter, Sky added silently.

Sky crossed her arms. She wanted the plan to work, but their luck could swing either way. She felt uneasy depending on something none of them had control over.

"I guess we'll have to risk it," Reine eventually said. "It's our only choice! We can minimize the risk of getting caught by getting rid of the illusions as soon as we're safe. All we have to do is get to the top floor, and—"

"I'll cause a distraction."

They stared at Asher, dumbfounded. Reine's mouth opened, then closed, and it was the first time Sky had seen her speechless. She was shocked too. Not to diss Asher or anything, but he didn't seem like the kind of guy to risk his own life.

"We can't just give up, and you're the ones fighting Tremor. That's gotta be at least as dangerous." Asher grinned. "I'm committed, guys. I can't wait to see Abby, or Isaac, or even Mr. Nidek's faces when we return as true metavillains."

Sky felt her budding sense of respect for him start to sprout even more. It *would* be pretty sweet to prove Abby wrong.

Reine finally recovered. "But that's suicide! You can't—"

"If I can make them think there's a threat somewhere else, then no one's even going to look twice at the Goethan signatures in the bathroom. You can turn me invisible, right? Just activate the illusion as soon as I finish, and I'll give them the slip in no time." He smirked, causing Reine to run a hand through her hair with a grudging scowl.

Sky ended the debate. "He's right, and you know it," she said, peeking through a slit in the bathroom door. "Now let's stop wasting time. Time to kick some ass!"

CHAPTER 28:
FINDING LIONS IN SNAKE CAGES

YEAR 2035

The plan, for once, unfolded beautifully. Reine growled and pushed at the Goethan, and she eventually managed to forge three perfect illusions around them. The one enveloping Asher was, of course, dormant. He needed to be able to use his Goethan unsuppressed.

"Say the words '*Wonder Abby*' and you'll activate the shield," Reine instructed, a thin layer of sweat shining on her forehead.

Asher chuckled nervously. "You are really obsessed with that show, you know that?" He groaned, shifting his feet. "Wow. I can't believe I'm actually doing this."

The approaching conflict bothered Reine more than she liked to admit. She gave Asher an encouraging nod as he exited the bathroom and then the building, then sagged with the effort of maintaining her connection to the Goethan covering her friends. It scared her that they had no special trick, no plan to defeat Tremor. What would happen if one of them was killed? Reine didn't like to get too attached to people, but Sky was different from the rest.

Even Asher. As corny as it sounds, I don't know if I can survive losing someone again.

"Hey!" a man shouted from outside the bathroom. Reine and Sky took that as their cue to sneak out into the reception area. They were just in time to catch a glimpse of Asher before he disappeared behind a cloud of dust.

The glass doors burst open and wind stirred, forming whispers around the reception area that gathered into a roar. Guards shoved their shoulders against the bulletproof doors as a tornado righted itself and crashed down into the middle of the room. Its gray-washed clouds twirled bits and pieces of the scenery around them into deadly missiles silhouetted by colorful lightning. The guards hesitated, and then backed away when the walls began to shake.

"Code red! All Units to ground leve—ah!" A guard tried to call for help, only to be cut off when a bolt of electricity erupted out of her chest. A few started to run. Reine noticed she was still alive, so they didn't have much time before everybody—about four guards left—recovered . . .

"They're gone!" Sky said. "The, uh, two creepy guards just left to check out the situation." She tried to see through the debris, but Asher was an indistinct figure in the distance.

Reine wished him luck. It was going to be hard to catch up when security was quadrupled. She opened the "For Emergencies" door a crack and slipped through with Sky. It was basically a fire exit, so there were stairs that led all the way up to the top.

Twenty-two floors. Fun.

She raised her left eyebrow. Reine entered the fifth level, and then bounded up the floors. She didn't have to break their invisibility yet because the Goethan powering their bodies was self-contained.

Better step lightly. Do they make these stairwells so echoey on purpose?

"There are guards there," Sky murmured, nudging Reine in the direction of the door.

They had reached the twenty-second floor, and unfortunately, someone had stationed five men in front of their only exit. The fire in Reine burned brighter. They were getting closer to their target.

"Save your Goethan," she said to Sky. "I'll deal with this."

She carefully accessed the fourth level so that no excess power slipped out, and then *drew* the Goethan out of the two illusions surrounding them. The burly men yelled in surprise, and she narrowed her eyes. These were no metahumans. She redirected her mass of concentrated Goethan into a ball of illusionary energy that hovered above her open palm. It split and shot out like light refracted by a prism. Smell, taste, hearing, touch, and sight: all senses were taken from them as her powers coordinated targeted strikes across their bodies.

This situation reminded her of the government takeover her mom had told her about. Humans were no match for someone who could steal the launch codes right out of a president's mind. She silently thanked Asher. *Metahuman guards here would have been a problem.*

Stepping lightly over the guards—they would recover later when the Goethan wore off—Reine and Sky tiptoed their way into a dusty corridor. Cobwebs, but no spiders, hung in the corners. It was as if they had stepped into a barren wasteland.

"Do you feel that?" Sky asked Reine, edging closer to her friend. Unnatural ripples of dread pulsed through the air, making it quake with foreboding. Tremors of fear forced themselves through her, and she clenched her jaw reflexively.

"Steady. It's not real, Sky," Reine answered. "We have to get closer."

Almost as if wading through quicksand, the two marched forward, the sound of distant shouting in the stairwell providing motivation. They could now hear people talking.

It's Starflight! Reine realized. *And Tremor.*

Their voices were coming from behind the closed door of a room with concrete walls so she couldn't be sure, but there was no mistaking the metavillain's distinct way of speaking. Tremor's tone was more suggestive than expressive—almost as if it were telepathically conveying malicious intentions through the undulations in the air. The sound reminded her of the hissing of a tarantula—not too disturbing—but the *intent* layered beneath it was what made Sky cling tightly to Reine.

"You refuse to give me the information now?" Starflight's voice drifted through the corridor, strangely distorted. "Disgusting worm. I thought we had a deal!"

The tremors of fear grew stronger.

"*Do not mistake our hospitality for trust . . . We will lead you to Pantheon's base when we deem it best,*" the villain replied.

What?

Sky took a step back. Reine gripped her hand.

"Seriously? You—fine," they heard Starflight reply, "but if your useless team doesn't give us back our money's worth—" she let the threat hang for a moment, "—you can consider our protection of your fake bank *gone*. Who knows? I might even send Gravedigger after you, just for the fun of it. Do we have an understanding?"

Oh no.

Reine dragged Sky into a dim corner to prevent the metahero from seeing them as she stormed out, not even bothering to close the door before flying away. She broke a hole in the building's wall on her way out.

"I swear," Sky said, "if I get surprised even one more tim—"

"STOP RIGHT THERE!"

One of the shadowy guards they had seen before pointed a gun at them. Another had a person—Asher—slung over his shoulder. As the duo watched, he threw Asher, cuffed and bruised, onto the ground.

"Your mission has failed. Surrender now, or we'll kill all three of you. Starting with him."

CHAPTER 29:
TREMORING WITH FEAR

YEAR 2035

"What is this . . ." a voice hissed.

As one, the squadron of guards bowed deeply. Sky could see their knees trembling, and she had to resist the urge to whirl around. If this . . . thing used fear as its weapon, she shouldn't feed it more fuel.

"Boss—I mean, master. We think this boy was sent as a distraction so that these two assassins could kill you."

Sky turned slowly—*this feels so awkward*—and glanced back. The closeness of Tremor set her on edge. Its wraithlike body, elongated and misty, hung over her head like some sort of deformed werewolf. The villain was more Goethan than human, with unnaturally long, stick-like limbs and a blank face. She felt a pang of respect for Starflight. *I can't even imagine being alone in a room with Tremor, let alone insulting it.*

A ripple of thought spread across the corridor. *"Turn around . . . girls . . ."* it said, *"show me the faces of my would-be assassins . . ."*

The thing reached down with a wide hand and rested it on Sky's shoulder, as if it could feel her discomfort. Reine glared daggers, batting the pitchfork-like appendage away. Tremor's guards immediately tensed, but her hand only passed through their master's body. It was no more solid than thick fog.

"Relax, men . . . I would hate to accidentally torture you while interrogating these wonderful villains here . . ."

His guards needed no clearer dismissal. Scrambling to get away, they managed to all cram into the elevator before Tremor's stick-thin arm shot out, spewing midnight-colored Goethan everywhere. Sky and Reine backed towards their only source of light: the hole Starflight had made in the wall. The metavillain's hand wrapped around Asher's entire body and lifted him up. Its noxious power soaked through the guy's skin.

What the hell? Sky wondered, dread descending like churning quicksand.

One second, then two, and Sky became confused when nothing happened. She saw Asher's face begin to twitch.

"He's waking up," Reine said. "Why—"

His mouth opened, but no words came out. Instead, a centipede the size of a small snake began to crawl through the opening. Sky flinched. Parasitic-looking slugs and other slimy creatures were oozing their way out of his pores, leaving no mark except for the constant twitching of his body. The insects were made of the same dark material as Tremor, but they were quickly becoming more solid as Asher's body contorted in terror.

"Stop!" Sky pleaded.

Reine dashed forwards, striking at Tremor's head with a wooden chair she had found discarded in the corner, but the furniture just passed through. She didn't have a chance to run before Tremor gripped her by the neck.

"Food . . . wonderful food . . ."

Infusing her with the same, pervasive Goethan, Reine fell limp as her kicking grew weak, then stopped. Sky panicked. She tried to enter the fourth level by snapping her fingers on her right hand, but even the physical connection couldn't help her when her mind was in such turmoil.

"Please . . ."

Tremor stared blankly at her, and she felt her feet near the edge of the broken wall. For the first time, Sky understood why people chose to jump from flaming buildings. The thing didn't care about interrogation. All it wanted was her fear, to use her greatest weakness against her. She would die before letting it succeed.

The outside. It's my only chance . . . I need to end this.

She prepared to jump.

Reine knew Tremor had gotten to her as soon as a vision filled her mind, removing all control of her body. She was able to feel but not move, hear but not listen—almost as if she was in an immersive virtual reality experience. She looked through her host's eyes. The scene was vivid, a direct replication from her memories. Reine would have sighed if she could.

It was the day her father had died.

"It's finally happening," Oliver whispered to himself. "I can't believe it's finally happening."

Reine put a hand on his shoulder, but not for the reason he thought. She hoped it would help him regain his sense of morality. These were innocent people they were about to kill, after all. Not just Starflight.

"Are you sure about this?" she asked him.

When Aahna had spilled the complete plan to them two days ago, Reine had been plagued by doubts. Now she was no less divided. She suspected that the woman was purposefully giving them less time to consider the consequences of their actions. Reine knew it was working on her. Having to push the button might cause her hesitation, but she wasn't sure if she could stop her dad when it would be so much easier to let him pull the trigger.

"Of course," he scoffed. "Worry about yourself—there's only five more minutes before it's your turn."

Reine shifted her feet.

They were standing in a storage room that was all furniture, except for a few hastily rigged wires and a button with a glass cover around it. Oliver had hidden the detonator behind a chair. Someone could chance upon it while they were distracted, and a light touch would detonate explosives all throughout the main hall of the bank.

"Four minutes."

"Alright. I'm going."

Dragging her feet, Reine took out a scary-looking knife. The job of her and a few other metavillains was to cause a big enough stir to draw Starflight herself. It eased her conscience that the action would scare some of the innocents into running away. At least she was doing something to help.

Her earpiece crackled. "Starflight is spotted. She, per her schedule, is having her 9:00 a.m. coffee."

Reine fiddled with the device to decrease its volume. The stupid thing better not give her away.

"Affirmative," she whispered back. "Should we proceed?"

"No need to be so formal, but yes. On my mark, we will fire the first shot in ten, nine . . ."

She ran her hand through her hair nervously. This was it. Reine waited for the exhilarating rush of cold competence, the joy of doing what she did best, but nothing replaced the doubt. Instead, she could have sworn the opposite was happening.

"Break some bones, team. Go!"

Swallowing her indecision, Reine charged into the lobby as one of the villains—only one had managed to get a gun—fired a shot into the ceiling. All attention turned to him.

"Move! Move! Move!" he roared, giving the bystanders a chance to escape.

She surveyed her surroundings. There were about thirty people she could see, and that was already plenty. She cursed. The civilians were being scared by their blades and Goethan attacks, but only five ran out of the bank. The rest just cowered behind pinewood desks and prayed.

"What are you doing?" she screamed at a couple. The woman's protective demeanor reminded her of Amy. "Can't you see it's safer to leave?"

The bank's rotating glass doors shattered, and a streak of purple shot through a metavillain near the entrance. She died with her head and limbs separated from a torso that wasn't there anymore. With renewed confidence, the husband stood his ground as his wife tried to pull him away. Starflight had arrived.

"Hah. Stupid villain. Where are you going to run to now?"

"Honey. Please . . ."

Reine was already backtracking, retreating as planned. It was easy with everyone distracted by the metahero's entrance. She watched as one of her father's friends created a ball of gleaming light, prompting Starflight to lunge for him. It was a trap. The villains pooled all of their Goethan through the outstretched hands of a bald man, and he brought them together to blast the hero, trapping her inside a block of pure force.

"Retreat!" someone shouted in Reine's earpiece. "Hurry. Oliver's about to blow the whole place to the ground, and Starflight isn't going to stay down for long."

Indeed, purple cracks were already spreading through her prison. It was lucky that her dad had infused the bombs with his Goethan-nullifying powers. They would definitely be able to destroy her. Reine ran outside with the others, thinking about the lives they were about to save . . . and end.

"We can't," she said.

"What?"

"Please. Just tell my dad to stop this. This is . . . wrong."

The other metavillains looked at her with fire growing in their eyes. She understood their frustration, but maybe . . .

The last speck of their compassion died.

"*They're only expendable humans . . . like you're an expendable human!*" the man who had trapped Starflight spat. "*Too soft. I knew we should never have let you join the group!*"

They started sprinting at full speed again, leaving Reine to stare into the bank by herself. The burning desire to follow them was maddening. She felt every survival instinct rise up inside her to beg their foolish owner to escape.

The villain called back to the girl when she didn't budge. "*Are you serious? You can't—you're—you're going to die if you stay! You know that, right?*"

It was the final straw. Without a backward glance, Reine ran back into the bank.

Sky stood frozen with indecision. The beautiful view that offered her freedom from Tremor's oppression was only a small step away, mocking her with its clear skies and city landscape. Even the slums didn't look too bad from a distance.

She laid a hand on the jagged edges of the broken wall.

"*Well?*" Tremor whispered from behind her, unbearably close. "*What will you choose?*"

Sky trembled. Behind her was all-encompassing fear, and the other option cost only her honor . . . and her life. She held one foot over the edge, basking in the afternoon sun and the summer wind. It almost negated the terrifying presence behind her, but she could still feel its glee, and something small within her rebelled against the idea of feeding it—of playing its little game. But that was a good price to pay for salvation.

Isn't it?

She remembered when Starflight had used her as bait for her father. Sky didn't have a choice back then, but now was different. She had the power to make a decision, and it would come with consequences that not even her father could save her from.

"I . . . I . . ."

"*Yes?*"

Pantheon damn you, Tremor.

Spinning around, Sky slapped the thing across its face with a Goethan-coated hand. The pained hiss that came with her attack almost made it worth it when Tremor's thin fingers grasped at her body, expelling corrupted Goethan like a factory. She entered the fifth, third, and fourth levels simultaneously. The deadly weapon only brushed her skin as she dodged, her heightened senses screaming at the *wrongness* of the villain's power. Its other hand flew at her.

That assha—

Sky slowed down the approaching attack in the stupidest way possible. She grabbed onto Tremor's pitchfork hand and *wrenched* its skeletal fingers away before they could wrap around her neck. She tried to break them, but they latched onto her arm instead.

Sky screamed as her Goethan clashed against the metavillain's. It had become a battle of strength. The third level protected her from the fear-creating effect of its power, but the thing was definitely submerged in much higher levels than she was. Hell, he was more Goethan than human, and she had to admit the former was way more powerful.

I can't brute force this. There's no way I'm ever going to beat it.

Letting go and ignoring the smell of burning flesh, Sky bought herself a brief moment as Tremor also recoiled. The thing recovered almost instantly, but she was already vaulting over it with a fifth-level assisted leap. Sky had trained with Goethan since the beginning of her life. She knew how to deal with the pain.

"*Come back* . . ." Tremor whispered as she sped towards the exit, all hints of the damage it sustained gone. "*Your friends need you . . .*"

Sky wished she had brought earplugs.

I'm sorry Reine, she thought and kicked the door to the stairway open, her damaged hands refusing to cooperate. *I'm not brave enough to stay, but I promise I'll try to get help. I believe in you. You guys just need to survive a little longer.*

She bounded down the stairs, not knowing that the guards had found where they'd stashed their backpacks in the bathroom— and therefore the emergency phone. It was going to be a disaster.

But for whom?

In the top floor's dark corridor, Tremor hunched patiently over the Asher boy. It watched as his mouth opened in a silent scream, fortifying its Goethan's effects with his fear. It waited for its appetizer to cook. The bugs crawling out of his body were still dissolving when they touched the ground: a sign that his meal wasn't quite ready yet.

"Parasites, little boy?" the thing whispered into his ear. *"What a boring fear . . ."*

Still, its meal wasn't completely spoiled. The ones that resisted longer always had a better taste, and there was the girl. Unlike the boy's soft, yellow light, her Goethan was more red, more violent. Her hands were balled into fists, and its power corrupted her weaknesses like pus bubbling in an open wound.

Tremor made no sound as it slid across the shadows to loom over its main course. It so admired the intricate history carved into her fears. In fact, it could almost see them, as if they were written across her tan skin. The other girl would have made a wonderful dessert too, but she had escaped. It glanced regretfully—or with as much regret as it could show, anyway—at the spot where she had stood. This one and her friend with the ginger hair would have made such wonderful, complementary flavors of fear laced with tragedy, but no use dwelling on what could have been.

Tremor crossed its long, stick-like legs together and waited for its food's mental defenses to break down. It had no worries about anyone escaping its web of fear. It was the only one here who could see the more subtle colors of Goethan: proof that its prey hadn't mastered any levels beyond the fifth. And without their bodies, trapped in their own defenseless little minds . . . their powers meant *nothing*.

Reine sprinted past the frozen Starflight, cracks still spreading around her as if she were breaking the prison by sheer will alone. She knew Oliver would wait as long as possible before detonating the bombs in order to allow his friends to escape.

"Dad!" she shouted, waving to the security camera she knew her father was using to monitor the situation. "Don't press the button yet!"

Reine could just imagine the panic Oliver was going through right now. She realized she was being irresponsible—what happened if Starflight broke free first and killed them all?—but she also knew that the sight of her was the only thing that was stopping her father from causing a massacre.

"Just wait!"

She frantically signaled for the civilians to leave, then ran like she had never ran before. Even on the night of Amy's death, Reine had been running for her own life. Now she ran for everyone else's.

"Flee while you can, villain! Starflight will deal with you soon."

Ignoring the jeers, Reine almost slammed into the disguised door that led into the storage room as she threw it open and crashed into her dad.

"Reine? Wha—" His expression turned from worried to surprised to mad. She tried to pull him away from the detonator, but Oliver jerked away.

"What are you doing, Reine? She's about to break free!"

She shook her head, positioning herself between him and the button. How could she get him to understand? She knew there had to be a better way.

"We can't just kill all these people too!" Reine said, and her dad's frown curled into a snarl. "Now that we know she can be trapped, we can always make another plan. How would you feel if I was the one who was in there?"

Oliver slapped her. Not a gentle, disciplinary pat like the ones he used to give her in order to correct her form during training, but a real, malicious smack across the face.

"LET ME KILL HER! DO YOU KNOW HOW LONG I HAVE PLANNED FOR THIS? AMY DESERVES TO BE AVENGED, AND IF YOU DISRESPECT HER LIKE THAT, THEN MAYBE YOU SHOULD JOIN HER!"

Reine stumbled out of the way as her dad lunged for the button, eyes wide at the sight of the fully shattered energy cage that no longer held Starflight. The world seemed to focus on his desperation.

"I'm sorry," Reine said.

She let her instincts take over and twisted her body, swinging both of her legs around and lifting them from the ground. She was stunned—her dad had just told her she was better off dead—but she had never let painful words get in the way of her actions before. Her body mirrored that of a butterfly in flight.

Reine's foot crashed right into his face, and she heard an audible crunch. Oliver rolled on the ground. His arm was still extended, his fingers grasping as he tried to shake off the pain. Reine breathed hard. The silence was only broken by the cracking sound of the wall.

Wait.

The cracking sound of the wall?

Starflight solved that mystery a moment later. She burst through the concrete and didn't even bother to glance at the young woman before hitting her dad so hard he shattered the chair stashed behind him. Reine was pretty sure he had broken half of his bones.

"*You useless worm.*" *The metahero seethed, for once without perfect hair or costume.* "*Yo—You almost killed me!*" *She seemed shocked as the words exited her mouth, and Reine was surprised too. Perhaps confronting the fact that even being one of the most powerful metahumans in existence didn't guarantee her immortality had knocked some humanity into her.*

"*Killed me . . .*"

For a moment, they shared a sense of déjà vu, the scene that had happened so long ago surfacing in their minds again. The room became a long corridor, and her dad's body became Amy's. Starflight even flinched as if expecting a Goethan bomb from Reine to detonate.

"*Again . . .*"

She stared at Reine, and she could only stare back as the cogs turned in the hero's brain. Reine knew she should be begging for mercy, or apologizing to the woman, but nothing came out. The fact that this was all her fault—that she had probably sealed her dad's fate—was finally enough to make her pause.

"*Starflight,*" *Oliver groaned, holding onto consciousness,* "*it was my fault. I wanted to kill you.*"

Both he and Reine knew there was no point in running; Starflight would catch them in a second. Reine hesitated, debating whether to argue against him. Wasn't she supposed to say that it was her fault, that she would rather die than let the hero kill her father? But Reine couldn't bring herself to say the words. Her emotions had been culled since the death of her mother, and if she were being truthful, Oliver hadn't exactly been the greatest father either.

"*He's telling the truth,*" *she found herself saying.* "*I was trying to stop him from killing the people in the lobby.*"

Reine was surprised at the anger—no, hatred—burning in her words. It was almost as if she was venting all of her frustration at the past few years in one sentence.

Starflight started laughing. "*Very interesting. Perhaps the little worm does have some potential after all.*"

She lifted back up into the air and started gathering purple light in her hands. It was disconcerting. Even with her civilian clothes on, Reine saw the metahero once again.

"But that doesn't mean I can say the same for her father."

Oliver lowered his head. Reine tried to catch his eye and caught a glimpse of fear, hatred, and pain—lots of pain. She didn't ask for forgiveness. Did she want to? Then Starflight thrust out her hand and incinerated her dad. It was too late. Purple was all Reine could see.

CHAPTER 30:
THE ONLY THING TO FEAR IS TREMOR ITSELF

YEAR 2035

When the light cleared, Reine realized she was still in the memory. But she was also . . . completely fine. That couldn't be right. Wasn't Tremor's power supposed to have dealt her a crushing emotional blow by now? And something seemed different, anyway. In the original version of the memory, Starflight had spared and ordered her cadets to keep an eye on her after killing her dad, but all she was doing now was pacing around.

"Little girl . . . Is it not time to die?"

She turned sharply towards the metahero, and noticed that she could control her body again for some reason. Starflight looked wrong. With a start, Reine realized there was a dark tinge to the glow surrounding her, as if she had been contaminated with some of Tremor's Goethan. She backed away. Maybe the real test had finally arrived. Reliving the memory was traumatizing, but Reine had been forced to confront her own actions so many times with Sky's help that they no longer held sway over her. Tremor's Goethan must have created this final obstacle to break her.

"I don't understand . . ." the metahuman that was not Starflight hissed; it was still ignoring her. "Why didn't the memory work?"

Reine bunched up her fists, gladly averting her eyes as Oliver's ashes and the rest of the scene crumbled away. Was fighting even an option? For all she knew, Tremor could trap her in her own brain forever, waiting for her to give in. She tried to feel for the cage around her mind, but there was nothing.

Reine eyed the imposter warily. It was still puzzled, and she was not about to explain her sudden lack of fear.

"Tremor," she said, drawing its attention away in case it figured out its mistake, "you've lost, and you know it. What kind of stupid scare tactic was that, anyway? I was never afraid of watching my father die."

The woman that was not a woman reacted like it had been slapped, "Impossible . . . my Goethan is never wrong . . . unless . . ."

The skin of its body began to bulge and bloat with some dark power. Reine could see Tremor's nightmarish shape trying to break out, but for some reason, it chose to keep the form of Starflight for a little longer. It manipulated her face into a ghastly grin. "Your greatest fear was Starflight all along."

Reine was almost bemused until the creature fired a purple beam of concentrated energy at her. It tore through the side of her shirt, leaving a line of black, charred skin in its wake. The area felt numb, but the fact that she couldn't feel the pain disturbed her.

"Is this even allowed by your Goethan?" she gasped after dodging another laser beam. "Starflight is definitely not my greatest fear."

Tremor ignored her, and Reine growled in frustration. Raising her left eyebrow and snapping her fingers on her right hand, she entered the fourth and fifth level. There had to be some way to exploit the villain's mistake. If its power worked best when targeting someone else's distress, then maybe it would be weaker without the right ingredients.

"Just relax, little girl . . ." the villain was whispering, "I promise your death will be painless. You won't even feel it when I consume your past."

Reine shrugged. "I doubt you'll like it. It's pretty hard to stomach."

Rolling, she dodged a lightning-fast attack from the fake Starflight. It made sense that dying in her head would lower her mental defenses and allow Tremor to . . . eat her? That part was still weird, but she had no intention of letting it go that far.

Wait, *Reine realized, coming to a stop.* If this is all inside my head . . .

Then Tremor blasted her with a fist-size bolt of death, and she vaulted away. Too late. She hit the floor with a thud, feeling the heat melt away flesh. The laser didn't miss this time; it didn't even skim past her skin. It went directly through her stomach and out the other end.

"Delicious . . ." the creature said.

Through a haze of pain-filled tears, Reine could see Starflight's legs melt and change into Tremor's form. It seemed to hover above her, like an angel of death waiting to collect her soul. She bit down on her lip to stop from screaming. There was no point in checking the wound. She knew it was fatal.

Thump. Thump.

Reine zeroed in on the sound of her heart and felt her life slip away. The blood-pumping organ was slowing down despite the boost of adrenaline in her desperate body, and it almost made her faint to direct the Goethan in her brain at it. She swallowed her exhaustion through sheer will. Dropping her control of the fourth and fifth level, Reine coughed out blood as she gave one final push in the direction of her heart.

Thump . . . Thump . . . Thump.

"At last . . ."

Her mind's body stopped working first, then her brain. The mass of neurons dimmed one last time, and then . . .

Reine's real body lapsed into true unconsciousness, ready to be consumed. Tremor put a tentative finger on the teen's cold forehead. The girl's red Goethan was a fading sunset that still refused to vacate her heart, but Tremor didn't care. It shivered with excitement, too exhilarated to even devour its appetizer, and then *breathed* . . .

Only to jerk back. Confused, the villain tried again to no avail. It tried to overpower her Goethan shield with its own, an act that it shouldn't even have to perform, but the girl's power matched its own.

"*Impossible,*" Tremor seethed. Even if the girl was accessing the third level, its seventh-level mastery should already have killed her.

Unsettled, Tremor prepared to stab one of its thin fingers into her heart. The source of her recovery was coming from there. She must have filled her heart—a conduit for the third level—with Goethan before letting her metaphysical body die.

The pitchfork-like hand came crashing down, flying towards Reine's prone body. It pierced the first layer of her shirt, and was just about to draw blood when . . .

Reine caught it. Muscles trembling, her eyes opened, flashing a golden red. Blood flowed from where her hand was cut by Tremor's sharp fingers, but she quickly returned the favor as her Goethan rebelled against its, igniting a deep pain that burned within both of them.

Tremor screamed. It was a high-pitched sound filled with more fear than hurt. Writhing like a worm, the thing tried to turn its hand transparent and pull away, but Reine's Goethan stopped it from escaping.

Then the girl punched it in the face.

Tremor recoiled, screeching again as fresh pain tore against its mask-like skin. How was the girl conscious? This shouldn't be happening. It shouldn't even be possible!

"*Stop* . . ." it thought, the sentiment echoing loudly. "*How* . . ."

But Reine never stopped, punching it again and again until Tremor couldn't take it anymore. It tore at its own arm, cutting the stick-thin limb off with a hiss and jumping away. The girl's bravery was like salt to a snail.

For the first time, the light coming from the hole in the wall paled in comparison to the murderous red of Reine's Goethan. The thing scuttled with a wince to the edge, and it looked down at the twenty-two-floor drop and back over its shoulder. She was still limping towards it, as resolute and unstoppable as ever. In fact, she actually seemed *more* blinding!

"*My guards . . .*" it thought, so afraid now that Reine could hear it. "*Where are my guards?*" Tremor trembled. The familiar emotion of fear was coursing through it.

"How?" it asked again, trying to buy time. "How?"

Reine continued to stumble forwards. The thing clung tighter to the sides of the hole in order to not fall down. Her mouth tightened in a grimace of concentration, and the lava-hot light burning within her suddenly brightened.

"You assumed I was scared of Starflight," Reine said, her eyes narrowing. It almost seemed like she was on the brink of touching the sixth level. "But that was never true. Not even close. I'm scared of the fact that I might have killed him, Tremor—that I caused the death of my father for nothing."

She settled into a drop stance, keeping both feet flat on the floor and straightening her arms to form a balanced blade. Blood dripped from the palm of one hand.

"But I know what I did was right. If you had shown me a scenario where I stopped him with no innocent lives at stake—" she shrugged. "—who knows, Tremor? It might have worked."

Reine flowed forward to strike . . .

And Tremor let itself fall.

CHAPTER 31:
DEATHSTINY

YEAR 2035

Hurtling through the air, the thing braced itself for impact. Desperation lent strength, and Tremor activated its seventh level power as it hit the ground. Dark Goethan swirled around it, taking the few bits of humanity it had left, but it had done it!

The villain sank through the earth and then surfaced, becoming corporeal again. It would have chuckled if it could. The villains may have thought they succeeded, but Tremor wasn't so easy to kill. No. It would have its revenge!

"*Reine . . .*" it thought, keeping the name for future use. "*Yes . . . Just wait till I come for you . . .*"

"**Tremor.**"

The thing jerked its head towards the noise, not caring about the sunlight stinging its beady eyes. There was the girl with the ginger hair again, and standing next to her was . . . **Pantheon.** His Goethan was captivating, harnessing the power of a thousand black holes—Tremor could feel its own body betraying itself, the dark Goethan yearning to join the villain's.

"Not so scary anymore, are you?" she said mockingly. Her eye was swelling, and the Goethan numbing the pain in her right arm had been tampered with: Pantheon's handiwork. It hung limply by her side. "You should fire your guards. They couldn't even stop me from making a phone call."

Tremor screamed and pounced at her, the knowledge that this would be its final act lending it courage. Its Goethan had failed on Reine before, but that was because it didn't know her true fear. This girl's was as clear as night. The thing almost drooled at the thought of the anguish its powers would cause her.

"Wha—What are you doing?"

Pantheon had gripped Tremor by its stick-thin neck, his hand not squeezing but holding with the firmness of granite.

"I normally wouldn't interfere . . ." the man said with a bored tone, **"but seriously, Tremor? Dealing with a metahero?"**

The villain sputtered and whined, trying to make up an excuse before giving up. Lightning-fast, its two arms shot out, wrapping themselves around his adversary's chest. Pantheon looked down without much interest and pulled his arm back. He aimed his fist at Tremor's face. It was like looking into a solar flare. He struck just as the villain dissolved into a cloud of dark Goethan, becoming incorporeal. The attack went through its transparent body . . . and burst into resplendent flames.

"No . . ." Tremor whispered.

"Yes."

EPILOGUE:
THE RETURN

YEAR 2035

Reine yawned, then Sky, and Asher did too. The thin, tall man standing in the unused parking lot put his hands on his hips, as if daring the yawn to spread to him. He yawned. Yawning really *was* contagious.

"So, your parents aren't coming to see us off?" Sky asked Asher.

"Yeah."

"I don't think they really like us," she confided.

Reine shrugged. "They probably expected more from the meta-villains who took down Tremor. We got to stay at their house for summer break, though, so I'm not complaining."

The thin man glared at them. He was constantly looking around the small, walled parking lot, as if ready to bolt the moment anything suspicious happened. Sky didn't think he had to worry. Virus, Pantheon's second-in-command, had sent two emails through separate domains to Asher's parents: one containing a description of the man they were supposed to find, and another for the code phrase to give him. It was only after meeting the first man in the indigo baseball cap that they had been directed to the thin man.

Sky rolled her eyes. She'd never seen Asher's parents more ecstatic than when they received those emails. *I wonder if they're proud that Pantheon's letting Asher start his junior year after holding him back as a freshman, or if they just really want to get rid of us.* For a pair of rich metavillains, they were stingier than Reine's parents had been.

"You kids ready to go?" the impatient villain asked.

They nodded, and the man narrowed his eyes at the empty parking lot one last time before he rubbed his index finger against his thumb. A moment later, he was grunting with effort as he gripped the air and tore it like he was peeling wallpaper. The space in front of him shimmered. A blurry image formed. The thin man held onto the air until the scene solidified and they stepped through. Sky felt her heart grow a little heavier. The dead bodies had been removed, and grass regrown, but there were still twisted pieces of metal and rock embedded inside the ground where Gravedigger had struck.

"Thanks," she said, pausing. "Um . . . you know, I never got your name."

The thin man hopped back through the portal. "And you don't need it."

He turned away, and the image of the parking lot dissolved into embers that fizzled out before Sky could touch one. She glanced at Reine. She was scowling at the students appearing around them. They were all accompanied by metavillains with teleportation abilities, and some materialized while others faded in like black-and-white photos. Sky waited for that familiar loneliness to burn, for their disapproval to wash over her, but she found . . . nothing. The students looked happy. Heck, they *were* happy—just friends chatting after a long summer away.

Sky touched Reine's shoulder. "You're gorgeous," she said, and she watched her friend's scowl turn from confused to a light blush that crinkled the edges of her eyes.

"And you're braver than you think you are," Reine said.

"Really?"

"Duh. Our classmates don't know what they're missing."

Asher looked around uncomfortably. "Ummm . . ."

"You're ruining the moment!"

"Sorry," he said, "but is it me, or does Virus seem to be walking towards us?"

"Why would he do that?" Sky scoffed.

They all turned to study the villain striding casually in their direction. He was slim but strong like a ballet dancer, and he wore round-eye tortoiseshell glasses that brought his smile to life. Then he was standing beside them.

Virus took off his glasses. "Walk with me," he said.

He folded his glasses and put them in his coat pocket while the trio whispered to each other. Following Virus, they approached the hill that contained the north entrance—it was a staircase cut deep into the earth with a retractable wall of unpolished rock that was currently open—but continued around to the back of the hill as the rest of the students descended the stairs into incandescent light. Virus closed his eyes, and when he opened them, a retinal scanner rose from the ground on a metal pole. He stared into it for a moment; the pole was spraying a watery, jelly-like substance onto the grass. Waving for them to follow, the metavillain jumped in the portal as he took out his glasses. He slid them on.

Sky landed on spongy ground: the default flooring of all simulations. Their surroundings were gray, and bright light emanated from within the mist, but another portal was right in front of them. Virus strode forward with more urgency.

This guy is like fifty! Sky thought, skipping to keep up. *Shame on me for being slower than him, but he has such long legs!*

They finally exited the simulation, the cold liquid of the portal making Sky shiver. Her feet touched glass. She looked down and instantly felt vertigo wash over her as the ground disappeared and the Goethan reactor spun below them.

"It's only transparent from our side," Virus said. "The glass, I mean. This is Pantheon's laboratory, and he finds it calming to see the Goethan reactor from above."

Asher and Reine were staring down with interest, but Sky felt sick at the thought of even standing. She sat down in an armchair; there were quite a few. She kept her eyes level with the granite walls, and studied the various paintings that made the room feel more like someone's home than a lab. There were glowing wires everywhere. Sky hadn't noticed them at first because they crept along the walls and the ceiling, but they converged on a single armchair . . . right behind the one she was sitting on.

Sky yelped.

Reine whirled around. She froze when she saw who Sky was staring at. His head resting against the armrest, Pantheon was slumped on an armchair with glowing wires sticking out of his arms and chest, pumping Goethan. They passed through his suit jacket as if it weren't there. The metavillain stirred.

"What happened to him?" Asher asked, tentatively reaching out to poke at a limp hand. "He looks like someone took the 'meta' out of 'metavillain.'"

Pantheon's eyes snapped open, and Asher stumbled backwards. Sky winced as he hit the glass floor with a thud. There was still a sense of gravity—of fate—surrounding the metavillain, but his presence no longer made reality bend to his will.

"I was **confident**," he said. "*Too* **confident.**"

Virus took over, pulling Asher to his feet. "He's injured from a . . . failed experiment." The vice-principal glanced at his boss. "Should we wait till the others get here?"

"**Just** tell **them.**"

"As you wish. At the start of summer break, Pantheon was growing unstably powerful. He's . . . unique. Each time he stole the life force of another metahuman, the extra Goethan would leak deep into his subconscious and coalesce until it started controlling *him*. It was subtle at first—just a few nudges to absorb a metahero's Goethan instead of snapping their neck—but it soon escalated into mass murder. You see, Goethan is attracted to sentience, which explains why animals and plants produce Goethan while rocks do not. His mass of Goethan became so large that *it achieved* sentience."

Sky blinked and mouthed, "Do you know what he's talking about?" to Reine, but she shrugged.

Frowning, Asher rubbed his face. "How is that even possib—"

"I'm not done. We believe, Pantheon and I, that Goethan is merely the separated body of a dead *god*, for lack of a better word. And as you know, gods don't like to stay dead—death is but a barrier they must overcome. In this case, it left a clump of Goethan large enough to retain its intent to live. As Pantheon absorbed more power, the little piece began to form its own ideas. It wanted to live again, but at what cost? Goethan has become an integral part of the ecosystem. Without it, all living beings will die."

Asher turned pale, and Reine pointed accusingly at Pantheon. "You knew about this, but you still helped it get stronger? What were you thinking?"

The metavillain glared at her, and she took a step back. Sky walked between them with her hands held out on either side. "Can we all calm down? This is a lot to take in, so let's get all the facts before we start making accusations. Sir, Reine makes a good point. Did you have a plan to stop this . . . god?"

"We **tried** and we **failed.** When I used the **ninth level** to take back **control,** half **of** my **Goethan** rebelled and **split** from me. It's **still** out there, growing **stronger.** It'll start **small**—plants are an **easy** target—but when it **starts killing** humans . . ." He sank back into his armchair, letting the implications sink in.

Pantheon defeated almost all of the metaheroes in that battle against Gravedigger. Hell, even someone with half his power could do a lot of damage if they aren't holding back.

"**Do** you know what **Pantheon** means, Reine? For the **Greeks** and Romans, it was a **temple** dedicated to **all** the gods of their **religion**. For us, it's the **shadow** of a god that will **consolidate all** the **bits** and pieces of its little **godlings** until it **is whole** again."

Pantheon closed his eyes. "We **don't** know what **killed** this god or how it **died**, but if **we** don't kill it **again** and kill it for **good** this time, our **lives** will be **nothing** more **than** the playthings . . . of a **God.**"

9 781525 571565